W9-CMU-177

THE TWO-FACED LORD

Lord Michael Anthony, the Earl of Davenchester, was the model of exquisite elegance and icy arrogance in the drawing room.

Who, then, was this man who stood in the moonlight looking down at Hetta? Whose strong arms pulled her hard against his tall, lean figure? Whose lips so expertly kissed hers while his thumb gently caressed the racing pulse in the side of her neck?

What kind of man was this lord who played the part of the perfect gentleman for the world to see, yet now revealed himself in this way?

And even more troubling to Hetta, as she felt herself respond in a manner as unthinkable as the earl's advances were shocking, what kind of woman was she. . . ?

LOVE'S
MASQUERADE

⦾ SIGNET

*Introducing a new
historical romance by Joan Wolf*

DESIRE'S INSISTENT SONG CARRIED THEIR PASSION THROUGH THE FLAMES OF LOVE AND WAR . . .

The Rebel and the Rose
JOAN WOLF

The handsome Virginian made Lady Barbara Carr shiver with fear and desire. He was her new husband, a stranger, wed to her so his wealth could pay her father's debts, an American patriot, sworn to fight Britain's king. But Alan Maxwell had never wanted any woman the way he wanted this delicate English lady. And a hot need ignited within him as he carried Barbara to the canopied bed, defying the danger of making her his bride tonight . . . when war could make her his enemy tomorrow. . . .

Coming in July from Signet!

Love's
Masquerade

Gayle Buck

A SIGNET BOOK

NEW AMERICAN LIBRARY

NAL BOOKS ARE AVAILABLE AT QUANTITY DISCOUNTS WHEN USED
TO PROMOTE PRODUCTS OR SERVICES. FOR INFORMATION PLEASE
WRITE TO PREMIUM MARKETING DIVISION, NEW AMERICAN LIBRARY,
1633 BROADWAY, NEW YORK, NEW YORK 10019.

Copyright © 1986 by Gayle Buck

All rights reserved

SIGNET TRADEMARK REG. U.S. PAT. OFF. AND FOREIGN COUNTRIES
REGISTERED TRADEMARK—MARCA REGISTRADA
HECHO EN CHICAGO, U.S.A.

SIGNET, SIGNET CLASSIC, MENTOR, PLUME, MERIDIAN AND NAL BOOKS
are published by New American Library,
1633 Broadway, New York, New York 10019

First Printing, June, 1986

1 2 3 4 5 6 7 8 9

PRINTED IN THE UNITED STATES OF AMERICA

1

Miss Hetta Stanton was given the thin violet-scented envelope when it arrived, and sat down with it in a straight-backed chair at a Sheraton writing desk. The somber gray skirts of her high-waisted frock fell in subdued folds about her slender feet so that only the toes of her slippers peeped under the hem. The letter from her godmother, Lady Beatrice Pelborne, came as a welcome surprise and she slit it open impatiently with a silver letter knife. She read the letter with eager eyes, but soon a faint frown appeared between her arched brows. When she reached the elegantly scrawled signature, she folded the parchment with painstaking care. Hetta fell into deep thought with the missive held between her slim fingers, her hazel eyes oblivious to the brilliant morning outside the study window. After a few moments she pulled a blank sheet toward her and took up a pen to write a short note. She sanded the freshly written sheet, then folded and sealed it with wax.

From across the room a short portly gentleman wearing a severe black frock coat and wig looked up from the weighty volume on his lap. He marked his place carefully with one finger, blinking owlishly through the spectacles perched on the end of his nose. "Urgent business, Miss Hetta?"

"Yes, Cheton, I suppose you may say so. It seems that my dear godmother is desperate for my company. She cites accute boredom as the root of her distress and begs that I visit her for the Season since I shall soon put off mourning clothes. She wishes to foot the bill for my

5

come-out, saying that she knows I may be relied upon to humor a decrepit old woman.'' Cheton hid a sudden cough behind his hand and Hetta laughed at him. ''I, too, discount that touch. I half-believe that she is ageless.''

''Lady Pelborne had frequently struck me as being very capable and shrewd,'' Cheton agreed.

Hetta lifted her brows and gave him a level look. ''Is that the reason you made free to solicit her help on my behalf without my knowledge, Cheton?''

Cheton blinked and a ruddy hue flushed his plump cheeks. ''Yes, my lady,'' he said quietly. ''My pardon if you are displeased, but I felt it to be my duty to yourself, and to the late lord, to appraise Lady Pelborne of your circumstances. I perceived the situation here at Meldingcourt to have become untenable for you since your father's death.''

Hetta was touched by her old friend's loyalty. ''Thank you for your concern, Cheton. I have always known that you held my father's interests, and my own, in the greatest esteem.'' She smiled and the faint frown eased between her brows. ''I do admit that the thought of a London Season is irresistible. These last few months have been extraordinarily unpleasant, quite beside Papa's absence. Cousin Jonathan is most persistent.''

''If you will permit my blunt speech, Miss Hetta, I consider the manner in which the Honorable Jonathan Markham has attempted to ingratiate himself an impertinence beyond belief,'' said Cheton roundly.

''How can you say so, Cheton?'' Hetta asked in gentle mockery. ''He has been at such pains to make himself agreeable and assures me that once we are wed, I shall take my place among the best of the *ton*. A country miss such as myself must be flattered to receive the notice of so fashionable a buck.''

Cheton snorted and firmly adjusted his spectacles. ''The Stanton family is one of the most respected in England, as well you know, miss! You may look as high as you please for a suitable husband. The good Lady Pelborne shall certainly introduce you to a score of gentlemen who shall be more than honored to escort the mistress of Melding-court.''

''And in London I need not endure Cousin Jonathan's importunities.'' Hetta looked across at him, her eyes dancing. ''I am certain that you must have painted a most lurid picture of my circumstnces for my godmother to bestir herself so suddenly, Cheton. Have you made me the princess beleaguered behind her own castle walls?''

''Indeed so,'' said Cheton with a faint smile. ''Though I never strayed from my natural reticence, I was able to make Lady Pelborne aware of the peculiar evils that beset the course of your days.''

Hetta stared at him in amazed awe. ''I perceive that I have grossly underated your talents, Cheton. Only a Banbury man could have appealed so expertly to Lady Pelborne's lowest instincts.''

''Indeed not, Miss Stanton.'' Cheton's voice was dry. ''I hold the Lady Pelborne in the highest regard. Her taste for the dramatic is known to be unparalleled.''

Hetta gave him a speaking look. ''I have penned an acceptance to Lady Pelborne for her kind invitation and shall have it posted immediately. I intend to post down to London myself as quickly as it may be arranged.''

''Then, with your permission I shall order out one of your father's carriages and instruct two of the footmen to ready themselves to accompany you,'' said Cheton, laying aside his volume and beginning to rise from his chair.

Hetta shook her head, staying him with a gesture. ''I shall not be using one of Papa's coaches. I intend to hire a chaise. There shall be no need for outriders from Melding-court.''

Cheton sank back in his chair, staring at her in surprise. ''But—''

She cut him short with a gesture reminiscent of the late lord her father. ''I have made up my mind. Papa's carriages are all so antiquated that it would mean another day or more on the road. A chaise shall be quicker by far. And I have a wish to travel in a different style than I have ever before done.''

''But a hired chaise will be most uncomfortable compared to a carriage," said Cheton hopefully. He saw the determination in her eyes. "At least take outriders with you, Miss Hetta. Lady Pelborne will most assuredly frown upon such an undistinguished arrival."

Hetta knew it to be true. Lady Pelborne insisted upon traveling in the style befitting her consequence and would expect no less from the late viscount's proper daughter. However, Hetta would not allow herself to be swayed. She smiled affectionately at her old friend's anxious eyes. "Dearest Cheton, I realize your concern is all for my safety and comfort. It is appreciated, believe me, but in this instance I am adamant. Come, Cheton! It is such a little change, after all. If it will make you rest easier, I shall take Papa's pistol with me for protection." From Cheton's expression this suggestion did not seem to have found much favor with him. Ignoring his long face, Hetta rang the hand bell on her desk.

The oaken door opened and a footman in dark-green livery stepped in. "Yes, my lady?"

Hetta held out the missive she had penned to her godmother and he came forward to take it. "Post this, please, and have someone send to the village for a hired carriage. Then have Maggie sent to me in my rooms." As she spoke, she rose from the desk. The footman bowed and went to the door, holding it for her. Her straight full skirt brushed behind her across the carpet.

"My lady!"

She turned in the doorway, a slender figure with magnificent chestnut hair plaited in an unfashionable coronet around her head. Her brows were raised inquiringly. Cheton was struck by the steady regard of her hazel eyes. It reminded him strongly of her father, who had been a man of generous heart and character. "Take care of yourself, won't you?" said Cheton gruffly.

Hetta smiled faintly. "I shall try, Cheton." She went out and the paneled door was gently closed behind her.

Cheton sighed to himself. He could not like it. Mister Stanton would have wanted his neck for allowing Hetta to override him. But the daughter was as headstrong as her father ever was. Cheton sincerely hoped that Lady Pelborne would prove equal to the task of conducting her goddaughter through her first London Season. He smiled; what he knew of the indomitable Lady Pelborne went far to reassure him. He adjusted the spectacles and bent once more to the volume on his knees.

In the hall Hetta was unsurprised by the sight of a familiar figure. Since her father's untimely death from a fall while riding, her cousin Jonathan Markham had made it a point to see how she went on. With uncharacteristic cynicism she sometimes wondered that his family feeling coincided so neatly with her father's death because she had never known him to visit before.

The gentleman was at that moment handing a footman his high-crowned beaver and brown kid gloves. "Good morning, cousin. What is this nonsense about hiring a carriage?" he asked, advancing toward Hetta. He was of a stocky medium build, shown to advantage in a blue superfine coat and top boots, and wore his red-brown hair cropped close.

Hetta nodded at the footman who had her letter to speed him on his way, then addressed her cousin coolly. "I suppose you have come to argue with Cheton again. You will find him in the study. You will excuse me, I know."

His rather hard blue eyes studied her face. "I shall see your esteemed man of business in a moment, my dear. Why is it that you require a carriage?"

"It is none of your concern, Cousin Jonathan," said Hetta, and made to brush past him to the stairs.

Markam took her elbow firmly so that she was compelled to stop. "Anything that concerns you, fair cousin, must concern me. Pray join me for a moment in the drawing room." He ushered Hetta in the drawing room and closed the door. Hetta moved away from him farther into the room. Markham looked across at her, his hand still on the knob. "Your attitude is quite shocking, my dear. Believe me, it is hardly good *ton* to brush off a visitor so rudely, especially before the servants."

Hetta raised her well-defined brows. "I am astounded that you consider yourself a visitor, Jonathan. It seems to me that you have been running tame at Meldingcourt forever."

Markham wagged a finger at her and moved to the fireplace. "You've a sharp tongue, cousin. Not every man would be so tolerant as I. However, we digress: let me understand why you have sent to hire a carriage when you have three that must be perfectly suitable if you wish to visit in the neighborhood or go to the village. Or perhaps I mistake the reason? Surely you have not anticipated my early departure from this charming place." He smiled as though it was an absurdity that she could ever wish to see his back.

"Quite the contrary. It is I who am leaving." Hetta had the satisfaction of seeing his complacent smile wiped away.

"What the devil are you talking about?" he asked sharply.

"My godmother is suffering an agitation of the nerves and requires my presence. Naturally I must go to her, and I have simply chosen to hire a carriage for my journey. I shall probably be departing for London within an hour or two," said Hetta calmly. She studied Markham's frown and said sweetly, "Surely there can be no objection, cousin?"

He looked up, still frowning. "This comes very sudden. You can not have considered the discomforts of such a journey. I fear that I can not allow you to wear yourself out for the whims of one selfish old woman."

"Your fears do not enter into it," Hetta said calmly. "Pray recall that though my father's will has left you some authority in the workings of the estate until my majority, you were not named my guardian."

Markham's lip curled. "Yes! I am most uncomfortably aware that my hands are virtually tied. Master Cheton opposes me on business at almost every turn while you consistently reject my advice. I truly despair of ever bringing you into fashion, cousin. You could be a taking little thing properly rigged out."

"Surely that duty falls on my guardian, Lady Pelborne. I am certain that you see that I but obey my lawful guardian's wishes in undertaking this journey," said Hetta with quiet pointedness.

"I find it preposterous that your father should have left his only daughter in the charge of a doddering old woman, who is known to be no more than a common actress," exclaimed Markham. "Surely he must have realized that a mere woman—and especially one such as Lady Pelborne—could not safeguard your interests as well as I."

"On the contrary, it was quite understandable," Hetta retorted crushingly. "Even though you were the sole remaining male relation to our family, you were personally unknown to my father. Naturally he felt easier leaving me under the aegis of one he knew could be trusted to care for me and sponsor me into the best of polite society. Even you, cousin, must admit that an invitation to a ball given by Lady Beatrice Pelborne is prized by any member of the *ton*."

"Yes, Lady Pelborne can be most influential in certain circles when she so chooses," said Markham slowly, his eyes narrowing in thought. He smiled at Hetta, dispelling the calculating look. "I most certainly see your wisdom, my dear. Assuredly you must visit our dear Lady Pelborne. Pray remember me to her kindly."

"I take it that you have no objection to my visit, then?" Hetta asked with irony.

"Quite the contrary, cousin, I wish you to have a most comfortable visit," said Markham. "I shall expect you back in a fortnight."

Hetta raised her chin. Her eyes held a dangerous sparkle. "You assume much, cousin. My godmother reminded me in her kind letter that it has been a year since Papa's death. She has offered to sponsor me into society this Season, and I have accepted. Wasn't that handsome of her?"

"What? Surely you jest," exclaimed Markham with a ludicrous expression of surprise.

Hetta smiled, delighted that she had at last thrown him off balance. "I admit that it came as quite a surprise to me as well. I had not really expected it of her, you see. Though I have always been aware that Lady Pelborne holds me in affection and that she fully intended one day to sponsor me, I have never deemed it practical to count

on that day. My godmother has always seemed to me to be
a bit whimsical.'' She realized how she must sound and
put a hand to her cheek. ''Oh, dear, I must sound perfectly
horrid.''

''Not at all, cousin. You were merely making an observation of reality. I, too, find it best to deal in practicalities
rather than chance,'' Markham said absently. ''However,
this is an event I had not foreseen.''

''Nor had I,'' Hetta said, wondering at his tone. ''I am
quite in spirits to think of the round of parties, but I am
most particularly anticipating the many new personages I
am sure to meet. This past year we rarely heard what was
happening until the news was quite stale. I shall be glad to
converse with those who have seen more of the world than
I.''

''I assume that you are referring to the dashing young
blades just home from their romp with Bonaparte.'' Markham gave a bark of laughter. ''My dear cousin, they shall
be dangling after the pretty young debutantes, not a country miss of almost one-and-twenty who possesses not a
whit of town bronze.''

Hetta looked at him, stung. Her voice was cold. ''There
are times when you try my good nature too far, cousin!
Pray excuse me. I have kept Maggie waiting long enough.''
She swept him a stiff curtsy and turned to the door.

''Hetta!'' He leapt forward to intercept her at the door
and, taking her hand, said softly, ''Dear cousin, can you
not understand and forgive me? It is my jealous ardor for
you that causes me to speak so. To be deprived of your
fresh and unspoiled company, even for a short while, is a
dismal prospect for me.'' His eyes on hers, he carried her
slender fingers to his lips. ''Could you not forgo these
pleasures until we may journey to London together?''

Hetta disengaged her hand and stepped back, opening
her eyes wide. ''Why, cousin, it was you who convinced
me that I should go. Often I have regretted my sad lack of
the town polish that you so admire. It is my hope that a
London Season will inspire me with a certain dash and
elegance.''

''I understand that I have angered you.'' Markham pulled

at his lower lip. "I quite see that you are set on this course; very well. I presume that you shall have outriders for protection? One hears rumors of unrest of late."

"I do not anticipate trouble, cousin," Hetta said shortly.

Markham bowed and stepped back, allowing her access to the door. "Of course not. Naturally I shall follow you with all speed."

"Certainly, if that is your wish. But pray do not fear that I shall trespass on our kinship, cousin," said Hetta. "I shall remember to treat you as I shall any other gentleman who may choose to call." She swept out of the drawing room, leaving Markham with an expression of brooding discontent on his face.

2

Hetta did not tarry long once the hired carriage had swept through Meldingcourt's iron gates and up the graveled drive to the front steps of the manor. There were last-minute instructions to be given to the housekeeper and a quiet word with Cheton, who accompanied her to the top of the front steps.

"Now, do not be anxious over the cost of the Season, Miss. Lady Pelborne long ago sent me stringent instructions, before this trip ever came about, that it would be she who would foot the bill. Your usual quarterly allowance may be spent in any manner you wish as pin money," Cheton said.

Hetta frowned from under the unfashionably narrow brim of her bonnet. "It is not quite what I like, but I know Godmamma would be displeased if I were to insist otherwise, so I shan't." She smiled and held out her gloved hand to her old friend. "I shall miss you most of all, dear Cheton. You have truly been a good friend and mentor to me, especially during the past year since Papa's death. Do not let my cousin tease you too much."

"You need not worry, my lady," said Cheton dryly. To Hetta's surprise he made a deep bow over her fingers. "I wish you a fair journey, Miss Stanton."

She smiled at him mistily before turning to the steps. Hetta glanced around, but there was no sign of her cousin, for which she was grateful. The unpleasantness of their last interview was still fresh in her mind.

The trunks and portmanteaus were strapped to the boot

of the chaise by a footman, and Cheton walked down to the carriage with Hetta to give the driver his instructions. Hetta gathered up the hems of her dress and cloak before stepping up into the carriage to join her tiring-woman, who had insisted on accompanying her on the journey. Earlier while Maggie did the packing, she had read Hetta a lecture on proper decorum. "For far be it from me to dictate to ye, but a respectable lady will not be journeying without her ladies' maid," Maggie had said in her soft Scottish burr. "Well, ye know what Master Stanton would have said about it, too! So I'll be going with ye that he might rest easy in his grave, and none of your nonsense! Bad enough it is that ye have taken it into your daft head to ride in a nasty hired carriage, but I'll not have it bandied aboot that ye're naught but a common baggage running up to Londontown without a chaperone. I canna ken what Master Cheton is aboot to allow it, but ye'll not be getting around me so easily." Out of breath, she had nodded decisively and glared at her serene mistress over the clothing she was laying out to be packed in a trunk.

"Of course you shall go, Maggie. I would not dream of it otherwise," Hetta said agreeably, and left her maid staring after her.

Not an hour after Maggie's declaration, Hetta settled herself on the seat inside the chaise and the carriage door was securely latched. Cheton motioned to the driver. The driver's whip popped and the carriage lurched into motion. Hetta waved a good-bye but soon put up the window as the chaise swept past Meldingcourt's iron gates and took the public road.

As the chaise put the manor ever farther behind them, Hetta felt her spirits rise perceptibly. She had not dared to contemplate a Season in London with any seriousness, but now that they had indeed embarked for London, she felt free to allow her imagination to soar.

Lady Pelborne had promised her a dazzling Season. As her goddaughter, Hetta knew that she would receive an invitation to every prominent function. Hetta's thoughts drifted into a familiar daydream. Lady Pelborne's newphew could possibly be in London and she might at least meet him.

Hetta could scarcely recall when she had not thrilled to
Lady Pelborne's tales of her nephew Michael. She had
described him as a dashing and gallant gentleman, one
who embodied all that Hetta desired in a suitor. Hetta had
come to think of him as her "sweet Michael," and the
possibility of meeting him excited her.

"Oh, Maggie, it will be marvelous to visit Godmamma,"
she exclaimed suddenly, her eyes sparkling. "I shall
make new acquaintances and dance at Almack's if Lady
Pelborne can procure vouchers for me. I have not been
away from Meldingcourt on even the most trifling social
calls since Papa died, only seeing our neighbors at Sunday
chapel; and with the exception of yourself and dear Cheton,
I have missed the bright wit of conversation most of all.
My tongue must surely have dulled from disuse. Lady
Pelborne will find me but a sad country mouse, I fear."

"Mayhap she will, but m'lady has a way of setting all
to rights," Maggie said, her knitting needles clicking above
the clatter of the carriage wheels. She cast a speculative
glance at her young mistress. "Mayhap ye'll meet up with
a nice gentleman who will be more to your taste than
Master Markham."

"I am in truth not unhappy about leaving my cousin
behind, although I sincerely pity poor Cheton," said Hetta
with a smile, her expression giving away nothing of her
true thoughts on the topic. Even Maggie was not to know
of the secret hopes she cherished for the outcome of her
stay in London.

Her companion snorted. "Your pity is wasted on that
one, but I'm thinking that Master Markham could be
spared a drop or two. I have yet to set eyes on a more
determined gentleman. Aye, ye canna but admire a man
who kens his own mind."

Hetta's eyes flashed before she turned to the window.
"The Honorable Jonathan Markham is of no consequence
at the moment." She leaned forward for a better view of
the unfolding countryside and its neat fields and hedgerows. "What a truly glorious day! I do hope this weather
holds at least for another day. I should like to go riding in
the park if my godmother can seat me from her stables."

Her maid cast her a shrewd glance. "Aye, miss, I saw the sparks in your eyes. Ye've been pulling caps with Master Markham again, have ye not?"

Hetta laughed and shook her head. "Truly you are the most provoking and disrespectful creature! I suppose it comes from knowing me from the schoolroom. If it will satisfy your curiosity, my cousin and I merely disagreed on the wisdom of this journey. There is certainly nothing novel in that, for we are forever at outs over one thing or another."

"Ye'll recall that your father had hopes for ye and Master Jonathan," Maggie said in a wooden voice.

"Papa did not know him, or he would never have contemplated such a ridiculous scheme. Indeed, Maggie, for Papa's sake I have tried to like him, but I cannot. He is so arrogant and so patronizing that it sets my teeth on edge," Hetta said. She lifted her shoulders in a dismal shrug. "It is odd, but though he presses his suit with such determination, I do not feel that he actually cares anything for me." She laid her head against the seat squab and her brow furrowed. "I am in a puzzle to discover his motive for pursuing me, for he can not be a fortune-hunter. Papa once mentioned that my cousin inherited a respectable fortune from a paternal uncle, though it did not include land."

"Mayhap ye wrong the gentleman, and he is desperate for love of ye," said Maggie, pursing her lips while she caught up a dropped stitch in her knitting.

Her own laughter surprised Hetta. "Oh, no, Maggie, there you are mistaken, for my cousin makes it quite plain that he finds me lacking in all respects as a woman. He holds me in utmost contempt for my lack of polish on the one hand, yet he mouths pretty speeches when he hopes to turn me to advantage. I cannot believe those to be the actions of a love-stricken man."

'Aye, ye're right," Maggie said. "If it were love, the gentleman would be swooning over your hand."

Hetta did not hear her. She slapped her palms together. "I wish I knew what to make of it, if only to route the man from Meldingcourt once and for all."

"The gentleman does seem to be forever underfoot," said Maggie. She reflected a moment. "Mayhap ye'll see clearer in London with m'lady to advise ye. I'm thinking that she has dealt with enough gentlemen in her lifetime to guide ye now."

"Oh, yes! I cannot tell you what a relief it shall be to be among different company," Hetta said. "Lady Pelborne has promised us a fine visit, Maggie. She has promised us tickets to Asterly's Circus if we wish, and so much else! Do you wish to go first to the shops or to the Tower?"

The Scotswoman shot her a glance over flashing steel knitting needles. "Have ye not thought of the wild beasties, miss? Ye wouldna want to be missing the sight of them, all ferocious and man-eating as they be."

Hetta quickly assured her companion that it had been the very next suggestion on the tip of her tongue. The conversation turned to recollection of every wonder or treat that was said to exist in London, and in this pleasant manner the miles passed swiftly. The chaise stopped only once for a change of horses at an inn and they stepped down to stretch cramped limbs. The innkeeper persuaded them that a cup of tea was in order and ushered them inside to the coffee room. The team was soon changed, and after hastily downing the last of their tea, Hetta and her companion returned to their seats in the chaise. It lurched forward, then once more settled into its rattling pace.

Hetta took off her bonnet with a sigh. She glanced out the window and saw that a low bank of clouds was slowly gathering on the horizon. "I fear that I shall not have my ride in the park after all. It appears that we are in for rain this evening," she said regretfully.

"Ye'll not be galloping around a strange place, then, and a good thing," said Maggie unfeelingly.

"Really, Maggie, you can be the most provoking creature," Hetta said. "And what, pray, is wrong with my wishing to go riding?"

Her maid shot her a look of triumph and took a deep breath. "Far be it for me to say a word, but—"

Suddenly a gunshot cracked. The chaise slewed over the

road and the two women were tossed over to one side of the carriage.

"Har there! Stand to!" shouted a rough voice.

The chaise rolled to an abrupt stop, jerking occasionally from the movement of the nervous team.

Hetta could hear the driver's fearful voice swearing at the horses. She hastily scrambled to the window. In the road stood a stocky horse straddled by a large ruffian with heavy black brows. A massive horse pistol was in the man's beefy hand, raised and pointed toward the front of the chaise at the driver. Hetta's eyes widened in incredulity. "Dear God . . ." she breathed, drawing back from the window. She dropped to her knees beside the seat and ran her hand swiftly under it, pulling out a flat leather case. Her fingers trembled as she worked at its catches and she could feel the cold sweat break out on her brow.

"What is it? What are ye doing?" Maggie's voice was sharp, and when she espied the case, she sucked in her breath. "Miss, ye'll not be shooting m'lord's own favorite pistol."

Hetta threw open the case and drew out the long-barreled firearm. Gingerly she checked the priming to see that it was loaded. Carefully she pulled back on the hammer. "I may have little choice, Maggie. He looks a desperate character."

"Och, we'll be murdered, then. If the rascal outside does not kill us himself, ye'll be certain to do it for him with that nasty thing," Maggie exclaimed.

Hetta heard a fumbling at the door latch. She whirled up onto the seat, kicking the gun box out of sight and hiding the heavy pistol in a fold of her cloak. Its weight seemed to drag on her arm. The window glass blurred with movement, then the door was jerked open.

The highwayman had dismounted and stood framed in the doorway, his pistol raised menacingly at the women. Hetta stared a fleeting moment at the wide black barrel, then her eyes flew up to his face. Small malevolent eyes glinted back at her like polished black stones, set in a rough face with a wild thatch of black hair and beard. The highwayman belched and the distinct odor of rotten gin

permeated the air. Without a word he reached out with his
free hand and yanked Hetta up from the leather seat. Hetta
bit back a startled cry, struggling against him.

A bloodcurdling Scottish war cry split the close confines
of the carriage. Maggie leapt at the highwayman, slashing
at his eyes with her steel knitting needles. He jerked back,
spitting an oath, and his grasp on Hetta's arm slackened.
She twisted free to fall beside the seat, panting. The
highwayman snarled a filthy word and leveled his pistol at
the blaze-eyed maid. In desperation Hetta swept up her
firearm and her finger tightened on the delicate trigger.
The gun roared, swiftly followed by a second shot. Her
arm jerked up with the recoil and the barrel struck her head
sharply as she was thrown back. The highwayman flung
wide his arms with an expression of surprise on his face.
His smoking pistol dropped from his hand as he fell backward onto the road. He lay still, his black eyes staring. A
spreading stain darkened the front of his rough frieze coat.

The carriage horses squealed in fear, plunging. The
driver swore, fighting desperately to control the team before they tangled in the leather traces and broke their legs.

The chaise pitched like a boat. Hetta lay stunned, her
ears ringing from the explosions. She felt Maggie's arm
about her shoulders, urging her up. The acrid smell of
exploded black powder burned her nostrils. Dazedly she
pulled herself to a sitting position beside the door. Hetta
stared down at the dead man, appalled. The pistol was a
heavy weight in her hand and she let it slide to the floor.
She closed her eyes against the sight of the dead man.
"Oh, dear Lord, forgive me," she whispered. Pain pulsed
dully behind her right eye.

Suddenly the maid clutched her arm. Despair shrilled
her voice. "Oh, miss, there's another!"

Hetta looked up, startled, and felt sick panic. A second
ruffian had swung his mount from around the front of the
chaise. Even as she reached for the pistol again, she knew
there would be no time to reload, and as she met the man's
hard eyes, she knew there would be no mercy. With hardly a
glance for his dead accomplice, the higwayman stared at Hetta
with flat expressionless eyes. Slowly he raised his pistol.

Thunder rumbled loud, becoming the swift beat of hooves. The highwayman slewed around in his saddle, his eyes narrowed in surprise. A shot whistled overhead. Instinctively, the highwayman ducked, swearing. He wheeled his horse with a savage kick and took off at a gallop. Barely a moment later two horsemen pounded past the chaise in swift pursuit of the fleeing highwayman.

Hetta scrambled out of the chaise, closely followed by Maggie. Both took care to skirt the dead man, holding their cloaks back so that the hems would not brush his body. They stared after the horsemen. "Did you see who they were, Maggie?" demanded Hetta, holding on to the chaise door to steady herself. Her head was aching abominably and she felt dizzy.

"Nay, miss. But I'll be knowing the scoundrel they are chasing," the maid said grimly. Hetta glanced at her in surprise. Maggie nodded, her lips thin. "He'll be your cousin's man, the one they call Lucus."

Hetta stared at her dumbfounded. "But surely you must be mistaken. Cousin Jonathan prides himself too much a gentleman to ever have such a villain in his employ."

"Be that as it may, I am not mistaken."

Hetta knew her companion's sharp eyes well enough to believe her. "Then I am obliged to inform my cousin, of course, even if it is unlikely that he will believe it. He shall not be amused to hear even a rumor that one of his servants takes to the roads, at all events." She smiled suddenly at her maid. "Thank you for your foolish bravery, Maggie. I could not have managed to shoot him otherwise."

Maggie sniffed and said gruffly, "It's I who should be doing the thanking, m'lady. Likewise I would be lying dead this moment."

Hetta reached out and squeezed her hand briefly. She looked off. "One of our gallant rescuers is returning now. He shall tell us if the ruffian has been captured. Cousin Jonathan will undoubtedly lend greater credibility to our story if his man has been thrown in jail."

The approaching rider was reining in beside them. Hetta stepped away from the chaise door to greet him. A stone turned under her foot and she stumbled. Sharp pain lanced through her head as she tried to catch her balance. She felt herself sway and half-turned toward Maggie.

The maid's eyes widened in horror. "Miss, ye're bleeding!"

Hetta's knees gave way despite Maggie's quick support. Before she crumpled completely, strong hands caught her and carried her gently to the roadway. She sat half-supported by a muscular arm, her face pressed against a masculine shoulder. A warm feeling of security washed through her. Hardly aware that she spoke, she breathed, "Oh, my sweet Michael!"

"Here, let me see that," snapped an authoritative voice above her head. Long fingers caught her chin and turned her face to the late-afternoon sun. She blinked up in confusion to see a lean browned face with piercing green eyes. "Who?" She put up a faltering hand to her forehead, trying to reorder her thoughts. "It aches abominably. So idiotic of me, but I felt so faint suddenly."

His glance flickered to hers. "The cut is not deep. You were fortunate. The recoil of a firearm can be dangerous if one isn't prepared for it."

Embarrassed, Hetta attempted to sit up. "I am fine, truly. Do let me stand."

"Lie still!"

Instinctively she obeyed the whipcrack order and looked up at him with wide eyes. The stranger took a fine linen handkerchief from his coat pocket with his free hand and on his bent knee folded it into a bandage. He pressed the pad to her brow and Hetta was impressed by his gentle competence as he efficiently fastened it around her head. Beyond his broad shoulder she could see the other rider, now returned and confering quietly with her driver. The rider held the reins of two horses with satchels tied behind the saddles. There was no sign of the highwayman." He has escaped," she said.

The gentleman kneeling beside her glanced toward the two men in conversation. "So it appears. Are you able to stand, ma'am?"

Hetta nodded, then wished she had not when her head

swam. She rose shakily with the stranger's help. Maggie put an arm about her waist to steady her and the gentleman stepped back. Leaning on Maggie for support, Hetta smiled at him wanly. "I must thank you, sir. Maggie and I would have fared much worse without your opportune appearance." She put out her gloved hand. "I am Miss Hetta Stanton and this is my maid, Maggie MacPherson."

He made a brief bow over her hand, then released her fingers. "Lord Anthony, at your service. I am happy that my batman and I could be of assistance, Miss Stanton. When we came upon your chaise and were in time to witness your valiant shot, we knew immediately what was afoot."

"It was more desperate than valiant, I fear. Had it not been for Maggie's brave attack on the man with her knitting needles I do not know that I could have raised my pistol at all," said Hetta, barely heeding the conversation. Involuntarily her eyes went to the highwayman's body lying beside the chaise. Quickly she looked away, shuddering. "It was horrible!"

Lord Anthony caught his batman's eye and jerked his chin meaningfully toward the dead man. His servant nodded in understanding. He tossed the horse's reins to the coachman with a quiet word and walked over to the body to catch it under the arms. He began to drag it from the road, the highwayman's heavy boots scoring twin trails in the gravel.

Satisfied, Lord Anthony turned back to Hetta. "I am certain that it was a most unpleasant experience, my lady. I will lay information at the nearest magistrate about the incident, of course. It astounds me that the highwaymen made so bold this near to London, and particularly on such a well-traveled road."

"So am I surprisèd, though there has been grave unrest since the war ended, and these scoundrels seemed desperate enough for any deed. I was certain that we were at our last prayers," Hetta said. She knew from the dragging sound what was happening and she swallowed the bile that rose in her throat. "Do you travel to London as well?"

Lord Antohny bowed slightly in assent. "I have but just

returned to England from the Continent after resigning my commission. I hope to give a pleasurable surprise to my aunt, of whom I am quite fond.''

"I feel that she could not be other than pleased," Hetta said with a frank smile that brought warmth to her lustrous eyes.

Lord Anthony's brow quirked. Fleetingly he thought that there was more to this drab little wren than he had first seen. He offered his arm to her. "Allow me to hand you to your carriage, Miss Stanton. If you will permit, I shall be honored to act as your escort for the remainder of the way to London.''

"Thank you, sir, you are most kind," Hetta said, surprised. She placed her hand on his arm. "I admit that I should feel more comfortable with an escort even though I know that highwayman will not return. Maggie believes that she recognized the man who escaped, and foolishly I feel a little uneasy.''

The gentleman shot a piercing glance at the maid, who was standing silent beside her mistress. "Indeed? And who might the scoundrel be, Maggie?''

"The one ye put to flight is called Lucus. He is in the service of Master Jonathan Markham, my mistress's own cousin," Maggie said with grim relish.

Lord Anthony's brows shot up.

Hetta flushed, embarrassed. "Really, Maggie, you have made it sound so sinister. I am certain that once my cousin learns of his man's reprehensible conduct, he will see Lucus justly punished.''

"That is as may be, miss, but meantime I wonder if we shan't see the rascal's evil face again. For be sure he'll not lightly forget how ye have killed his partner when the spalding tried to pull ye from the chaise," said Maggie. She nodded sharply. "Aye, and how does he know that we didna recognize him? Be sure he knew the two of us. I saw it in his eyes. He'll not be wanting tales to get back to Master Markham, who is known to be a hard master.''

"Be still, Maggie. You have let your imagination run away with you, just as I did for a moment. But we stand in no danger. The man would be mad to contemplate seeking us out to do us harm. He is far more likely to disappear from Cousin Jonathan's employ,'' Hetta said. She pressed her fingers against the dull throbbing of her brow. The headache was steadily worsening and began to sicken her. ''Pray let us hear no more such nonsense.''

Lord Anthony observed her keenly. ''I fear that you are still suffering from the blow, Miss Stanton. If Maggie will be so good as to precede us, I will walk you now to the carriage. I am persuaded that you shall wish to reach London as speedily as possible, and I suggest that you have a physician examine you for concussion.'' He looked at the maid and she nodded, hurrying to the chaise.

Hetta was grateful for the support of Lord Anthony's arm as they walked to the chaise. He handed her up the iron step into Maggie's care. Hetta settled back onto the seat with a sigh, putting her head back against the seat squab, the white bandage standing out stark against her dark hair. She shut her eyes. Maggie's lips thinned when she saw how white her mistress's face had become.

''My batman and I shall ride alongside until you reach your destination, so you may both rest easy,'' said Lord Anthony, preparing to close the door. He caught sight of the discharged pistol on the carriage floor and retrieved it. He handed it butt-first to the maid. ''I suggest this be put safely away, Maggie.''

''Aye, m'lord.''

He closed the door and it caught with a quiet click.

Beneath her, Hetta felt the chaise roll forward and then begin to pick up speed. Faintly over the whir of the wheels she could hear the clipping hoofbeats of riders close by. ''Though I had wished for an adventure, Maggie, I am so glad that it is over,'' she murmured.

''Aye, Miss.''

3

The sway of the carriage was monotonous and Hetta slowly relaxed. The sound of rain, when it began, was a soothing accompaniment to the carriage wheels. It was not long before her head slipped to Maggie's bony shoulder and she slept, comforted by the knowledge of their escort.

The riders outside turned up their collars against the rain and stoically ignored the wetting of their coats as evening drew on. They did not notice the horseman shadowing their course from behind the hedgerows alongside the road.

Sometime later when the light rain had ended, Hetta started awake, feeling Maggie's hand on her arm. The interior of the chaise was dark and she blinked, puzzled. "We're in London, miss, and as I judge it nearly to Pelborne House," said Maggie.

Hetta sat up and stretched, covering a yawn with one slender hand. "Oh, Maggie, I feel that I could sleep forever."

"Time enough for rest once ye've properly greeted Lady Pelborne," said her companion tartly. The chaise was slowing. "Aye, we've come to m'lady's now. Here is your bonnet, miss. It won't do to give Lady Pelborne a fright straight off at sight of that bandage."

"Certainly not," agreed Hetta, putting on the bonnet over her plaited hair. She finished tying the ribbons under her chin as the carriage rolled to a stop.

A moment later the chaise door was opened by Lord Anthony. He let down the iron step. "I trust the journey passed agreeably enough." He handed Hetta out of the carriage to the wet pavement and looked at her searchingly. "Are you feeling better, Miss Stanton?" She inclined her head and he turned to hold out a courteous hand to Maggie. The maid gave him a rare smile and allowed herself to be handed out.

Hetta walked to the flight of steps to stare up at an imposing brick town house ablaze with light. Excitement surged through her, dispelling the last remnants of drowsiness. Feeling someone come up beside her, she turned to find Lord Anthony standing at her side. He was staring up at the town house with a queer expression. "Is there aught troubling you, my lord?" asked Hetta curiously.

He glanced down at her quickly. "Why, no, Miss Stanton, far from it! From all appearances one would suppose your godmother to be at home. I hope that your headache has dissipated somewhat?"

"Indeed, yes." Hetta smiled up at him, warmed by his solicitude. "I am indebted to you for seeing us safely to our destination, Lord Anthony. Pray won't you come up with me for a few moments? I am persuaded that my godmother will wish to express her gratitude as well."

An odd smile crossed Lord Anthony's face. "Certainly, Miss Stanton. It would give me great pleasure to make the acquaintance of your godmother." He turned his head to address his batman, who stood nearby with their mounts. "James, pray see to the horses a while longer while I meet this lady's godmother."

His servant eyed him with a sour grimace and Lord Anthony laughed before offering his arm to Hetta. She glanced up at him in puzzlement, wondering what had struck him as so humorous. Together they climbed the steps. Maggie followed closely behind, carrying a slim leather case that she felt best not to entrust to anyone else.

Lord Anthony pulled the bell and stepped aside, casually pulling the brim of his beaver well over his brow. The door was opened immediately by the butler in black and silver livery, and light bathed over Hetta. "Welcome, miss! Lady Pelborne has been expecting you," he said, standing aside for Hetta and her companions. The butler glanced sharply at Lord Anthony when he passed by, but that gentleman ignored him.

Hetta glanced around, curious to see Lady Pelborne's town house. Several paneled doors led off from each side of the hall and at the far end was a magnificent sweeping staircase with intricately carved balustrades. The door opposite her was flung open. A tall woman gowned in a deep violet and silver chemise robe buttoned from neck to hem stepped into the hall. "Erwin, is that Hetta? Drat the girl, she should have been here hours ago."

Hetta laughed and went forward, holding out her gloved hands. "My dear ma'am! Indeed, and I would have been but for an adventure. Pray don't scold or I shall tell you nothing about it."

Lady Pelborne clasped Hetta's hands and kissed her lightly on the cheek. "Dear creature! How happy I am to see you! I knew that you would put life into the place; you've not been here about five minutes and already you are speaking of adventures. I see that you have Maggie with you. How are you, Maggie?"

"Would I have let my mistress come alone, then?" asked Maggie brusquely, nodding with a slight smile at Lady Pelborne, who laughed.

"Of course you would not!" She turned to her goddaughter once more. "Do but come into the study where we may be comfortable, my love. Erwin will see that your trunks are taken up and show Maggie where your rooms are to be." Her eyes went beyond her goddaughter to the quiet gentleman clad in a rain-streaked military coat and trousers. His tall beaver was pulled down at an unfashionably low angle across his brow, partially hiding his face. "But who is your tall companion? Surely this cannot be your cousin!"

"Indeed not," said Hetta with a revealing emphasis. "Pray forgive my rude manners, ma'am." Quickly she turned, stretching out her hand to Lord Anthony. With a brilliant smile, she said, "Godmamma, I wish you to meet the kindest of gentlemen. If it had not been for his timely appearance, I fear Maggie and I would have been shot by a highwayman."

"Well, this is something indeed. It seems that we stand in your debt, sir," exclaimed Lady Pelborne.

"I desired him to come up, for I knew that you would wish to make his acquaintance," Hetta said. "Lady Pelborne, allow me to present Lord An—"

The tall gentleman came forward, removing his beaver with a flourish. "The Earl of Davenchester!" His green eyes were alight with mischief as he made an elegant leg. "Your devoted servant, ma'am."

Lady Pelborne uttered a shriek and flung herself upon him. Stunned, her goddaughter watched as she fervently embraced Lord Anthony. Laughing, he return her embrace. Lady Pelborne plucked at his sleeve with her long fingers. "You have given me a shock, dear boy. What ever are you doing here, and with Hetta?" She shook her head reprovingly at Hetta. "Really, child, I could have expected such a trick from Michael, but I never dreamed it of you." She did not notice her goddaughter's expression of shocked astonishment but linked an arm with each of them. "But come into the study, both of you. I wish to hear how it comes about that you have met." As she spoke, she drew them through the doorway of the study and closed the heavy door behind them, cutting off the footmen's curious stare.

Hetta had a fleeting impression of the sofa and chairs done in warm red upholstery and a mahogany desk and bookcase before she turned with a questioning look to her godmother. "Lord Anthony is your nephew? But you did not tell that he was . . . That is, I never realized . . ." She floundered, tangled helplessly in her confusion. She should have known the moment Lord Anthony introduced himself, but she had been so rattled by all that had happened that his name had made little impression. She spied the growing amusement in Lord Anthony's eyes and flushed. Mortified, she demanded, "Godmamma, why did you never tell me that Captain Anthony had become Lord Anthony, the Earl of Davenchester?"

Surprise etched Lady Pelborne's face. "But did you not know? He has but recently come into the title, of course. I must make it a point of addressing him as

Davenchester now!'' She realized that her goddaughter's color was uncomfortably heightened under Lord Anthony's amused eyes, and she gave a merry laugh. ''Oh, my poor dear, it was too bad of him. He has deliberately kept you in the dark. All unwitting you have introduced a nephew to his only aunt. But there! He has always been a shameless scapegrace.''

''I must cry pardon, Miss Stanton,'' said the earl, his grave tone belied by the twinkle in his eyes.

Still flushed, Hetta studied him momentarily before bestowing on him her sweetest smile. ''Of course, sir. Your sterling qualities must surely outweigh any lack of shame.'' He gave a crack of laughter and Hetta responded with a smile of genuine warmth. She said shyly, ''Indeed, I will not soon forget your gallantry this evening, my Lord.''

His eyes suddenly glinted. ''Nor shall I forget your touching trust in me.'' There was an indefinable inflection in his voice that held Hetta still, her eyes caught by the enigmatic expression in his eyes.

Lady Pelborne sensed the byplay and her glance flickered sharply between them. She demanded suddenly, ''Tell me of this adventure on the instant. I am all curiosity to hear of the villainous highwayman.''

Hetta seated herself on the sofa, suddenly trembling. Even though she was no longer looking toward him, she could feel Lord Anthony's continued regard. With an effort she put brightness into her voice. ''Actually there were two highwaymen. We did not know of the second until he came from around the chaise after I had shot his accomplice with Papa's favorite pistol.''

''My dear!'' Lady Pelborne was disconcerted and cast a swift look of astonishment at her silent nephew. ''But how brave of you to do so. I am certain that if I had been in your place, I would have been frightened out of my wits.''

''So I was, but there was no time to consider. He was about to shoot Maggie.'' The horror she had felt suddenly overwhelmed her and her eyes glimmered with tears. ''I killed him, Godmamma!''

Lady Pelborne swiftly went to sit beside her on the sofa and patted her hand. ''Of course it was a great shock to you, my love, but you have done only what you must. If it had not been for you, Maggie would in all likelihood be dead now. The scoundrel undoubtedly knew the risks of such a lawless life, and yet he persisted. I do not see that you should be held to blame for his stupidity." She turned her head toward Lord Anthony. "But then, how is it that you are credited with saving their lives, Michael, if Hetta vanquished her foe?"

"You have forgotten the second highwayman," said Lord Anthony, leaning at his ease against the high mantel of the fireplace. He withdrew from his pocket a slender cigar and match. He lit the end of it, gently inhaling.

His aunt watched this leisurely procedure with growing exasperation. "Really, Michael, you would try the good nature of a saint. What happened to the other rascal?"

"He took flight when my batman and I came upon the scene. We gave chase, naturally, and I believe we winged him. But in the end he managed to escape," said Lord Anthony shortly.

Lady Pelborne looked at him in disgust. "You disappoint me, Michael. The least you could have done was to catch the man by the heels. It would have made a far better tale, believe me."

"My abject apologies," Lord Anthony said, his expression one of mock humility.

Lady Pelborne snorted. "I suppose I should be grateful that neither of you were harmed by this night's work."

"Unfortunately that is not quite true. Miss Stanton did suffer a blow to the head when her pistol recoiled on her," said Lord Anthony. He glanced at Hetta with the same enigmatic expression that had so disconcerted her a moment before. "Upon examination I found the wound to be superficial, but there exists the slight possibility of concussion. Miss Stanton has suffered from a headache since it happened."

As he spoke, Hetta's eyes had widened in horror at her recollections. Surely she could not have actually addressed him as her "sweet Michael," and burrowed her face into his shoulder in so intimate a fashion. She cast a fleeting glance up at the earl, hoping that it was an imagined occurrence, but his amused expression told her otherwise. Clasping her fingers together tightly, Hetta knew beyond doubt that for some peculiar reason of his own he was prepared to enjoy her discomfiture. With a sinking feeling she wondered how he intended next to ridicule her. She realized he had her at a distinct disadvantage in that unless she wanted to reveal her lack of discretion before Lady Pelborne, she could do nothing short of leaving the room to put an end to his needling.

"My dear Hetta!" Hetta jumped guiltily at her godmother's exclamation. Lady Pelborne was studying her with an expression of genuine distress. "I wondered a trifle at your pallor, but I had put it down to the shock you had sustained in this unpleasant incident. I had no idea that you were injured. You should have told me."

"Pray do not distress yourself, ma'am. The headache is truly m—much better," said Hetta, slightly stammering. She suddenly realized a way of gracefully escaping from Lord Anthony's too-knowing eyes. "I do own, however, that I am sadly worn." She avoided meeting Lord Anthony's gaze, her color rising.

"Of course you are, child. I should have seen it sooner," exclaimed Lady Pelborne. "Obviously you are fagged to death. I insist that you go upstairs directly and rest. We shall visit longer on the morrow." Lady Pelborne rose from her seat as she spoke, and pulled a bell rope hanging on the wall near the sofa. She turned as the study door was opened by a footman. "Please ask one of the maids to show Miss Stanton to her rooms, John."

"Of course, my lady." The footman bowed and waited, holding open the door.

Hetta rose to her feet and held out her hand to Lord Anthony. She said coolly, "I know that my godmamma shall enjoy the chance to visit with you in private, so I shall wish you good night with a good grace, my lord! Perhaps we shall meet again one day, however."

Lord Anthony bowed over her hand. He held her fingers for a moment longer than necessary and said softly, "So formal, ma'am? I had quite thought us already to be the oldest and most intimate of friends after our adventure together!''

She realized that he was aware of her discomfiture and was again making a deliberate attempt to put her out of countenance. She raised her brows and returned his regard as steadily as she was able. ''Indeed, my lord? But we have barely met, so that must be my excuse for maidenly reticence.''

His smile was quick and warm. ''Undoubtedly we shall meet again, Miss Stanton. However, I do not plan an overlong stay in London, so you may consider yourself safe from my graceless manners for a time.''

Hetta made him a polite, if somewhat stiff curtsy, acknowledging him with a cool nod even though her heart was beating fast. His smile had the oddest effect on her. She turned away from him to kiss her godmother's finely lined cheek with real affection. ''Good night, dear ma'am. Thank you for your kind invitation. I am certain that I shall enjoy every moment.'' She knew full well that Lady Pelborne had been an interested observer of their exchange and wondered what that lady had made of it.

Lady Pelborne gave her a quick hug. ''There, child! It is I who shall have the pleasure of your fresh young company. Rest well, for I've planned a rigorous schedule for you this Season, and I mean to begin it tomorrow. I hope that you may stand the pace, for I shall accept no excuses for crying off.''

Hetta laughed. ''I hope that I may hold up, then.'' She went to join the footman at the door. It was closed behind them, leaving Lady Pelborne alone with her nephew, the Earl of Davenchester.

''It was bad of you to tease the girl,'' said Lady Pelborne, her eyes twinkling.

''She will survive it, I think,'' said Lord Anthony, gently tapping ash from his cigar into the fireplace.

''Indeed, I believe she will. Hetta has a lively intelligence and is not afraid to use it to advantage. She does not poker up as so many of our young ladies do,'' Lady Pelborne said casually. She had been sharply aware of the undercurrents between her goddaughter and nephew and wondered at the cause. But she knew Lord Anthony well enough to know when not to indulge her inquisitiveness. She was content to let her curiosity lie for the moment, for she thought the chances were excellent that it would all come clear with time. Her goddaughter had always been a confiding little thing. She seated herself in a wing chair near the hearth and looked up at her nephew. "Well, Michael, how long may I expect you to visit with me before you are off again on some jaunt or other?"

"Not above a fortnight, and then I am traveling down to the family estate. My man of business has written me regularly for almost a year that it needs tending and now is as good a time as any," said Lord Anthony.

"Then you have sold out at last?"

He grinned down at her from his superior height. "Indeed I have, Aunt. What alternative did I have, with Boney caught neatly by the heels at last? The army life became so cursed flat afterward that even the thought of England appeared less of a bore. Mind you, though, I hardly expected to find it much livelier than when I left."

Lady Pelborne snorted. "I understand you well enough, I think. You have always been an irrepressible young devil. Coming into the title has not sobered you one whit."

Lord Anothony threw up his hand in mock protest. "Aunt, you do me a grave injustice. I assure you that I have become a pillar of respectability. No longer do I course the countryside with an eye out for the stray adventure or fox."

"Hah! I predict that within six months your man of business will be in flat despair," said Lady Pelborne. She wagged her finger at her nephew when he laughed. "You may make merry, my boy, but you'll not gammon me so easily. We two are too much alike; staid respectability soon bores us. Why do you think I enjoy the theater and politics so much? And this piece of knight-errantry of yours this evening merely proves my point."

"This is ungrateful of you indeed, ma'am! After all, I have rescued your own beloved goddaughter from villains most foul," Lord Anthony said, a teasing gleam in his eyes. "Surely you would not have had me leave her to their tender mercies? It is too bad of you, ma'am."

"Certainly not," said Lady Pelborne, ruffled. "I merely wish you to consider before you leap. Yes, and so should Hetta! I fail to understand what possessed the girl to travel without an escort, as I feel sure she did, for otherwise there would have been no need of your gallantry. Most likely she could have been spared this unpleasant episode if she had done so."

"Indeed, ma'am. Yet I do not believe your goddaughter will brood overmuch upon it," said Lord Anthony. "She has backbone and is not easily rattled under fire. I have seen that much tonight, and I respect her for it. And I may say the same for her maid. The woman actually attacked the first highwayman with her knitting needles, diverting him long enough for Miss Stanton to bring up her pistol."

"Did she indeed?" Lady Pelborne said, amused. "I have always had a high regard for Maggie, and her loyalty to her sometimes flighty mistress is unquestioned. Hetta is not always the most sensible of girls. She favors her late father in that regard. I respected him highly but on occasion he was known to let his intelligence go begging. His provision for Hetta's future in his will is a prime example. It has placed her in an untenable position, and that is the reason I have asked her to come to me for the Season."

"May I inquire into the circumstances?" Lord Anthony asked curiously.

Lady Pelborne waved a hand in obvious irritation. "I am disgusted each time I reflect upon it. The girl has been shamefully pressed to marry a cousin whom Stanton named as one of the trustees of her inheritance. She has literally been forced to flee her home to escape his insidious attentions. Thus her presence in London. I do not go so far as to accuse the man of being a fortune-hunter. Indeed, it is said that he possesses a respectable inheritance of his own. But I find it highly repugnant that a young woman is hounded toward the altar not a week after her father's death and on every day since. Never have her inclinations or desires been consulted, nor was she allowed consideration for her grief." Lady Pelborne drew breath, shaking her head. "Naturally as Hetta's guardian, though it is not a role that I particularly fancied for myself—another one of Stanton's extraordinary lapses, I feel certain—I could not allow her to remain where she was, subjected to such outrageous pressure. So I thought to have her up for the Season since she is out of black gloves. I hope to show the poor chit a pleasant time and perhaps even to see her married off credibly. *That* would certainly put her ramshackle cousin's nose out of joint."

Lord Anthony was frowning. "One wonders that Miss Stanton did not appeal to you sooner if her situation was so unbearable. It sounds to me rather fantastic. Perhaps Miss Stanton is given to exaggeration?"

"You have mistaken the case. She has not applied to me at all. She is as willful and proud as her father ever was," said Lady Pelborne with an exasperated sigh. "I learned the whole from Cheton, who was her father's man of business and trusted friend. He also happens to be the second trustee of Hetta's inheritance, and a more close-mouthed man I hope never to meet. Believe me, if Cheton wrote to me, the case was indeed desperate."

"I see." The earl was silent a moment, recalling the maid's assertion that she had recognized the escaped highwayman as being in the employ of her mistress's cousin. If Maggie's identification was correct, it placed Miss Stanton's narrow brush with the highwaymen in an unexpectedly sinister light. "Of a sudden I find this business of the highwaymen rather intriguing," he said slowly. "My batman gathered from speaking with the driver of the hired chaise that it appeared as though the chaise had been stopped for the express purpose of taking Miss Stanton out of it. There was apparently no demand ever made to hand over her valuables. The maid unwittingly corroborated his story. She stated that the highwayman attempted to bodily pull her mistress from the carriage. After what you have related to me, one might gather that the highwaymen's true motive was not robbery."

"But what else could it have been?" Lady Pelborne asked, startled. She stared intently at her nephew's thoughtful expression and demanded sharply, "What have you not told me, Michael?"

Lord Anthony inspected the glowing tip of his cigar. "Maggie recognized the highwayman who escaped as one Lucus, whom she claims to be in the service of the Honorable Jonathan Markham."

"Markham! But that is the mawworm who has besieged Hetta so stringently. Surely you do not suspect that he is the perpetrator of that holdup." Lady Pelborne's mind raced, and suddenly bright patches of angry color appeared high on her cheeks. "I gather that you are implying an attempt at abduction?"

"So it would appear," said Lord Anthony calmly. A strange sixth sense whispered to Lord Anthony that adventure lurked just beyond his vision, and the challenge was irresistible.

"Then the man must be a lunatic," exclaimed Lady Pelborne, appalled. "What could he possibly hope to achieve?"

"That is precisely what intrigues me," Lord Anthony said. There was a faintly quizzical expression in his eyes when he looked across at his aunt. "Would you consider it too irresponsible of me to embroil myself in one last adventure, Aunt? I suddenly have a great curiosity about this gentleman and his intentions toward your goddaughter."

"Of course I would not! Indeed, I shall feel better knowing that you are watching out for dear Hetta's interests," Lady Pelborne said. "But what do you propose to do? The man can hardly be accused of an abduction that never took place, and especially by yourself. You are not a member of Hetta's family, after all, and your involvement even as her rescuer tonight may create talk. The stir it would cause if you were to challenge Markham would embroil Hetta in such speculation that I would not dare to wager on her chances of being accepted into polite society. Her reputation would literally be ruined."

Lord Anthony smiled faintly at her. "My dear Aunt, when have you not known me to act with discretion?" He ignored her snort of derision. "Actually, I hardly know myself what my plan of action will be. However, I have decided to open my town house here, since I intend to stay in London, where I may keep an eye on your goddaughter. Perhaps the Season will not prove altogether dull if Markham chooses to stage another attempt on Miss Stanton's virtue.''

Lady Pelborne frowned and tapped her fingers on the chair arm. ''Ah, yes, your town house.''

At her intonation the earl raised his brows. ''One gathers that there may be a problem?''

Lady Pelborne shrugged elegant shoulders. ''You may recall that you gave Edmond's widow leave to use the town house as her own until your return to England. Loraine came back to London from the country not a week ago. She won't have heard of your arrival.''

''Then Lady Anthony is in for an unlooked-for pleasure,'' said Lord Anthony, flicking his thin cigar into the fireplace with casual fingers.

Lady Pelborne chuckled. ''Your appearance will undoubtedly come as a shock to Loraine, especially when she realizes that it will mean her removal from such a prestigious address. You're aware of what construction she may put upon that.''

''However disobliging my sister-in-law believes me to be, I have no intentions of casting her homeless into the streets,'' said Lord Anthony. ''I intend to post down to my estate in the morning. My business there should take no more than a fortnight to conclude. Lady Anthony should find that ample time in which to make other arrangements.''

''I have often wondered why you never cared for the woman,'' Lady Pelborne murmured.

Her nephew's smile was humorless. ''I find my sister-in-law difficult to respect. Loraine was a beautiful ninnyhammer with no sense of the proprieties and she knew nothing of how to conduct herself when Edmond married her. She has not changed. I never understood why he chose someone so obviously unsuited to become the Countess of Davenchester.''

''So it is her lack of propriety and pride that offends you,'' said Lady Pelborne. ''Those are hardly major sins, Michael.''

"It is more than that," Lord Anthony said, frowning. "I have too often seen her badly dipped at the card tables. As for her outrageous flirtations, I wonder that Edmond did not strangle her in their first year. More than once I saw him beside himself with jealous rage. I think the pain she inflicted upon my brother is what I cannot forgive."

"Nevertheless she suited Edmond, who, I may remind you, was not behind in his own extravagances. Loraine can admittedly be a trial, but at heart I believe her to be a decent woman. I believe she truly mourned Edmond's death," said Lady Pelborne, "but do not expect her to be still in black gloves. It has been nearly a year and she is a butterfly and always shall be."

Lord Anthony laughed shortly. "I do not expect it, ma'am. It is my belief that Edmond's worldly possessions are what rendered him particularly attractive in her eyes. As you say, she will not care to set up housekeeping elsewhere. However, she should have no difficulties in letting another town house for the Season. I will of course make ample provision for her as my brother's widow."

Lady Pelborne shook her head. "Loraine would find hunting up a residence a tremendous task, and in the end she would only apply to me for help. No. I believe I shall invite her to stay here with Hetta and myself instead. She will provide amusing company for my goddaughter and may prove of help to me in bringing the girl out. Even you, Anthony, must allow that Loraine is a superb hostess."

He shrugged. "As you wish, ma'am. I know only that it is not my concern. I trust, however, that you shall spare the time from your arduous duties as duenna to play hostess once or twice for me. I shall wish to put on a ball or soiree to mark my advent on society. At the very least I may discover that I enjoy the newly exalted social position to which I have fallen heir."

Wisely Lady Pelborne forbore to point out that it was properly Lady Anthony's place to act as his hostess. There would be another more fortuitous opportunity to do so at a future date. "Perhaps you shall," she said, "but beware that you do not find yourself snapped up as a prime matrimonial prize by one of the simpering misses who grace Almack's these days. Pray choose someone with a little more dash if you can."

"Leg-shackled?" The earl shook his head, smiling. "No, thank you, ma'am. I am a confirmed bachelor. Even if I were interested in finding a bride, the chase holds little appeal for me. You forget that I cut my eyeteeth in London."

"Believe me, dear boy, an earl is of infinitely greater worth in the marriage mart than Captain Michael Anthony, a younger son with few prospects," Lady Pelborne said with worldly cynicism. "There shall be more than one cap set at you this time."

"I have no intentions of settling into dull domesticity so easily," said Lord Anthony.

"Then have you become reconciled to the thought of Sir Rupert Sikes stepping into your shoes?" asked Lady Pelborne silkily, her eyes suddenly faintly taunting.

Her nephew's lips tightened. "My contemptible cousin would reduce the earldom to penury within a year of succeeding to the title, and well you know it. The thought of that loose screw as my heir nauseates me."

"Then pray do not dismiss the possibility of your own nuptials so quickly, my dear," said Lady Pelborne. She smiled at him and continued gently, "You were a youth when this war began and you have returned unscathed, thank God, a man of nine-and-twenty. You are of an age now when you must soon give serious consideration to your duty to marry and set up a nursery."

"Damn, you're right, of course. But I never thought it would fall to me to further the family line." Lord Anthony smiled rather sadly. "It was always the joke between my brother and me that he would father the heirs and I the bastards. I never dreamed Edmond would be killed at Waterloo, or that I would succeed him. He seemed always to have the devil's own luck on the battlefield, not once being wounded during the entire Spanish campaigns." He shrugged and grimaced at her. "Very well, Aunt, I give you my word that I shall give serious consideration to the choosing of a suitable bride. However, do not press me too hard, I beg you. I mean to enjoy my last months of freedom to the hilt.''

"Certainly, Michael," said Lady Pelborne, giving him her hand as she rose from the chair. Her glance was sly. "Perhaps by solving dear Hetta's plight you shall discover an answer to your own."

Lord Anthony cracked a laugh as he opened the study door and escorted her through. He shook his head, a glint of humor in his eyes. "Doing it too brown, ma'am! I am too experienced in matchmaking ploys to be snared for your goddaughter. Fairytale romances happen only behind the footlights.'' As he spoke, they walked down the hall to the staircase and Lord Anthony lent his arm to his aunt as they started up the stairs.

"You could do worse for yourself," Lady Pelborne said, abandoning subtlety in favor of a frontal assault. "Do but consider the convenience if you were to ask for Hetta. She is of good family and is unspoiled by the demands of society. Moreover, her portion, though not huge, is nonetheless handsome. It seems to me that your gallant role tonight has placed you in a suitably romantic light that would appeal strongly to any young female. I would not be astonished if she were not already half in love with you.'' She caught the derisive gleam in his green eyes, and sighed. "It would make too convenient a solution, would it not? I suppose that I shall simply have to make the best of things. I do detest the role of guardian! Believe me, nothing is more boring than rubbing elbows with jealous hatchet-faced mamas who are presenting their newest crop of simpering, dim-witted daughters. I shall be so short of temper that there will be no living with me.''

They had reached the landing outside Lady Pelborne's door. Lord Anthony turned to his aunt and raised her hand to his lips in affectionate salute. His eyes held humorous understanding. "You shall manage splendidly, ma'am. I have never known you to refuse a challenge or fail to overcome it.''

She gave his fingers a brief squeeze and laughed, pleased at the compliment. "You've a honeyed tongue, my boy. Take yourself off to bed before I give you the set-down you so richly deserve. You have the same rooms you have always had, of course. I doubt not that you shall be gone before I rise, so I shall wish you a fair journey now."

"Good night, dear lady. I will endeavor to return with all possible speed." He bowed to her and, with a wave, went on down the long hall.

Smiling, Lady Pelborne shook her head and proceeded into her room, where she knew her dresser would be patiently waiting up for her.

4

From her bed, Miss Hetta Stanton heard her godmother's throaty laugh and then the quick masculine footsteps that passed her closed bedroom door. Warmth flushed her face. The muffled closing of two bedroom doors hardly registered with her. She stared into the dark, her thoughts in a turmoil.

Despite her real fatigue, Hetta had lain awake for the better part of an hour after Maggie had snuffed out the candle and left her comfortably settled for the night. It had shocked her to learn that Lord Anthony was her godmother's nephew, whom she had always heard referred to as Michael. If she had stayed with them any longer in the study she feared that the Earl of Davenchester's baiting would have led her to betray more than she already had. Her godmother's powers of observation were acute. Lady Pelborne would have soon become aware of undercurrents and would probably have demanded an explanation. Hetta did not think she could have borne such probing. Her deepest feelings were torn and quivering. If only Lord Anthony were not her godmother's nephew!

"Michael." Softly Hetta tested the beloved name as she had so often done in the past. She had been a child when Lady Pelborne had first spoken of her best-loved nephew. Her subsequent glowing accounts of Michael's exploits, the winning of his captaincy, and his gallantry on the field of battle had been encouraged with time and the awed interest of her young goddaughter. Hetta could not remember when she fell in love with Michael, but her romantic

dreams had long been woven around his shadowy figure.
He was always the gallant hero who swept her off her feet
and placed her safe before him in the saddle. In those
dreams he inevitably vowed his everlasting love for her as
their lips met in a sacred kiss of burning promise.

Hetta turned restlessly on the down pillow. Her beloved
Michael and the Earl of Davenchester were the same man.
Lord Anthony had naturally acted properly in coming to
her rescue. That was to be expected of a gentleman as
gallant as the hero she had come to admire through Lady
Pelborne's tales. But she had always pictured Michael as
fair, his ways gentle and respectful, whereas Lord Anthony was dark-haired and possessed a set of green eyes
that seemed to burn her with derision. He was certainly
virile and could even be called handsome, but Hetta thought
he was leaner and harder than any romantic figure had a
right to be.

Hetta frowned, remembering the aloof amusement in
Lord Anthony's eyes when they had rested upon her. She
bit her lip. He had appeared to dismiss her as a figure of
fun. And though Hetta was charitable enough to admit that
she had been unusually tongue-tied and gauche upon learning his identity, she nonetheless felt humiliation at his
indifferent behavior.

She found it impossible to reconcile the imperturbable
Lord Anthony with the compassionate, vibrantly alive man
of her godmother's stories. Lord Anthony had been unfail-
ingly polite and considerate when she required assistance,
but only once, when he first greeted Lady Pelborne, had
she seen his urbane manner warm. For herself, he had
reserved a subtle provocative manner that Hetta found
maddening, and the more so since she could not retaliate
as she would like. He definitely seemed to lack the sensitive and life-loving nature Lady Pelborne had claimed for
her nephew.

With deliberation Hetta smoothed a wrinkle in the cov-
erlet. She was beginning to realize how great a fool she
was to have expected so much from this visit to London.
The man who had stolen her heart was actually a figment
of her own imagination. Her beloved Michael did not

exist. Tears filled her eyes. Angrily she dashed them away. Suffering regret for a shattered dream served no purpose. Romantic fancies were for schoolgirls, not for a young woman of nearly one-and-twenty, and should have been put aside long ago. But despite the logic of her conclusion, her tears persisted in spilling over.

Hetta threw back the bedclothes and reached for her wrapper. Earlier she had noticed a bookcase in the study. Perhaps if she found a dull novel it would act as a sleeping potion. She belted the robe tightly around her small waist and lighted the candle on her bedside table. Shielding the flame with her palm, she cautiously eased open the door, hardly daring to breathe when it softly creaked, but the hall remained quiet. She sped swiftly down the hall, her bare feet soundless on the carpet.

On the stairs she moved more cautiously, feeling her way down. Suddenly a stair creaked loud underfoot. She froze, her heart pounding. Straining her ears, she could detect nothing out of the ordinary disturbing the silent dark. It struck her that she was reacting much as a house-breaker must, and on a breathless laugh she continued her descent. She traversed the deserted front hall, her steps quick and short on the icy marble tiles, and entered the darkened study.

Hetta glanced over to the wall on which she remembered the bookcase. Moonlight filtered through a part in the drawn draperies over the window so that even without the aid of her candle she would have had no difficulty in making out the placement of the furniture. Hetta set her flickering candle on a library table, In the uncertain light she struggled to decipher the titles of the books on the shelves and recognized the latest title by Mrs. Radcliffe. She smiled to herself. Her godmother's taste in literature would naturally include popular authors. Hetta pulled free one of the more slender volumes and straightened, half-turning to pick up her candle.

Out of the corner of her eye she saw the figure of a man in shirt and breeches watching her from the shadows. The novel slipped from her nerveless fingers to the carpet and her throat tightened. The man moved swiftly. A hard palm clamped over her mouth, stifling the scream that rose in her throat. He yanked her back against him, pinning her against his chest with his arms. Hetta twisted, fighting to be free. His hand shifted slightly and she sank her teeth into his thumb, drawing the salt of blood.

His hand jerked and he swore sharply under his breath. "Be still, vixen, or you will have the house down around our ears! Do you wish to be found under such compromising circumstances?"

Through her terror Hetta dimly recognized the furious voice as Lord Anthony's. She sagged against him, shuddering in relief. Her pulse raced madly, and wide-eyed, she stared up into his shadowed face.

Slowly he took his palm from her bruised mouth. "It was not my intention to frigthen you, Miss Stanton," he said softly. "Please accept my humble apologies."

Hetta moistened her lips and nodded jerkily. She brought her hands up flat against his chest. His arms loosened but did not fall from around her. She was acutely aware of the rapid rise and fall of her breasts pressing against his shirtfront. "Please let—let me go, my lord," she whispered breathlessly.

Lord Anthony's quick ear caught the nervous quality in her voice. A fleeting smile crossed his face. Obviously Lady Hetta had recovered sufficiently from her fright to be aware of her compromising position. He himself rather enjoyed the sensation of her soft curves in his arms and was reluctant to release her so quickly. It occurred to him that it was the perfect opportunity to teach Miss Stanton her first lesson in propriety. His voice was ruminative. "I seem to recall an instance earlier today when you were not unhappy to be in my arms."

Hetta's cheeks flamed. Thankful for the concealing darkness, she choked, "It is infamous of you to remark on it, sir."

"So it is, but then I am known to be shameless," he said softly. His hand lightly caressed the slender curve of her back, and warm shivers went up her spine.

"Pray let me go," she implored desperately, very much afraid that the strange weakening of her bones would communicate itself to him. Her mind was in an odd state of confusion. Her only coherent thought was that this was not her beloved Michael, and she clung to it.

"You are trembling. Do you think that you are capable of standing without my support?" His voice held a trace of amusement. "I am not unwilling to prolong my assistance."

She stiffened and made an attempt to pull free of him again. His unyielding arms tightened, drawing her closer until she could no longer ignore the flattening of her breasts against the lean tautness of his broad chest. With a half-sob Hetta pounded him with an impotent fist. His point having been made, the earl freed her with a slow deliberation that made her cheeks burn.

She backed away a few steps, folding her arms around herself. She was unaware that a shaft of moonlight caught her. Spun silver tangled in her hair and cast mystery into her dark eyes; slivers clung to breast and thigh in a way that made the man watching her pull in his breath sharply.

"What—what are you doing here, Lord Anthony?" Her voice was a whisper of sound, reinforcing the ethereal aura bathing her slight figure.

It was a moment before he found his voice. "My soldiering days have left me with a habit of sleeping lightly, so when I woke, thinking that I had heard a sound in my sleep, I left my room to investigate." His teeth glimmered briefly. "I saw candlelight in here and naturally I followed it with the intention of surprising the intruder. Imagine my amazement when instead I discovered a beguiling wraith cloaked in moonlight." He had moved toward her and now reached out a hand to touch a silken strand of the long hair that flowed over her breast. Hetta stood frozen, hardly daring to breathe, her widened eyes on his shadowed face. His fingers played with her hair, once brushing the point of her breast. "And what of you, ma'am? How came you to the study?"

The prosaic question startled her from her seeming paralysis. "I—I could not sleep. I thought perhaps if I read for a short time . . ." She stopped, wondering at her feeling of breathlessness. He unnerved her in a way she could not understand. Instinctively she sought to retreat.

"It is late. Pray excuse me, my lord," she said. She made to go around him to retrieve her candle.

Lord Anthony's fingers tangled in her hair, sliding around to warmly cup her nape. His thumb gently massaged the racing pulse in the side of her neck. Hetta's breath caught, and without thinking she raised her hands to ward him off. Laughing softly, triumphantly, he folded her hands together in his larger hand and pulled on her wrists to draw her up to his chest, effectively trapping her. Hetta stared up into his lean face so close to hers, trembling with mingled fear and a flutter of strange excitement in her stomach. His eyes gleamed at her. "I believe you owe me payment for the injury to my thumb, fair vixen," he said, his breath warm on her upturned face. Slowly he lowered his head. His questing lips found hers, soft and warm, and he took rough possession. He moved his mouth hard on hers, demandingly. Hesitantly her lips parted in sweet response.

His fingers tightened crushingly on her wrists, then fell away, and his arm slid around her slender frame. His other hand bit cruelly into her back, molding her against his hard length. Spreading his fingers wide, he slowly traced the curve of her spine through her thin wrapper to the flare of her hips. With expertise he molded her to the swell of his taut thighs.

His touch was burning and powerful in its sensuality. Hetta swayed into him. A slow-stirring fire awakened in her racing blood, a melting in her limbs. Her hands slipped over his shoulders of their own accord. His mouth gentled, drawing her into a deepening response. Her senses reeled. Then she was clinging to him as though drowning.

She never knew how long it was before Lord Anthony suddenly raised his head and released her, his breath coming quickly. Hetta staggered, and if she had not caught herself with one hand on the library table, she would have fallen. She steadied herself against it with a pounding heart. Numbly she stared at him, incapable of coherent thought. As though in a trance she watched him bend down to retrieve from the carpet the novel that she had long since forgotten.

After noting the title with raised brows, Lord Anthony held it out to her. "Pleasant dreams, my sweet lady." Her heightened senses discovered a thread of mockery in his voice and she recoiled from it, throwing up her hand in a pathetic gesture of defense. Lord Anthony was startled by the wounded look reflected in her wide dark eyes. With a muttered exclamation he stepped quickly toward her, his hand held out. With a low cry Hetta whirled away from him and fled from the study. "Hetta!" She did not check at his soft urgent call, but flew up the dark stairs as though hounded by her blackest dreams.

Lord Anthony stood where she had left him. He had seen fear and bewilderment often enough on the battleground to recognize it in Miss Stanton's face. He felt disgust for himself. He had kissed her purely on the impulse of the moment. He had not meant it to go further, and it would not have if it had not been for her reaction. She had surrendered to him with a passionate innocence that was different from any other woman he had ever known.

He swore softly, wondering how he was to make his apologies. A public apology would fatally compromise Miss Stanton's reputation. The servants would be certain to gossip outside the household and then even his aunt's influence would not be able to save her goddaughter from disgrace once the tale was around London. His eyes fell on the novel in his hand and his lips tightened in decision. When he left the study, he carried the novel with him.

5

Hetta woke and blinked sleepily at the bright morning light slanting warm across her bed. A housemaid was just pulling back the curtains and she smiled shyly at Hetta before quietly leaving the bedroom. Hetta stretched her arms over her head and then lay back again on the pillow. She felt surprisingly well-rested despite the rigors of the day before and an indifferent night's sleep. Some of her lazy contentment abruptly faded. The awkward problem represented by her cousin and the violence associated with her journey seemed to pale to insignificance beside what had passed between her and Lord Anthony in her godmother's study.

She touched tentative fingers to her tender lips and wondered that they were not branded. She could still feel the bruising sensation of the earl's hard mouth. Despite herself, she vividly remembered the caressing warmth of his hands through her thin wrapper, molding her to the contours of his hard body.

The thought left her trembling. Mortified, Hetta sat up and pressed her palms against her burning cheeks. Even now she did not feel terror or disgust, but rather a fluttering of fearful anticipation that was at once pleasure and pain. Her behavior had been totally abandoned. She had not protested; instead her body had seemed to welcome Lord Anthony's expert lovemaking. Drawing up her knees and wrapping her arms around them, Hetta closed her eyes against the memory of her own response. She had clung to him without shame, as though he had been no stranger but her lover.

When she had fled from him to the safety of her bedroom, she had swiftly locked the door and fallen against it weak and trembling. She had feared pursuit and strained her ears for any sound. She had not known what to expect of a man like the Earl of Davenchester. Would he dare to scratch at her door for entry? The thought had brought her hand to her throat. But she had heard only the soft closing of a door down the hall and she knew that Lord Anthony had passed silently by in his stockinged feet to resume his interrupted slumber. Inexpressibly weary, Hetta had turned away from the door and crossed the room to her own bed. The sheets had been icy when she slid between them. Shivering, she had pulled the bedclothes close under her chin. She had closed her eyes, but her thoughts had refused to allow her to sleep.

For a wild instant she had thought herself in Michael's arms and had responded with ardent passion to his lovemaking. Lord Anthony's words had been like a douse of cold water, sobering her instantly to what she had done. She felt that she could easily hate him for being the cause of her self-betrayal. It had left her innermost yearnings completely naked and vulnerable. She had stared long into the dark, her thoughts confused and painful, until gray exhaustion claimed her.

The bright morning did not bring her any closer to an understanding of herself than she had possessed a few hours before. Hetta still found it incredible that she had responded to a stranger's lovemaking. She had cause to feel gratitude to this man, but only that. Yet the hunger of his kiss had stirred her senses in a way she had never before known. Hetta could not make sense out of it, but instinctively she recognized the danger. The thought of it happening again, and her possible reaction, made her shudder; but whether from fear or anticipation she could not tell.

The connecting door between her room and Maggie's opened and the Scotswoman bustled in. "Well, miss, ye have at last decided to leave off your dreaming." Her

mistress started violently at the sound of her voice and
Maggie slanted a bright glance at her as she crossed to the
wardrobe. "It is nae cold enough to have ye shivering.
Have ye a bad conscience, then?"

"It—it was nothing, only the remnants of a dream,"
stammered Hetta, a faint blush rising to her face.

"Oh, aye, that journey was such as to trouble the
dreams of the hardiest soul. I myself had a fitful night of
it," Maggie said.

"What o'clock is it?" asked Hetta. She wondered if
Maggie had heard anything unusual in the night, but she
did not dare to inquire.

"Late enough that Lady Pelborne has been waiting on
ye for this half-hour or more in the breakfast parlor," said
Maggie blandly, taking from the wardrobe a blue muslin
frock with long sleeves whose cuffs buttoned tightly at the
wrists.

Hetta threw back the bedclothes and slid out of bed.
"Why did you not wake me sooner, Maggie? Help me
dress at once!"

"Aye, miss."

The maid's voice was unusually meek and Hetta looked
at her with suspicion. There was a familiar gleam of
anticipation in Maggie's eyes so Hetta did not comment on
the maid's unnatural display of respect. Maggie's disappointment was palpable. She grumbled incessantly under
her breath as she dressed her mistress, but Hetta stead-
fastly ignored her.

Within a very short time Hetta was making her way
downstairs. It was not until she was halfway down that she
remembered the Earl of Davenchester. Her step faltered. It
was probable that he, too, would be breakfasting with
Lady Pelborne. As though her thoughts had conjured him
up, Lord Anthony appeared below her in the hall. He was
attired in a sober coat of military cut, over which was
carelessly thrown a caped greatcoat that set off the breadth
of his shoulders, and buff pantaloons smoothed smartly
into a gleaming pair of top boots. He was engaged in
drawing on a pair of doeskin driving gloves and did not
immediately perceive her.

Rooted to the stair, Hetta wondered rather wildly how she was to face him after having made such a complete fool of herself in the study. Assuredly the earl would have formed a hard opinion of her character, for naively she felt that she had behaved no less wantonly than a tawdry opera dancer.

Suddenly Lord Anthony looked up as though he had felt her dismayed regard. His smile was disarming. "Good morning, Miss Stanton. I trust that you passed a tolerable night?"

His gentle barb struck home. Stung out of her cowardice, Hetta forgot her dread and stared down at him with an air of defiance. The man was insufferable. She had naturally earned his scorn, but it could hardly be any greater than the feelings of revulsion she harbored for him. He was far more to blame for that shameful episode than she. In any event, his opinion of her could hardly be thought to matter to her, for she positively detested him. She recalled that the earl was soon to be leaving London. Perhaps she would meet him but a few times more, a situation that could not but please her. On that worthy thought, Hetta summoned up a stiff smile and returned his cordial greeting with restraint. "Good morning, my lord." With her head held high she resumed her descent.

The earl watched her progress with a glint in his eye. He had been amused by the fleeting play of emotions across her expressive face, and now he had no difficulty in deciphering her cold nod as she passed him. He flexed his fingers, smoothing the soft leather of his gloves. "It was kind of you to see me off, ma'am," he drawled lazily.

Hetta's eyes were drawn to his hands, and it dawned on her that Lord Anthony was dressed for travel in beaver and caped greatcoat. Her startled eyes flew to his imperturbable face. "You take your leave suddenly, my lord. I had quite understood that you meant to stay a few days to visit with Lady Pelborne before leaving London."

"My plans have of necessity been changed. Lady Pelborne shall undoubtedly offer an explanation if one were to express curiosity," said Lord Anthony with a faint smile.

Hetta opened wide her eyes and said sweetly, "Why

should I? I do not deem the reason for your departure worthy of any but the most cursory notice. We barely know each other, after all, and it is unlikely that we shall further our acquaintance to any degree.''

"As you say," said the earl gravely, only a twitch of his lips indicating that he acknowledged her hidden message. "I have this moment come from taking leave of my aunt; you will find her in the breakfast parlor. I wish you a most pleasant stay in London, Miss Stanton." He sketched her a short bow before he turned and strode toward the front door. He paused on the threshold to glance back at Hetta with an amiable nod.

Hetta did not wait to watch him bound lightly down the steps, but turned on her heel and entered the breakfast parlor. Lady Pelborne sat alone at the table. Her cup and saucer had been pushed to one side and she was busily scratching a list on a long sheet of paper. Hetta noted with a quick glance that there was only one other place set. "Good morning, Godmamma," she said cheerfully, dropping a kiss on her godmother's lined cheek.

Lady Pelborne returned her salutation fondly but with an abstracted air. She informed Hetta that their first visit of the morning would be paid to a modiste. "For your wardrobe is sadly outmoded, my dear. We shall need to order a number of gowns before you may be said to be decently attired for the Season. I wonder that Cheton did not write me sooner, but naturally the importance of a young lady's wardrobe never once entered his methodical mind," said Lady Pelborne, who was beautifully attired in a new morning frock and frilled mob cap. She critically eyed her goddaughter, who had seated herself across the table and was in the process of pouring a cup of steaming tea. "You've a dainty figure and good regular features. One could wish that your mouth were not so generous, but your nose is wonderfully short and straight, which makes up for a great deal. Indeed, your countenance is quite pleasing to the eye. With a little effort I believe you may pass off very well."

Hetta laughed, shaking her head. "Now I know how a filly up for auction must feel." Following her thoughts aloud, she continued, "My estimable cousin would be amazed to hear such a favorable assessment."

Lady Pelborne stared at her, her pen poised in midair. "Do you mean to tell me that Markham has had the audacity to criticize your appearance? That is outrageous!"

Hetta was regretting her unruly tongue. She said reluctantly, "Jonathan is quite set in his expectations and thus far I have fallen far short of fulfilling them in any way." The topic of her cousin was distasteful to her because it reminded her of the unpleasant situation he had created for her at Meldingcourt. She felt that to discuss it at all made her appear a self-pitying creature, an image she abhorred, but at the same time an explanation was certainly owed her godmother above what she had learned from Cheton. She looked over at Lady Pelborne with frank eyes. "I know that you must suspect me to be an abominable flirt for my cousin to have attached himself so thoroughly to me. But pray believe me, I have not once encouraged the Honorable Jonathan Markham in his obstinate pursuit. On the contrary! I have done all in my power to dishearten him, yet he continues to insist that we are to be wed. I am at a loss to understand his insistence, for I am certain he bears no particular liking for me, while I have made it quite plain that I do not care for him."

Lady Pelborne was frowning, but she patted Hetta's hand comfortingly. "Cheton wrote me the particulars, my dear. You need not enlarge upon that. I must confess, Markham's motives puzzle me as well. However, in my opinion, your dear father protected you too well from the wolves of our society. One has now descended upon your doorstep and you do not know how to oust him. Truthfully it is a wonder to me that you have been able to withstand the man at all. But I suppose that is the inborn obstinacy that you inherited from both of your progenitors."

Hetta smiled at her godmother over the rim of her teacup. "In short, I have little sense of fashion and even less of the ways of society, and am too willful to ever learn. You must think me a veritable country bumpkin."

"Certainly not a bumpkin, child. Merely a walking anecdote," said Lady Pelborne promptly.

Hetta made a wry face. "Thank you, ma'am. I may at least prove to be an *entertaining* anecdote!"

Lady Pelborne chortled, delighted by her quick humor. "I shall enjoy bringing you out much more than I once thought possible, Hetta. You have a charming wit that captivates one, and I anticipate that you shall set a few tongues wagging, but that should not overly concern you. Indeed, I recall now that Michael commented you were steady under fire. It is a quality that will stand you in good stead in the coming months."

Hetta felt her face grow warm. She concentrated on spreading marmalade on a piece of toast. With a casualness she was far from feeling, she said, "Whenever did Lord Anthony make such a nonsensical statement?"

"After you had gone up to bed, he and I spoke awhile of your misadventure. He quite admired your presence of mind." Lady Pelborne noted with interest her goddaughter's averted eyes and heightened color. Raising her cup of tea to her lips, she said as if in afterthought, "I shall enjoy having Michael with us in town this Season."

Hetta's head came up, her expression startled. "But surely I understood that Lord Anthony did not mean to stay in London?"

Lady Pelborne dismissed her nephew's character with a wave of her hand. "He has always been the most whimsical of creatures. It quite tries one's patience, I assure you. He took it into his head only last night and has posted down to his estates already this morning to attend to his most pressing affairs so he will be left free for the Season. I am sure I do not know how he expects to have his town house readied for him when he means to return in only a fortnight."

The unexpected news left Hetta speechless. She had successfully steeled herself through the awkward first meeting with the unrepentant earl, but only because of her anger. Once he had informed her of his imminent departure, she had thought her defenses to be unnecessary and had thrown down the gauntlet to him. She feared that she would not be so well prepared when next they met, as they

must during the Season's social whirl, for she had the most
lowering feeling that he meant to take up her challenge.

"Pray, where have you gone, my dear? I do not believe
you have attended to a single syllable I have said." Lady
Pelborne allowed a touch of exasperation to color her
voice. She had seen her goddaughter's unguarded surprise
and dismay over the earl's plans and shrewdly she played
to it. "Can you not at least make a show of interest? I had
thought you possessed of more wit than that."

"I am sorry, Godmamma," stammered Hetta, taken
aback by her godmother's unusually baleful glare.

"One must naturally forgive you," said Lady Pelborne
with a magnanimous air. She picked up a leather-bound
volume beside her elbow that Hetta had not noticed before.
Without breaking stride, she said, "By the by, Anthony
requested that I give this novel to you. I am sure I do not
know why, for as I recall it was a rather disappointing tale.
One always knew what was to happen next. I would not
have thought it in Anthony's style at all, but perhaps you
will understand his reason for choosing it for you." As
Lady Pelborne handed the novel across the table to her
goddaughter she observed with surprise twin flags of deepening color in Hetta's face. She wondered what could
possibly have passed between the two to warrant Hetta's
hot blush, but dismissed her suspicions. It could be no
more than romantic imagination at work, and it was no
wonder. Anthony must appear a knight-errant to the girl
after her rescue.

Lady Pelborne was satisfied that she had discovered the
cause of the tense chemistry she had noticed the night
before between her goddaughter and nephew. The unguarded vulnerability in Hetta's clear hazel eyes betrayed
her to the world. Lady Pelborne frowned. It would not do.
The chit must learn to disguise her feelings or have the
heart torn out of her by the gossips. As for Michael
himself, it would be disastrous if he were ever to see that
expression directed at him. She thought he might have
already suspected that Hetta was enamored of him. It
would explain his teasing behavior toward her, as though
she were his younger sister. But that look of hers would

only confirm his suspicions. Reflecting upon her nephew's
probable course of action, Lady Pelborne's frown deepened.

Hetta had accepted the novel with the utmost reluctance.
With an almost morbid curiosity, she opened the book. On
the flyleaf an arrogant hand had inscribed the words, "My
apologies." The bold scrawl fairly leapt from the page at
her. She knew it intuitively to be Lord Anthony's hand.
Hetta laid the novel aside on the table as though its leather
cover scorched her fingers. She misread Lady Pelborne's
serious expression and with a sinking sensation braced
herself for the inevitable questions concerning herself and
Lord Anthony. Though her mind darted quickly back and
forth, she could not devise a plausible explanation for the
earl's extraordinary gesture in leaving her a tale of romance. Certainly it had been the stroke of a devil to
remind her even in his absence of their clandestine meeting. Hetta felt herself go hot, then cold, at the thought of
trying to explain what had happened. It had been positively fiendish to place her in a position where she must
either satisfy Lady Pelborne's curiosity with the shocking
truth and more than likely be sent straight back to
Meldingcourt in disgrace, or spin a patent falsehood. She
wished heartily at that moment that there were some way
in which she could roundly repay Lord Anthony for the
mortification he had caused her. Wistfully Hetta wondered
if she possibly could confide in her godmother, who was,
after all, a woman of the world. But she knew it to be
impossible. She could not bring herself to tarnish Lady
Pelborne's cherished image of her favorite nephew, the
Earl of Davenchester. Unconsciously she sighed, her
thoughts gloomy. Lord Anthony was too near the lady's
fond heart.

Lady Pelborne started and came out of her reverie to
find her goddaughter eyeing her with an odd expression.
She realized immediately that she had been silent too long
with her own uneasy thoughts. Hastily she said the first
thing that came to mind. "I am concerned that you may
have suffered injury due to that regrettable holdup, Hetta.
Anthony mentioned concussion. It may be wise to have a
physician in to look at you."

Hetta could not help laughing, dizzily relieved by the turn of the conversation. "Really, dear ma'am, there is no need. I am much more the thing this morning, I promise you."

"Regardless of how you may feel, child, I am persuaded a visit from my own physician, who is a particularly dear old friend, is in order," said Lady Pelborne, warming to her unpremeditated notion. She wondered that she had not considered it before, and felt a twinge of guilt. "Concussions can sneak up on one all unawares, you know. I shall rest easier knowing that you will not faint or some such thing just as you are trying gloves."

"But truly, Godmamma—"

Lady Pelborne interrupted her by raising an imperious hand. "I must insist, Hetta. You appear unusually drawn and pale this morning and I wish to satisfy myself that it is not due to any ill effects."

Hetta was silenced, well aware that her wan complexion owed more to lack of rest due to a certain gentleman's disturbing influence, but she could not very well explain that to her godmother.

Lady Pelborne sensed Hetta's hesitation and pressed her advantage. "Now, do pray be a sensible chit. Practicing medicine is why I pay the rascal such exorbitant fees, after all. And not another word against it, or I shall ask him to prescribe the most vile draft to settle your nerves."

Hetta looked upon her with mingled outrage and amusement. She had forgotten her godmoher's high-handed manner. With laughter plain in her eyes, she capitulated but added, "Really, Godmamma, must you resort to blackmail? It is too bad of you."

"So it is," said Lady Pelborne affably. She apparently considered the subject closed, for she bent her head once more to the composition of her list.

Hetta eyed her with fond exasperation. Her gaze fell on Lady Pelborne's list of activities, and for the first time its growing length impressed itself upon her. She suspected that if she were to survive the day's outing it would be prudent to fortify herself with an unusually large breakfast, so she turned her attention to a platter of kidneys and eggs and served herself a liberal helping.

The companionable silence that fell between the ladies was broken only by desultory remarks, particularly those of Lady Pelborne, who bethought herself of several items she had planned for Hetta. "And I had almost forgotten to tell you, Hetta. We shall in all probability have Michael's widowed sister-in-law staying with us," said Lady Pelborne. "Lady Anthony's usual custom is to put up at the town house during the Season, but since Michael now intends it for his own use, Loraine must naturally make other arrangements. I sent around a missive earlier this morning to inform her of Michael's arrival and to invite her to come stay with us. Shall you mind a stranger here with us, Hetta?"

"Of course not," exclaimed Hetta warmly. "Quite the contrary, for I shall be delighted to make Lady Anthony's acquaintance. I do not know anyone in London and I should feel easier at my come-out if there were to be one or two familiar faces among the company."

"I had hoped you would say that," Lady Pelborne said. "Loraine has scarcely turned nineteen and may prove a welcome companion to you since she is so much closer your age than myself."

"I have always considered you to be ageless, ma'am," Hetta said, smiling fondly at her godmother.

"Dear child! I realize now why I am so inordinately fond of you," said Lady Pelborne with a laugh. "I shall count myself royally entertained with two young ladies to keep me company. Loraine cannot help but make one laugh, flitting here and flitting there as though she were an ornamental butterfly. She has a flair for enjoying all that is offered her in a manner that makes one feel generous. Needless to say, Loraine has become much petted and cosseted by the *ton*, and especially by the gentlemen. She is frightfully spoiled, but however exasperating her ways can be on occasion, I can honestly think of but one person who holds her in active dislike, and that I believe to be mere prejudice."

"When may we expect Lady Anthony to arrive?" Hetta

asked, thoroughly intrigued by her godmother's eloquent description of the lady.

"I haven't the faintest notion. I expect that we shall have had some word by the time we have returned from our shopping expedition," said Lady Pelborne with complete unconcern. "Unless we chance to meet Loraine at one of the shops, of course. She enjoys nothing so much as a new gown or a dinner party."

"But surely Lady Anthony will have had your note by now," said Hetta, somewhat surprised. "Should we not wait until we hear from her before we depart?"

"Certainly not. She will not have risen yet," Lady Pelborne said absently as she looked over her list once more.

Hetta glanced at the clock on the side table. "But it is already half-past ten of the clock. Surely she is not still abed."

Lady Pelborne glanced up at her goddaughter, snorting in derision. "My dear, Loraine rarely rises before noon and never before she has had her chocolate."

6

Scarcely had these words left Lady Pelborne's lips when
the door was flung open and a vision of loveliness stood
dramatically poised on the threshold. Her pale-mauve pelisse was strikingly trimmed in black ribbons and frog
closures, its cut closely outlining a well-rounded figure.
Perched upon her ash-blond curls was a ravishing high-
crowned hat, set off by a trio of black plumes gently
curling over the narrow brim, which immediately kindled
Hetta's envious admiration. The young woman clutched a
dainty handkerchief worked in lace to her heaving bosom,
and when her brilliant blue eyes fastened on Lady Pelborne,
she exclaimed, "Oh, Aunt Beatrice, I have been in such
terror. You do not know . . ." To Hetta's horified amazement the visitor flung herself into the older woman's arms
and promptly burst into tears.

The butler had come to the open door and hovered
there, obviously shaken by the visitor's manner of entrance. Lady Pelborne addressed him calmly over the quivering crown of the fashionable hat buried in her lap.
"Erwin, pray see that the east rooms are made ready for
Lady Anthony. She is obviously come somewhat earlier
than one had anticipated. You will know what to do with
her baggage when it arrives."

The butler glanced over his shoulder and said woodenly,
"It has arrived, my lady, and is swiftly filling the front
hall."

Lady Pelborne raised her brows in surprise. "Lady Anthony was quite taken with my invitation, then. My trust in

your capabilities remains unshaken, Erwin." He bowed in acknowledgment and was preparing to close the door when his mistress stopped him with a soft word. "Pray see that we are not disturbed." They exchanged a look that spoke volumes.

"Very good, my lady," said Erwin. He closed the door smoothly.

Lady Pelborne caught Hetta's expression of frozen astonishment, and she rolled her eyes heavenward, shrugging. Hetta wondered that she could react so calmly with Lady Anthony's heartrending sobs in her ears. Lady Pelborne disengaged herself from Lady Anthony's clinging hands and addressed her in a voice of the greatest indifference. "Pray do me the favor of drying your eyes, Loraine. I have never found swollen, blotched faces to be particularly attractive."

Hetta was taken aback by her godmother's callousness, but her instinctive gesture of protest was stilled when Lady Anthony at once straightened and with a small shriek ran to the glass hung above the side table. Standing on tiptoe, she anxiously studied herself and dabbed daintily at her eyes with the tiny scrap of linen and lace in her hand. Hetta glanced at her godmother, who winked at her audaciously. She realized that Lady Anthony's emotional outburst must not be an unusual occurrence.

Lady Anthony turned away from the mirror, clasping her hands together at her breast. "Is it so obvious, Aunt?" Her anxious eyes were surrounded by lashes of ridiculous length and appeared enormous in a delicate heartshaped face that bore not a trace of the ravages of her weeping. If anything, Hetta thought with a twinge of rueful envy, the young Countess of Davenchester gave all the appearance of a lovely flower after a gentle spring misting.

"It will have to do, Loraine," said Lady Pelborne gravely, a smile lurking in her eyes. "Hetta, you have doubtless gathered that this nonsensical little creature is my niece-in-law, Lady Loraine Anthony. Loraine, allow me to present to you Miss Hetta Stanton, who is my goddaughter. She will be staying with me for her comeout."

"I am most happy to make your acquantance, Lady

Anthony," said Hetta in a friendly manner. "I had heard
so much about you from Lady Pelborne that it made me
eager to meet you."

Lady Anthony's face lighted with a shining smile. "I
am honored, Miss Stanton, and so glad that you are staying
here. Aunt Beatrice positively dotes on you. I know that
we shall soon be fast friends. Do you play faro?" While
she spoke, she drew off her kid gloves and seated herself
at the table across from Hetta.

Hetta shook her head. "I am afraid that I am a rather
indifferent cardplayer. My father used to say that I had
absolutely no card sense."

Lady Anthony clapped her hands, exclaiming in delight.
"Oh, famous! We must play together, for I am forever
losing also, you know. It was such a trial to poor Edmond,
but he did not wish me to give up any of my little
pleasures, ever. He would not have liked me in black
ribbons, but there! One feels it only proper to make a show
of respect for everyone to comment upon. Do you not find
tradition to be stuffy and rather tiresome?"

Hetta was at a loss as to how to respond to Lady
Anthony's artless banter and glanced swiftly across the
table to her godmother for a clue. But Lady Pelborne, who
had leaned back in her chair to leave the younger women
to their conversation, merely lifted her hand to cover a
bored yawn. Her eyes gleamed with sudden amusement at
Hetta's helpless expression and she took pity on her. "Will
you not join us for breakfast, Loraine?"

"Breakfast!" Lady Anthony shuddered delicately. "You
must know that I never take it, Aunt Beatrice. Why, I
should be as wide as a coach if I were to touch as much as
a slice of toast in the morning."

Hetta could not help glancing down at her empty plate.
She could well imagine Lady Anthony's horrified reaction
to the repast of eggs and kidneys she had so thoroughly
enjoyed but moments before. She met her godmother's
gaze with laughter on her face.

"How truly thoughtless of me," murmured Lady
Pelborne, a quiver in her voice.

The butler chose that moment to enter the breakfast

parlor with a tray upon which was a service of fresh tea. He set it down on the table beside Lady Pelborne. Lady Anthony gave him a dazzling smile. "Poor Erwin! He did not know what to do with me. I quite thought he meant to cast me out, but of course, dear, dear Erwin would not serve me such a turn."

"Indeed not, my lady," said the butler, relieved by the restoration of her good humor. He allowed the faintest of smiles to flicker over his stern countenance.

"One hopes you are not so chickenhearted with some of my other visitors, Erwin," Lady Pelborne said tartly. The butler's smile broadened; then, almost immediately, he remembered himself and became once again poker-faced. He asked gravely if there would be anything else. Lady Pelborne waved him out, and as the door closed behind him, she said with wicked satisfaction, "One does not often seduce Erwin into displaying a human expression. You may depend upon it, Erwin was merely overwhelmed by the moment. I had not advised him to expect you so soon, Loraine, nor with your worldly possessions in tow."

Lady Anthony was reminded abruptly of her grievances. Her beautiful eyes filled and she clasped her hands together in a renewed display of agitation. "Oh, it is too horrible! I saw how it would be, of course, so immediately I threw together all I possessed and hurried to you. He is a beast and so I shall tell him to his face. Indeed, indeed, I cannot think what I am to do."

Hetta perceived that Lady Anthony's mercurial nature had once more taken a plunge toward the tragic. She turned to the tea service, murmuring, "I will see to the tea, shall I?"

Lady Pelborne sent Hetta a grateful look before addressing her agitated niece with marked resignation. "I apprehend that you are referring to Michael's return to England."

"Yes! So unexpected! I was never more shocked," exclaimed Lady Anthony. "And I am excessively obliged to you for your kind warning, ma'am. I stood quaking in my boots when I read it, for I imagined him to be on my very step."

"Then it was mere vaporishness on your part, my dear,

for I intended no warning, as you call it," said Lady Pelborne. "Michael merely sold his commission and has come home as we have all expected him to these many months."

"But it is so awkward. I was to have my first dinner party this very week, and now everything is to be ruined. But there!" Lady Anthony sniffed and had recourse to her handkerchief. "It is all of a piece. He takes such fiendish delight in my discomfiture."

"I fail to comprehend how you could possibly interpret Michael's return to be deliberate malice on his part. Indeed, one must be forced to conclude that you have taken leave of your senses, Loraine," said Lady Pelborne roundly.

"Oh!" Lady Anthony's rounded chin quivered. "But he has always been detestable to me, you know that he has! He is a bully and a beast and I hate him."

Hetta paused in the act of passing the tea, embarrassed by Lady Anthony's outburst. Surely it was a childish ill humor that provoked her to speak so immoderately about the earl, especially before his aunt. However, the passion in Lady Anthony's declaration was not lost on Hetta, and she shot a glance at her godmother, wondering if there were not some truth in the condemnation of the earl.

Lady Pelborne was visibly pained, but she replied with admirable composure, "I understand perfectly how you must feel, child. You and Michael have ever struck sparks between you, but surely you must realize that there is nothing in it. He can be quite intimidating when he chooses, as even I have occasion to remember." This last was a patent falsehood, for Lady Pelborne hoped she knew her nephew too well to be set back by what she termed his occasional crotchets. She therefore ignored her goddaughter's disbelieving expression, accepted the cup of tea Hetta offered her, and turned back to the onerous task of soothing over Lady Anthony's heightened sensibilities. "Do but consider a moment, Loraine. How could he possibly have known of your dinner party? He has no deliberate intention of complicating your life, of course. Why should he?"

Lady Anthony did not vouchsafe an answer. She sat with lowered eyes, pulling her handkerchief tightly through her slender fingers until Hetta thought it must be quite shredded. Hetta placed a cup of tea before her, but she shook her head quickly. Lady Pelborne sighed and her voice was cajoling. "Come, Loraine. Michael himself approved the notion of your staying with myself and Hetta, rather than see you burdened with the task of seeking out a new address. Surely you can credit him with that much thoughtfulness."

"I shan't be gulled, Aunt Beatrice." Lady Anthony raised eyes brilliant with unshed tears. "It was you who thought of it. *He* would rather by far seen me wander the streets in my chemise."

"Don't be caper-witted," snapped Lady Pelborne. "Michael would never—"

"Oh, one might have known you would defend him and, yes, even excuse him," exclaimed Lady Anthony, jumping to her feet. Her chair overturned. The tears rolled down her cheeks unchecked. "He has always been your favorite and could do no wrong. You were always glad that it was Edmond who was killed at Waterloo and not your precious, beloved Michael."

Hetta gasped, letting her cup clatter in its saucer. Her eyes flew to her godmother's whitening face. Lady Pelborne clutched the arms of her chair, a blaze of anger in her eyes. She leaned forward to deliver a blistering retort. Lady Anthony fell back a pace, frightened by her rage. Then with a sob she whirled and raced to the door. She pulled it open and left it standing wide behind her to the dumbfounded gaze of the footmen in the hall. Lady Pelborne fell back in her chair and covered her eyes with one hand.

Appalled, Hetta sat frozen until she sensed movement at the doorway. She looked up quickly and met the concerned gaze of the butler. They exchanged a long glance of understanding, then he bowed slightly and waited for her, doorknob in hand. Hetta rose from her chair with the intention of leaving her godmother to the privacy she undoubtedly desired to collect herself. As she went around the corner of the table, Lady Pelborne looked up.

The older woman straightened. "How right you are, my

dear. It is past time that we attended to our business," she said in a cool voice, rising with her list in hand.

Hetta stared at her in amazement. There was no sign in Lady Pelborne's face of the distress of a moment before. "But surely you do not still wish—"

Something flickered in Lady Pelborne's eyes but was quickly gone. "Certainly I do. I shall rejoin you in the hall. The landaulet will already have been brought around to the front steps for our shopping expedition. We have dallied long enough. Pray see that you are ready to accompany me in a very few minutes." Lady Pelborne swept out of the breakfast parlor with her head held high, sparing not a glance for the curious servants in the hall.

Hetta hurried after her, sending a questioning look at the butler.

He shook his head and turned into the breakfast room. His eyes fell on the novel at Lady Hetta's place and he picked it up. Undoubtedly she had forgotten the volume in the confusion of the moment. He would have one of the housemaids take it up to Maggie to give to her mistress.

Hetta caught up with her godmother on the stairs. The sudden whirlwind of purpose the older woman exhibited left her speechless. Lady Pelborne seemed unaware of her company as she glanced down with a frown at her list. "Yes, I have put it down. Hetta shall need silk, of course," she murmured.

"What will I need, Godmamma?" asked Hetta gently.

Lady Pelborne glanced around as though surprised to find Hetta beside her. "Some silk chemises, naturally. It has long been my experience that even the finest linen in a lady's undergarments may ruin the lines of a truly exquisite gown."

All thought of the recent scene fled Hetta's mind. Her mouth dropped open in astonishment. "Silk, ma'am! You cannot be serious. Surely it is too outrageously dear."

"My dear Hetta, do not dare to count the cost. It is my pleasure to have you gotten up as a genteel young woman of fortune and breeding," Lady Pelborne said. With a fleeting smile, she added, "However, I must admit that silk in a chemise is a device of my own making. Some would accuse me of borrowing too liberally from the ladies of the theater. But I have a penchant for silk. It is so deliciously wicked against the skin.''

"But silk, ma'am," said Hetta helplessly.

"Believe me, my dear, only silk will do justice to the most stunning of gowns. Anything less will most assuredly prove disastrous to the effect one hopes to achieve," Lady Pelborne said firmly.

Hetta suddenly recalled having seen a London beauty a few years before at one of her more dashing neighbor's weekend parties. The lady had worn a gown so gossamer that Hetta had stared, wondering what the woman could possibly be wearing underneath that would not have ruined the gown's lines. She had overheard with interest the hostess give her opinion that the lady had not an extra stitch to her credit and only the pale blush of her pink stockings showed a proper trace of shame. With the oddest sensation, Hetta now wondered if this was the sort of gown to which Lady Pelborne referred. She could not imagine herself in such attire. "I begin to wonder what I have agreed to," Hetta said slowly. "If I am not on my guard, I may well find myself made over from a quiet country miss to a brazen London smart whom no one, and least of all myself, shall recognize!"

"Fiddle! Despite the new trimmings you shall remain the same warm young woman you have always been." Lady Pelborne paused outside her bedroom door to smile reassuringly at Hetta. "You have my word that we shall not lose Miss Hetta Stanton. One simply wishes to bestow a little polish and widen her horizons a bit. Now, do go and change quickly, child."

Hetta was only partially reassured, but she could not help feeling a slowly burgeoning excitement as she sketched a curtsy and sped to her room. She was hardly in the door before she called impatiently for Maggie, her fingers fumbling with the row of tiny buttons down the back of her gown.

The maid looked around from the open wardrobe whose door had hidden her from view, and tartly recommended that her mistress calm herself. She drew out a dark-gray merino walking dress and shook out its skirts. "Och, ye're in a rare dither over naught. M'lady Pelborne will wait on ye if she must. She'll not fret over ten minutes more when the carriage has waited this half-hour or more while ye dallied over breakfast." She swatted Hetta's hands down and capably finished unfastening the buttons Hetta had found so uncooperative. Still scolding, she slipped off the muslin frock and deftly threw the walking dress over her mistress's head.

Accustomed as she was to Maggie's lectures, Hetta smoothed her hair and bent a deaf ear to the maid's monologue, until she heard Lady Anthony's name. She looked in the mirror at her companion with a renewed interest. "What did you say about Lady Anthony bursting into my room?"

The maid shook her head as she began to button up Hetta's dress. "Aye, I was close to leaping out of my skin when she burst through the door, weeping in such a way that would twist the heart of a stone. She was that wild-eyed, and I couldna say which of us was the more surprised to find the other, for she whirled around in a twinkling and was gone. I didna ken who she was, but I am told it was likely m'lady's niece. She appeared a sensitive creature, and no wonder, if she was widowed but a year ago and her so young! She is laid down now in her darkened room with a migraine and her hartshorn, puir lady."

"Perhaps it is just as well, for I cannot imagine that she and Lady Pelborne will be able to meet each other with civility for some time," said Hetta, taking her bonnet from the maid's hands and adjusting it on her head before the mirror.

Maggie cocked an eyebrow at her. She picked up a pair of kid gloves from the dresser and held them ready for Hetta. "It's that way, is it? The rumors one hears of a terrible argument are true, then?"

"Oh, Maggie, it was truly horrible," exclaimed Hetta, tying the ribbons of her bonnet under her chin in a neat bow. "Lady Anthony flung the most chilling accusations at Lady Pelborne, who then grew chalk-white and positively shook with rage. I have never before seen her in such a state. Indeed, I feared that she would have apoplexy before Lady Anthony fled from the room. I would far rather not have been witness to it, but then, I would not have believed the oddest part of it all.''

''And what may that have been?'' asked Maggie, her eyes snapping with curiosity. She held out the gloves to Hetta.

Hetta took them and began to ease them on. She frowned slightly. ''The oddest part of it was that Lady Pelborne did not then seem the slightest upset. She has insisted upon continuing with our original plans. I cannot imagine how she was able to put it away from her so easily, for she was very much affected.''

Maggie smiled thinly. ''M'lady Pelborne was ever one for the disguising of her true feelings. It was said that in her prime she could command the very tears of the playgoers whenever she wished.''

Hetta's eyes flew to the maid's in the mirror. ''Then it is true that godmamma . . . Cousin Jonathan charged that she was once a common actress, but I had put it down to spite.''

The Scotswoman clicked her tongue in disapproval. ''Common she never was! Oh, aye, a bit headstrong and ever ready for a lark, but traipsing the footboards was all to win a certain gentleman. Erwin was with her then, and though he does not tell all, I have pried loose most of the tale from him these many years.''

Hetta was wide-eyed. ''But whatever happened, Maggie?''

The maid's eyes narrowed in amusement. She said primly, ''It's not for me to be filling your head with ancient history, miss. What ever would m'lady think to discover us with our heads together?''

Suddenly reminded of her godmother's strictures not to keep her waiting, Hetta allowed the topic to lapse, but not before she vowed to Maggie to have the whole from her later. Her companion only laughed and shook her head.

Hetta had fastened the tiny pearl buttons at the wrists of her kid gloves and now glanced into the mirror to give a final inspection to her appearance. The dark-gray merino walking dress and her matching bonnet, with its single black feather curled primly over the rim, were eminently suitable for the damp chill of February in London and fashionable enough in their half-mourning to pass even Lady Pelborne's critical eye. Yet Hetta realized that the excellent cut of the high waist and straight full skirt did not enhance her appearance as she had hoped when she packed it for the journey. Making a face at herself in the mirror, Hetta thought it small wonder Lady Pelborne had decided to bring in her own physician to examine her, for even to her own eyes she appeared more pallid than she had the day before.

Hetta pinched her cheeks in an effort to bring some color into her face, but the pink faded almost immediately.

Watching her from behind in the mirror, Maggie shook her head. Her burr was strong as she said softly, "Och, I'll not be knowing what is to be done for ye, miss. Ye're that whey-faced from the day ye put on mourning and locked away your bleeding heart. I am reminded of the burns in blackest winter locked fast in ice."

"I thank you, Maggie." Hetta sighed, knowing there was some truth to Maggie's words. Since her father's death she had retreated from close emotional attachments. It was for this reason above all others that she found Jonathan Markham's possessiveness so repugnant. The question came unbidden to her mind what would she have done if she had truly found the man of her dreams. Would her fears have disappeared like the morning mist? Or would she have run from him as she had from Lord Anthony?

Her wide hazel eyes stared back from her reflection and she abruptly turned away from the mirror. She smoothed her kid gloves over her wrists and said brightly, "Never mind, Maggie. I expect I shall get over it one day. Even the coldest winter cannot imprison the burns forever." She started across the bedroom to the door, picking up her cloak from the back of a chair as she went.

"Aye, I'm thinking in the end it will take a most fiery gentleman to warm ye to spring again," muttered Maggie, beginning to straighten the wardrobe. Her mistress missed a step and turned startled eyes on her. Flushing suddenly to the roots of her hair, Hetta whisked out of the room and the maid stared after her in astonishment. "Now, what do ye suppose I could have said?" she asked herself, pursing her lips while she turned the matter over in her mind.

Pausing only to throw the cloak about her shoulders, Hetta hurried downstairs. She found her godmother before the gilt-edged mirror in the hall, adjusting a high-crowned hat decorated with a number of waving plumes. Lady Pelborne glanced around at her, noting with approval the faintest pink in her cheeks. "My dear Hetta, you are breathless. Most unbecoming to a lady's image. However, it has put color in your face and so I shan't scold you. There was no need to rush, you know. We shall have the remainder of the day to junket about town," she said, forgetting that it had been she who had admonished her goddaughter to hurry. She gave a brisk, satisfied nod at herself in the glass before she turned to Hetta and, drawing on her lavender kid gloves, asked, "Are you quite ready, my dear?"

"Yes, Godmamma," Hetta said demurely. The faintest of smiles played about her lips as she looked with fond admiration at her godmother. Obviously the terrible scene with Lady Anthony was to be put aside completely and their original plans followed with the greatest good nature. Hetta could only admire such extraordinary resilience of spirit.

"Then let us depart," said Lady Pelborne, starting for the door.

The porter standing in stiff attendance threw it open and the ladies passed through. A footman ran down the front steps before them to the landaulet below and stood ready to hand them up into the carriage.

Stepping up into the landaulet, Hetta seated herself at the far window and Lady Pelborne settled beside her. The footman latched the carriage door and signaled the driver.

As the landaulet rolled forward, Lady Pelborne said, "I do not wish to urge you to anything you particularly dislike, Hetta, but I insist that we at least have your hair done differently. Earlier this morning I noticed a greenish cast to the bruise on your brow and I fear it will soon be quite spectacular. I believe a shorter cut with curls falling about your face will be just the thing. Also, I am persuaded a touch of powder would be in order until the bruise disappears.''

Hetta gently touched the tender swelling high on her forehead. ''Powder, Godmamma? But surely only actresses and opera dancers wear cosmetics?''

Lady Pelborne smiled at her goddaughter's naiveté. ''Quite the contrary, my dear. A lady of quality must make use of the rouge pot to be truly à la mode. I do myself. The only rule one should follow is to apply it with a careful-enough hand to make one's countenance distinguishable from the heavily painted faces of our more gauche young ladies and a few of our ancient society dames. Many of those could well take note of the example set by our more attractive actresses and opera dancers on that score.''

Hetta laughed and said, ''How strange that Papa should tell me otherwise. He was quite adamant on the subject of rouge and insisted that no lady of quality would stoop to artifice of that sort.''

Lady Pelborne chuckled and patted Hetta's arm. ''Your father was an intelligent man but somewhat naive about the female sex, Hetta. We all have our tricks and artifices to show ourselves attractive and at the very least worthy of notice. Your education shall begin this very day and I wager that you will be as eager a pupil as any in learning the art of becoming a desirable woman.'' Her goddaughter made no response, and after a pause Lady Pelborne chatted on about the plans she had made for Hetta's enjoyment. She was unaware that she had struck a responsive chord deep within her goddaughter.

Hetta contributed an occasional monosyllable to Lady Pelborne's revelations, but her thoughts had returned to the previous evening when she had first encountered Lord Anthony's eyes, their expression amused and somewhat bored as they rested upon her. His sly torment of her under Lady Pelborne's nose had been galling. She had wished to erase that tolerant amusement from his face and she had inadvertently done so in the study, but the resulting flare of passion in his eyes when he took her in his arms had tripped off alarms in her head. She was now better able to examine the incident with some measure of objectivity, and she realized that Lord Anthony had not felt desire for her as a particulr woman; rather, she had been to him merely an available female whom he had found momentarily pleasing. Hetta's very nature revolted from the thought. Surely she was worthy of more. Surely a woman could expect far more from her life than brief episodes of passion or the cold loveless marriage that Markham had offered her.

Maggie's poetical black winter had lain long on her heart, but a yearning restlessness was wakening within her. She should at least thank the Earl of Davenchester for that much. His fiery caresses had stirred her to an awareness of her own sensuality that the romantic dreams of her phantom lover, her beloved Michael, had never done. Hetta knew beyond doubt that she could never again turn away from life and its hurts. She wanted far more than either Lord Anthony or Jonathan Markham had offered her, and she was willing to reach out for it. And perhaps through Lady Pelborne's guidance and instruction she would learn one means of how she might achieve her heart's desire.

"Here we are, Hetta," said Lady Pelborne, breaking into her goddaughter's reverie. Hetta started and found that the landaulet had come to a stop before a small unpretentious establishment in Regent Street. Above the door to the shop a modest sign proclaimed simply LEBONNIER. Lady Pelborne was already stepping down from the carriage and Hetta hastened to follow her.

The tinkling of a bell announced their entrance into the dressmaker's shop. Hetta looked around her curiously and immediately realized from the abundance of fine fabrics and laces on display that Lebonnier catered to a select clientele. She suspected that many of the velvets, satins, and sheer muslins had seen the inside of a smuggler's barrel or pack before they had ever reached London. It had not been so very long ago that the best fabrics were rarely to be found because of the war's embargo laws.

A saleswoman curtsied to Lady Pelborne and uttered a

quiet word of greeting before hurrying to the back of the shop, which had been partitioned off with a heavy brocade curtain. She disappeared behind it. A moment later the curtain was swept aside by a diminutive woman attired completely in black. Her hair was drawn back from a high brow like heavy raven's wings, bringing into prominence a narrow face of inbred arrogance. Followed by her saleswoman, the woman advanced on Lady Pelborne and Hetta with a ramrod carriage that was intimidating. Her husky voice was heavily accented. "It is good that you have come, my lady. How may I be of service to you?"

"Ah, Madame Lebonnier!" Lady Pelborne smiled warmly at the proprietress of the shop. She gestured toward Hetta. "Allow me to introduce to you Miss Hetta Stanton, who is my goddaughter. She is visiting with me for the Season and shall require some suitable gowns for her come-out." Lady Pelborne gave a meaningful look to Madame Lebonnier and added, "One naturally wishes her to appear at her absolute finest."

Madame Lebonnier's thin plucked brows flicked skyward. "But of course, my lady." She turned her cold eyes on Hetta and studied her for a brief moment. Unconsciously Hetta raised her chin and returned the woman's stare. Heavy lids drooped lower over Madame's black eyes. She suddenly snapped her fingers, issuing a stream of orders in French to the saleswoman standing behind her. The woman hurried away. To Hetta, Madame Lebonnier said, "We must first discover how to go. Be so good as to remove the bonnet and to be seated in the chair below that window."

Hetta was astounded by the woman's peremptory orders and looked to Lady Pelborne for guidance. Her godmother's smile broadened. "Why so surprised, child? Madame Lebonnier is an unparalled genius and therefore must be allowed her eccentric manners. There is no other who knows better what will become one."

Madame Lebonnier smiled thinly and her dark eyes conveyed more warmth than Hetta would have believed possible but a moment before. "*Oui*, I shall make of you the extraordinary debutante. When you enter a crowded room, the gentlemen will notice. And that is the desire of every woman, *n'est-ce pas?*" Without waiting for an answer, she graciously motioned Hetta to the chair set under a window hidden from the majority of the shop by displays. A slatted partition extended halfway up the windowpanes to give privacy from passersby and yet allowed warm sunlight to fall directly onto Hetta's face when she had seated herself and removed her bonnet.

Hetta smiled shyly at the deceptively small modiste. "I admit that the notion of gaining the admiration of a roomful of gentlemen is attractive, Madame Lebonnier. I should very much like to learn how it is done."

Her godmother chuckled, but it was Madame Lebonnier who nodded approval. "*Bien*, we shall begin." She turned to her assistant, who had returned to her side with several swaths of fabrics in different hues. With Lady Pelborne as an interested spectator, the Frenchwoman chose a velvet of a soft gray-green and flipped it around Hetta's shoulders so that it covered her cloak and dress. Her eyes narrowed again and she nodded in satisfaction. "It is as I thought. The pewter gray she wears is too severe for her. Do you see it as well, Lady Pelborne?"

Hetta looked up at her godmother in inquiry. Lady Pelborne wore a pleased expression. "Indeed, Madame! Her complexion appears much brighter now. Hetta, I forbid you to wear that particular walking dress and cloak again. They make you appear positively haggard, and the quicker you are rid of it, the better. Madame, we shall want a pelisse of that same velvet." The dressmaker nodded as though the order were expected.

Hetta shook her head and plucked at the velvet lying soft around her throat. "But how can it possibly make such a difference? This velvet is also a sort of gray."

Madame Lebonnier picked up a mirror and held it up before Hetta's face. "Look, *chérie*, and you shall see what we do."

Hetta glanced at herself and then stared intently. To her astonishment she appeared more alive than she ever remembered. Her wide hazel eyes were alight and becomingly flecked with gray-green, and her hair was a lustrous

rich chestnut. But most astonishing, her complexion had
smoothed and glowed a soft creamy peach. While she
looked, the soft muted velvet was whisked away from her
shoulders. She stared in disbelief at the dulled luster of her
hair and the sudden deadened pallor of her cheeks. Hetta
was stunned by the swift transformation. Her reflection
was once again that of the drab, pallid creature she had
come to expect.

"You must understand, *chérie*, it is the color that is
most important to a woman. Every work of nature demands its own special cloaking to bring it to magnificent
life. The greatest painters understood this truth," said
Madame Lebonnier, putting aside the mirror. "Before we
are done, you shall understand how to use colors to become the magnificent desirable woman you so wish to
appear."

Hetta looked over at Lady Pelborne. "I was actually
pretty, Godmamma! Could I possibly . . . Oh, do you
think it too much to ask?"

Lady Pelborne smiled gently at her. "Why do you
suppose I have brought you to Madame Lebonnier if not
for this? My dear child, nothing could delight one more
than to observe the blooming of a young girl into a stunning young woman."

Madame Lebonnier was arranging a teal-blue gauze in
folds over Hetta's shoulders. She cautioned, "It will demand much work, much concentration. You must have
patience, for it cannot all be done in one day."

Hetta nodded, once again examining herself in the mirror the dressmaker handed her. She touched the gauze in
wonder as the color at once wrought a miracle and brought
life to her face and eyes.

Madame Lebonnier questioned Lady Pelborne with a
glance as she gestured at the gauze and Lady Pelborne
nodded. Madame laid aside the gauze carefully before she
reached for a deep-jade-green satin.

"The Season begins in little more than a month," said
Lady Pelborne. "It is my hope that my goddaughter shall
be able to make her bow soon after."

"Calm yourself, my lady. Miss Stanton will make her

bow, I promise you," said Madame Lebonnier, her eyes narrowed in concentration as she draped the satin over Hetta's shoulders.

Lady Pelborne smiled in satisfaction. "Then I shall leave it in your capable hands to decide all she will require. Send the bills for the gowns around to me."

"*Bon!* It will go much more quickly thus," said Madame Lebonnier, her fingers deftly arranging and rearranging bombazines, sarcenets, and satins in such swift succession that Hetta had hardly absorbed the effect of each before it was whisked aside and replaced. "We shall soon discover which colors most favor Miss Stanton and then she shall be measured. Then both of you shall go away, heh?"

"Of course," Lady Pelborne agreed with a laugh. "We have several other visits and I wish to accomplish as much as possible this afternoon. One hopes that my goddaughter can be turned out with a semblance of decency before the week is out?"

"Of a certainty, my lady," said Madame Lebonnier with her thin smile.

For the next hour Hetta listened intently while Lady Pelborne and Madame Lebonnier discussed fabrics and fine laces and debated the merits of a particular design or cut of gown that would best flatter Hetta's figure. She was dazzled by the number of gowns, pelisses, and walking dresses that were thought to be essential to a young lady's wardrobe, but Lady Pelborne brushed aside her protests. Twice Hetta felt impelled to interject a different opinion on a particular design. Madame Lebonnier was surprised by her instinctive fashion sense and once unbent so far as to compliment her.

When Lady Pelborne and Hetta eventually made ready to leave the shop, it was to Madame Lebonnier's assurances that two of the gowns and a pelisse would be finished in little more than a week. She detained Lady Pelborne and Hetta with an imperious gesture. "But a moment more, if you please. There is something I must show to *mademoiselle*." She turned to her assistant and spoke low in her ear. The woman disappeared, soon re-

turning with a gold-striped bandbox overflowing with white
tissue paper. Madame Lebonnier turned back the fragile
tissue and gently drew forth a dazzling length of gold silk.
Sheets of tissue drifted away to the carpet when she freed
its folds shimmering with the light of old gold.

Hetta gasped at the sheer beauty of the domino, and
before she was conscious of it, she reached out to brush
the cool silk with the tips of her fingers.

"It is my gift for you, *mademoiselle*," said Madame
Lebonnier in her dry voice.

Hetta raised startled eyes to the dressmaker's arrogant
face. "Madame Lebonnier, you could not possibly be
serious. Why, it is much too costly to be given away.
Surely you must have it in mind for a particular customer,
for I cannot imagine it for simply anyone."

Madame Lebonnier allowed herself a sly glance toward
Lady Pelborne. "Do not fear that I shall not somehow
retrieve the cost, *ma petite!*"

Understanding her perfectly, Lady Pelborne chuckled in
appreciation. "My dear Hetta, pray do accept the domino.
One may always find a use for it. Madame Lebonnier is
rarely given to such magnanimous gestures, and to refuse
her would be quite unpardonable."

Hetta wavered, her eyes returning to the magnificent
domino. She had never possessed such a gorgeous garment.

Seeing her hesitation, Madame Lebonnier nodded sharply
and gave the domino over to her assistant. "Thérèse shall
once more fold it in the box for you, my lady. Then you
must both go, for I am very busy."

7

Moments later Lady Pelborne and Hetta emerged from Lebonnier. Hetta carried the gold box containing the carefully folded silk domino. "I cannot yet believe that she has given it to me," Hetta said, dazed.

"She has apparently taken a rare liking to you," said Lady Pelborne dryly.

Her driver had been patiently walking his horses up and down the block for the past half-hour and now espied them. Immediately he returned to the curb with the carriage and let down the step for them. Lady Pelborne gave orders for their conveyance to a certain milliner's shop in Oxford Street and thence to Mayfair, where Lady Pelborne assured her goddaughter they would be certain to find all else they might need that afternoon. She and Hetta entered the landaulet, their conversation easy and amiable.

The coachman expertly maneuvered the carriage through the tangle of tilburies, curricles, landaulets, and brave pedestrians. It was not long before he turned into Oxford Street and reached their destination. At the milliner's shop, Hetta spent a delightful hour trying on various bonnets and hats, the latter being whimsical confections made of straw and decorated with feathers or bunches of artificial flowers and satin ribbons. She was particularly enchanted with a gypsy hat that tied under the chin with a wide ribbon that passed first over the crown.

When she and Lady Pelborne emerged onto Oxford Street again, they both carried hatboxes, one of which contained the gypsy hat, and Hetta sported a new poke bonnet. The deep-crowned bonnet was trimmed with russet plumes and tied in a bow under the chin with gray satin ribbons of the same shade as her walking dress. Lady Pelborne had pointed out with what Hetta thought to be extraordinary practicality that the gray ribbons could later be replaced with a more flattering color, but in the meantime the russet plumes added a much-needed touch of sophisitication to her sober outfit. Hetta agreed readily, for her visit to Lebonnier had made her acutely aware of how dull her present attire was.

When the landaulet had carried them to Mayfair, both ladies agreed that it would be a pity to waste the rare afternoon sun, and after depositing their hatboxes with John Coachman, they strolled arm in arm down the street. Lady Pelborne was hailed by several acquaintances who glanced at Hetta in cool appraisal. Once she was introduced to them, the ladies' manner warmed markedly and they extended cordial invitations to her. Hetta shyly thanked each of them, though she was surprised by their immediate friendliness. Lady Pelborne remarked that one's connections and depth of pocketbook could only be assets in a cynical world.

Lady Pelborne had commented that many of the items on her list could be found in Mayfair, but Hetta was still impressed by the number of the shops and their variety. Every imaginable item was on display in the windows of linen drapers, haberdashers, silk mercers, and dressmakers. At the establishment of a plumassier Lady Pelborne discovered a trio of dyed purple ostrich feathers that she pronounced perfect for a fan arrangement and promptly bought.

The two ladies drifted leisurely from one shop to the next, making the occasional purchase of odd lengths of ribbons for refurbishing of one's bonnets or gowns; an exquisite ivory comb with gold inlay, a gift to Hetta from Lady Pelborne; silver netting to be knotted into a reticule; delicate hand-stitched lace handkerchiefs; and a large fur muff that came very dear and that Lady Pelborne insisted on purchasing for Hetta. At a glovier, Hetta stood in admiration of a pair of soft kid gloves of the palest oyster

gray, and with little urging from Lady Pelborne she tried
them on. The supple leather slipped up around her slender
wrists in a perfect fit, and she succumbed to temptation.

Hetta thought to purchase gifts for those dearest to her
and deliberated long over her gift for Cheton. At last she
chose a pipe carved from a fine-grained wood, for Lady
Pelborne had pointed out with worldly wisdom that an
elderly gentleman who spent his days in thought would
certainly find contentment puffing on a pipe in the eve-
nings. For Maggie, Hetta purchased a pretty locket on a
sturdy gold chain. The locket was of simple design, which
Hetta knew would appeal to the maid's somewhat austere
taste.

The ladies eventually emerged from their last stop in
Mayfair, a bootier where Hetta had been persuaded to order
several pairs of kid slippers and boots. They were laden
with wrapped parcels of every size and shape. Though
obviously fatigued, Lady Pelborne expressed herself satisfied with the day's outing. "For even if by some chance
Madame Lebonnier is unable to deliver some of your
gowns on time, the quantity of ribbon and lace we have
purchased may be used to refurbish two or three of your
present gowns. I am pleased to have accomplished so
much during our first day. I suggest that we now return
home for a well-deserved tea."

"I for one welcome the suggestion," said Hetta gratefully, flushed slightly from the activity. She was glad to
give her parcels to John Coachman, but during the exchange the small parcel containing Maggie's locket slipped
out of her hands and fell to the pavement. Hetta bent
quickly to retrieve it, anxious that it might have been
damaged. As she touched the narrow parcel, her fingers
brushed those of a stranger.

"Allow me, ma'am."

Hetta rose to her feet as the gentleman straightened with
the package in his hand. He was quite tall and carried
himself well, with shoulders thrown back and a proud tilt
to his chin. When the gentleman smiled amiably, weary
lines radiated from the corners of his bright-blue eyes. He
bowed to her and spoke in a mellow voice. "Your parcel,

ma'am.'' He wore a blue morning coat over a contrasting waistcoat and buff pantaloons strapped under the insteps of his top boots, presenting an altogether attractive picture.

Hetta stared up at him with a startled recognition. The angular construction of his face, the fine lines around his world-weary eyes, and his gentle manner belonged to the phantom of her dreams, her beloved Michael. But here he stood before her in the flesh, leaning at ease on his elegant walking stick. Hetta came back to awareness with a start, flushing when she realized the gentleman was still holding her parcel and was regarding her with a faintly quizzical expression in his eyes. She stammered her thanks and took it from him with a slight tremor in her fingers.

''Well, Rupert, I apprehend that you have dared to return to London. Wasn't your sabbatical to your liking?'' asked Lady Pelborne, stepping up beside Hetta.

The gentleman immediately turned to the older woman and made an elegant leg. He waved a negligent gloved hand at her question and once more slouched on his walking stick. ''Always a delightful treat to see you, dear lady. Alas, I found the bucolic countryside rather deadening to one of my particular tastes. Strangely enough, I missed the wicked pursuits and pleasures of London. One fails to comprehend why, for one day is quite like another. But then you understand me somewhat better than most, do you not, dear lady?''

A fleeting expression of distaste crossed Lady Pelborne's face. ''Indeed, and to my sorrow I might add. I assume you are fixed for the Season, then. One wonders at your audacity, Rupert. The gossip is yet flying thick over your last indiscretion.''

''Perhaps I have returned to consternate the gossipmongers, ma'am,'' said the gentleman with a quick grin meant to be disarming. Lady Pelborne continued to regard him with eyes that were decidedly cool. His lips tightened momentarily, then he turned toward Hetta with a weary, rueful expression that touched her heart. ''I do not believe I have had the pleasure of your acquaintance, ma'am?''

''This is my goddaughter, Hetta Stanton,'' said Lady

Pelborne shortly. "This gentleman is Davenchester's cousin, Sir Rupert Sikes."

Hetta shyly laid her hand in Sir Rupert's and murmured a polite greeting.

Gently releasing her fingers, Sikes raised a brow at Lady Pelborne. "Must you point up my connection with the Anthonys, ma'am? My cousins and I were never bosom pals, and I fear family feeling is particularly lacking between myself and Cousin Michael. Poor Edmond was at least a tolerable-enough fellow, but Michael—" He reflected a moment, then said softly, "Of course I must now address him as Davenchester, mustn't I? How truly annoying. He has ever possessed an inordinate sense of worth, I have thought. One wonders if the title will have gone quite to his head."

"You must be sure to ask him, Rupert," Lady Pelborne said. She motioned Hetta before her into the landaulet, herself pausing a moment. "Michael has sold out, you know." She had the satisfaction of watching Sikes' face harden in an expression of surprise and unease. "Good day, Rupert," she said gently, and stepped up into the landaulet.

As the landaulet pulled away, Hetta looked back to watch Sikes' tall figure until he was no longer in sight through the intervening traffic. She turned forward again with a sigh, her eyes alight. "Sir Rupert is a rather handsome gentleman, do you not think so, Godmamma? So tall and personable."

"Some people do find him attractive, I believe," said Lady Pelborne noncommittally. An undercurrent of dislike was patent in Lady Pelborne's tone.

Hetta glanced curiously at her godmother around the rim of her new poke bonnet. "Surely you do not condemn the man because he is not on terms with Lord Anthony? I am persuaded it is only a cousinly rivalry. Come, ma'am, this is quite unlike your generous heart."

Lady Pelborne snorted. "Rupert's envy for Michael is hardly the point, my dear. I find him objectionable on his own account."

"How odd, for I found him quite the gentleman," Hetta

said softly. A warm smile played about her mouth as she remembered how he had included her in his ruefulness, as though she would understand what he was thinking.

Lady Pelborne glanced at her goddaughter and her brows rose at Hetta's softened expression. The chit was by far too impressionable for her own good. She laid her gloved fingers lightly on her goddaughter's slender wrist. "Put him out of your mind, child," she said softly. "He is not to be thought of, you know."

Hetta was somewhat startled to have her thoughts read so easily. Blushing, she asked, "But why? Is—is Sir Rupert already wed, then?"

"No, not wed," said Lady Pelborne. She looked away, frowning as though undecided.

Hetta remembered what her godmother had said to Sir Rupert. "What was the gossip attached to Sir Rupert, ma'am? It must surely be at the root of your dislike. Can you not tell me what it is?"

"I would not stoop to repeat such a tale to you. Once you are out, you shall doubtless hear enough to realize why I have warned you of Rupert," said Lady Pelborne shortly.

"That is hardly satisfactory, ma'am," Hetta said.

Her godmother turned toward her with a stern cast to her features. Her eyes were the color of hard steel. "You need be aware of but one fact, Hetta: Sir Rupert Sikes is tolerated by the *ton* solely for the sake of his family connections and out of respect for myself and the Davenchester name." Her tone hardened, brooking no compromise. "You will oblige me by bestowing upon him only the commonest civilities—nothing more! And otherwise, if you value your reputation, pray keep at a wise distance from him."

Quickly Hetta lowered her lids to hide the flash of anger in her eyes. Only Jonathan Markham had ever spoken to her in such a peremptory manner, and instinctively she bridled against it, but she said only, "I understand, Godmamma."

Lady Pelborne searched her goddaughter's profile but found nothing to criticize in Hetta's calm expression and lowered eyes. Satisfied that her warning had been heeded,

Lady Pelborne relaxed into her corner of the seat with a sigh. She was completely unaware of the undutiful thoughts chasing through her goddaughter's mind.

Hetta thought it likely that her godmother's uncompromising attitude was not based solely on a dislike of Sir Rupert. Lady Pelborne was usually so open-minded. The emotional scene with Lady Anthony must surely have exacted a far greater toll on her patience than Hetta had realized, and to pursue her curiosity about Sir Rupert at that moment would naturally be the height of folly. She was unwilling to risk further displeasure, for she feared Lady Pelborne would feel herself compelled to order her to have nothing at all to do socially with Sir Rupert Sikes, and this Hetta did not want.

Hetta felt that whatever Sir Rupert had done to earn public censure was not as unpardonable as her godmother had hinted, and she thought it spoke well of him that he had returned to London despite the gossipmongers. Hetta was of the opinion that Lady Pelborne's personal animosity had led her to exaggerate the blackness of Sir Rupert's character. If she was to meet him again among polite society, which seemed likely when even Lady Pelborne admitted that he was accepted everywhere, Hetta intended not to spurn a friendly overture if one were made. She could not imagine anyone like Sir Rupert to be a scoundrel. He was so gentlemanly, so personable and fair—in short, so like her beloved Michael . . .

Hetta brought herself up short. A faint crease appeared between her fine brows at the preposterous thought. Of course it was nonsense that she would allow that consideration to persuade her to deliberately flout her godmother's wishes. She was simply dealing fairly with Sir Rupert, as she would with anyone, in choosing her friends and acquaintances by her own standards rather than someone else's. She meant to make her own decision concerning Sir Rupert with her eyes open and her heart free of prejudice.

The return drive to the town house in Grosvenor Square was covered in a subdued manner, neither lady stirring herself to offer more than the most desultory of observations. When the landaulet came to a stop and they had alighted to the pavement, it was to see a hired hack standing at the curb. Lady Pelborne and Hetta exchanged a look of mutual curiosity before they ascended the front steps. The front door stood open, unattended. Lady Pelborne's brows rose.

The ladies entered unheralded into the front hall, only to stop short at the extraordinary scene that met their incredulous eyes. Half way down the staircase the porter and a footman were engaged in a valiant struggle to maneuver a large heavily corded trunk to the ground floor. Beside the newel post at the bottom of the stairs stood a second trunk with three or four smaller portmanteaus gathered about it. Countless bandboxes were scattered in every direction over the hall's marble tiles, and in the midst of the confusion was Lady Pelborne's stolid butler, a red-and-white-striped bandbox dangling by their strings from each of his hands. Erwin wore an unusually harried expression as he bent his head courteously to Lady Anthony, who was clutching his sleeve in entreaty. She was attired in a traveling dress and pelisse with frogged closures and black ermine trim and carrying a matching ermine muff. On her head perched a poke bonnet with a ridiculously high brim, which tied with wide satin ribbons in a huge bow under her rounded chin.

"What the devil?" The mannish oath sounded strangely appropriate on Lady Pelborne's lips. She stepped forward, sweeping her hand around the hall. "Loraine, what is the meaning of this chaos?"

Upon hearing his mistress's thunderstruck voice, the butler's expression changed ludicrously to one of relief. Lady Anthony whirled away from him with a startled cry. She stared at Lady Pelborne and Hetta with dread in her eyes. "I—I am going to a hotel, Aunt," she said in a small defiant voice. "You cannot want me here any longer. I was insufferably rude and I know it, and indeed, indeed I am sorry."

Lady Pelborne's face softened. "You are a peagoose, Loraine. Of course you shall not move to a hotel. I would not hear of it."

"Oh! Are—are you certain, Aunt Beatrice?" faltered

Lady Anthony. She twisted her fingers together in suspense and there was the hint of tears in her eyes.

"I fear I must insist, Loraine," said Lady Pelborne, removing her gloves.

"Oh, you are too good to me." Easy tears started from Lady Anthony's eyes. Lady Pelborne sighed and put an arm around her niece's shoulders while she murmured soothingly. Lady Anthony's hiccoughing sobs drew curious glances from the footmen and porter. The door that led to the servants hall was pushed open a crack and the head of an inquisitive maid appeared.

Hetta became aware of their audience and touched her godmother's elbow to gain her attention. "Perhaps it were better to allow Lady Anthony to make herself comfortable on the sofa in the drawing room," she murmured with a meaningful glance around the unusually well-inhabited hall.

Lady Pelborne flashed her a look of instant understanding. "You are undoubtedly correct, my dear." She swept around on the butler and spoke in firm command. "Erwin, drop those idiotic bandboxes at once."

"Oh, no, no! Aunt, my very best straw," protested Lady Anthony, starting up from Lady Pelborne's shoulder. Her tearful plea went unheeded as the butler allowed the bandboxes to drop with a satisfying thud at his feet.

Lady Pelborne did not seem aware of the interruption. "We shall take our tea in the drawing room. Miss Stanton's purchases and my own are to be brought up directly. You will know how to dispose of them. As for this outrageous example of disorder . . ." She raked the cluttered hall with a scorching look of disdain and made a pungent observation on the vagaries of her household, adding that perhaps there should be certain changes made in her domestic staff. The half-hidden spectators stirred uneasily and Lady Pelborne seemed to take notice of them for the first time. She inquired in clipped accents if she had suddenly become a sideshow attraction. The servants edged quickly away. Lady Pelborne's eagle eyes fell on the hapless footman and porter who had successfully deposited Lady Anthony's trunk at the foot of the stairs and now stood uneasily glancing at each other. Their mistress issued a peremptory order that Lady Anthony's belongings were to be reestablished in her rooms, then inquired somewhat acidly if it was now the custom to leave one's street door open wide as an invitation to every jackanapes who chanced to pass by. The porter, suddenly recognizing his danger, sidled past Lady Pelborne and hurried back to his neglected post. The front door was closed with a resounding finality.

Hetta was hugely enjoying the sweeping skill of Lady Pelborne's performance and had to swallow her amusement when even the door to the servants hall was eased carefully shut. Hearing her gurgling laugh, Lady Pelborne rounded on her and addressed her in a voice of unmistakable command. "Pray be good enough to accompany Lady Anthony and myself, Hetta. I shall wish you to pour the tea when it comes." Hetta was taken aback by the force of her godmother's personality and could only nod mutely.

The butler sprang forward to open the drawing-room door for Lady Pelborne, who still had her arm around her niece's shoulders though that lady was no longer weeping. Lady Pelborne swept through the doorway with Lady Anthony without a glance right or left. Hetta followed and the door was closed immediately after her.

"Bravo, Godmamma," exclaimed Hetta softly, a little in awe of Lady Pelborne's high-handed performance. She thought it unlikely that the servants who had come under Lady Pelborne's sharp eyes and scathing tongue would give Lady Anthony's behavior more than a passing thought and the tale would therefore not find its way around London before the week was done.

Lady Pelborne turned twinkling eyes to her and gave her a broad wink. She waved the two young women to a comfortable sofa done in black-and-silver-striped silk and seated herself opposite them in a matching wing chair. "Now, Loraine, I wish to know why you had decided to remove to a hotel without vouchsafing a word to anyone," said Lady Pelborne quietly. "Surely you must realize that you are welcome to stay under my roof as long as you like."

"And I was certainly looking forward to your company,

Lady Anthony," said Hetta, "for I do not know another soul in London outside yourself and Godmamma."

Lady Anthony gazed questioningly at each of them in turn. She sighed and shook her head. "I have been foolish again and made a scene. I quite thought . . . But we quarreled so horribly and so I knew positively that you would not want me, either of you, because I was so unpardonably rude."

"My dear child, I may have my quirks but I hope I am not such an ogre as that," said Lady Pelborne.

"Oh, no, no! I would not have you think that I . . . Not but what I do not wonder at times—" Lady Anthony stopped in confusion and made a helpless gesture. "It is just that you have always sided with Michael and it so put me out that . . . But I shan't say another word on that score."

"I sided with Michael in this instance because of the gossip it would be sure to rouse if you were to remain together in the same residence," Lady Pelborne said.

"Such stuff! As though I care twopence for that." Lady Anthony tossed her head and the feathers swooped across her bonnet. "None of my true friends would regard it for a moment, for they all know how I feel about Michael's much-vaunted charm. Indeed, I cannot understand how any woman could succumb to him. Have you met my brother-in-law, Hetta?"

"I . . . Yes. We met but once, and that but very briefly," said Hetta, startled.

"Then you must surely have noticed how domineering and arrogant he is," exclaimed Lady Anthony. "I cannot comprehend what one may see in him, for he is not the least bit attractive or gentlemanly or—or anything else a lady must admire. I do not speak of his mistresses, of course, though I have never heard that he is particularly one for keeping a string of light-o'-loves."

Hetta gazed at her hands folded in her lap. She was startled by a stab of jealousy at mention of Lord Anthony's conquests. She did not consider it wise to demur with Lady Anthony's assessment of the Earl of Davenchester even though she felt it to be grossly wide of the mark. She could but wonder when the bare mention of his name would cease to conjure up bone-shivering memories. When he had kissed her . . .

Hetta pulled herself up short, recognizing the direction of her thoughts. She must be the wickedest creature alive to dwell upon such a scandalous encounter, and especially with any sort of pleasure! She felt someone's eyes on her and looked up quickly, meeting the speculative gaze of her godmother. The betraying heat rose in her face and her heartbeat skipped in fearful anticipation of the older woman's remarks.

But Lady Pelborne had already turned back to Lady Anthony. "Nevertheless, my dear, it is best never to give the tattlers any cause to bandy it about that you are setting your cap at Michael. Some would find it an irresistibly spicy tale to hear that the beautiful bereaved Lady Anthony was bent on finding consolation in the arms of her dashing brother-in-law. Michael is an extremely eligible *parti* in the eyes of the *ton*, you know."

"But how ridiculous! I *could* not care for him in that way, for he is not in the least like my poor Edmond," exclaimed Lady Anthony. Her eyes suddenly lit with a fiery expression that was astonishing in one so fragile in appearance. "Yes, and I should defy anyone to say differently. Edmond was the kindest, most generous creature alive. But as for Michael—"

Lady Pelborne hastily intervened. "Oh, I quite agree with you, my dear. Edmond was possessed of a much more predictable disposition. He was indeed very dissimilar in nature from Michael."

Lady Anthony nodded, satisfied, and threw out her hands toward Hetta in an expressive gesture. "There, you see! Even Aunt Beatrice, who adores him, will agree that Michael is a beast."

Lady Pelborne fell back in her chair, rolling her eyes expressively. Hetta started to laugh but quickly covered it with a cough behind her hand when Lady Anthony looked over at her in innocent inquiry. She was spared from offering an explanation when the drawing-room door opened and a footman entered carrying a serving tray with the tea ordered by Lady Pelborne. He arranged the plates of cold jellies and watercress sandwiches and the pot of tea on an occasional table standing beside the sofa; then he withdrew from the room, leaving the ladies to serve themselves. The next few moments were agreeably passed in making their selections and the pouring of the tea.

While mulling over the choice between a biscuit or a jelly, Lady Anthony suddenly sighed. "I was to have my first dinner party of the Season just days from now. Everything is ruined, for it was to be at the town house. It is simply too provoking. I have spent positively hours this morning wheedling the florists for their best baskets and now they must be canceled."

"I now understand how you came to have my note so speedily," murmured Lady Pelborne ruefully. "You must have risen at a most uncomfortable hour to have accomplished such a coup, Loraine. Of course we cannot allow your efforts to go to waste. You must direct the florists here instead and hold your little party as planned."

Lady Anthony clapped her hands. "Oh, may we, Aunt? I should be so happy. And it will be just the thing for Hetta. She shall be able to make the acquaintance of a few of our friends before her come-out. I shall naturally make over the guest list just a trifle." She turned to Hetta with sparkling eyes. "I know that you should enjoy it tremendously, dear Hetta, for I throw simply delightful parties; but it does not do to brag, of course! How extraordinary! I feel that I have known you forever, and we have just become friends."

"I hope that we may be friends," said Hetta, captivated by Lady Anthony's childlike goodwill. She listened as Lady Anthony chattered with lively enthusiasm and felt a growing amusement. She could only liken that lady to a merry lark, swooping and swaying from one topic to the next. Lady Anthony's occasional absurdities surprised a bubble of laughter from her ever more frequently.

Lady Pelborne watched her goddaughter's expressive face, noting in particular her dancing eyes. She congratulated herself upon the inspired notion of asking Lady Anthony to stay with them. Hetta had been made nervous too long by that paltry fellow Markham, about whom she meant to make particular inquiries. Her goddaughter had always possessed a natural vivacity, but Lady Pelborne had noticed a somewhat brittle quality about her since she had arrived in London, and she disliked it thoroughly. However, Loraine's nonsense seemed in a fair way to be acting as a tonic upon her. Smiling faintly, she wondered what Michael's reaction would be to find that the respectable Miss Stanton had become fast friends with his flighty sister-in-law. She hoped Michael did not take long in the country, for she already sorely missed the young devil.

As he had each afternoon since his arrival at Davenchester Court, Lord Anthony was conferring with his man of business. The solicitor took up the account books he had been showing to the earl. "I believe that we have discussed all that requires your attention today, my lord. Is there anything else I may do for you?"

"Yes, Sedgewick. You know, of course, that the contractor has informed me that it will cost a fortune to repair the original wing of the manor, and I have given my permission for it to be done," said Lord Anthony. "I also desire to have the gardens restored to what they were in my mother's day. Have I the blunt available from the rents for that as well?"

Sedgewick looked at the earl in surprise. "Why, I should think so, my lord. Forgive me if I seem startled, my lord, but I was not aware your lordship had an interest in gardening."

Lord Anthony smiled faintly. "I don't, Sedgewick. However, I do have a keen interest in the happiness of the future mistress of Davenchester. I have never yet known a woman who disliked a garden in riotous bloom."

The solicitor's sparse brows shot up. "My lord! I had no inkling of an engagement. Allow me to be among the first to offer my felicitations."

The earl's expression became pained. "Pray do not. I am a free man, Sedgewick, and hope to remain so for a little while yet."

Sedgewick wondered if he was being peculiarly dense in

not grasping his employer's meaning. "I beg pardon, my lord?"

Lord Anthony's eyes gleamed. He said gravely, "You must have had the honor of my aunt's acquaintance, Sedgewick. You may then imagine my feelings upon being admonished by Lady Pelborne that it is my sacred duty to marry and beget heirs, and that the sooner I do so, the better. Her arguments were quite persuasive."

The solicitor was seized with a fit of coughing that he quickly muffled behind a thin hand.

Lord Anthony seemed to take no notice, though his green eyes held a decidedly wicked light. He allowed a doleful sigh to escape him. "Alas, Sedgewick, I am resigned to my fate and dutifully make my plans. Yet, strangely enough, I find myself reluctant to make a hasty choice in my bride." The earl paused, then lowered his voice to a confidential level. "The truth of it is that I shall make the devil of a husband. I fear I shall be the cause of a grand disillusion for some poor unlucky creature. No, my chosen lady must not care a snap of her dainty fingers for my lack of character. But where am I to find such a paragon, Sedgewick? You may now guess the depth of my distress."

Sedgewick's dry voice cracked. "Your reservations do you vast credit, my lord."

Lord Anthony's sudden grin dispelled his exaggerated look of gloom. "My aunt would consign my noble reservations to the devil's keeping." Thought of Lady Pelborne brought to mind her guest, Miss Hetta Stanton. "By the by, Sedgewick, in all your many business dealings, have you ever heard aught of a gentleman called Jonathan Markham?"

The change in the solicitor's expression was dramatic. Through compressed lips, he said hastily, "That mountebank!" At Lord Anthony's look of astonishment, Sedgewick reddened. Clearing his throat, he said in his usual precise voice, "Forgive me, my lord. The Honorable Jonathan Markham is known to me only by reputation. An associate of mine had dealings with the gentleman while

serving as solicitor for Sir Giles, Markham's uncle. I fear
that Markham did not leave a favorable impression.''

The earl stretched out his long legs, top boots crossed at
the ankle, and settled himself in his chair. ''You interest
me. In what way, Sedgewick?''

His solicitor's face lengthened. ''I do not wish to slan-
der an acquaintance of your lordship's.''

Lord Anthony laughed. ''Have no fear, good Sedgewick. Markham and I are hardly likely to become fast
companions. On the contrary, I should be indebted to you
for any light that you may shed on the gentleman's
character.''

Sedgewick's smile was thin. ''Very well, my lord. My
associate related to me his genuine distress for the family
after Sir Giles died. A codicil was discovered to have
been appended to the will by a solicitor unknown to my
associate, which invalidated any previous dispositions and
made the Honorable Jonathan Markham sole heir to the old
gentleman's fortune. There was naturally an outcry that the
codicil was a forgery, and when that could not be proven,
certain family members accused Markham of coercing the
elderly gentleman into adding the codicil. My associate
believes Markham is at the very least guilty of undue
influence, for Sir Giles was in a frail state of mind for the
last year of his life. In short, my lord, it was a very nasty
business.''

''Surely Markham had the decency to try and smooth
things over,'' exclaimed Lord Anthony.

''On the contrary, my lord,'' Sedgewick said shortly.
''Though Markham received Sir Giles' fortune, my associate was able to preserve the manor house and lands for the
family because of the codicil's peculiar wording. When
Markham was informed, he behaved in a manner totally
unworthy of a gentleman of breeding. He denied the family access to any of his uncle's estate over which he had
control, and rescinded a small allowance Sir Giles had
made to his maiden sister. The unfortunate lady has been
forced to give up her small cottage and reside with cousins, which I understand is not a happy arrangement.''

Lord Anthony was stunned. Markham had acted with a

cruel malevolence that was utterly foreign to his own nature. Lord Anthony felt a burgeoning contempt and loathing for the man. Lady Pelborne had a right to be concerned for her goddaughter, he thought. If Miss Stanton reconsidered her decision and consented to Markham's suit, it was highly likely that she would bitterly regret it. A man of Markham's stripe did not turn saint when the marriage knot was tied. But even the astute Lady Pelborne could not be expected to divine the true depravity of Markham's character without warning. Lord Anthony felt himself duty-bound to drop a word in her ear. However, Miss Stanton herself was another matter. She was too great an innocent to heed any word of caution of his. Lord Anthony's thoughts flashed to his encounter with the naive Miss Stanton in his aunt's study, and his lips tightened. She would be like fragile porcelain in the hands of a man like Markham. Alone, she would be no match for him. Her gallant spirit would be utterly destroyed by his cruelty.

Lord Anthony realized where his thoughts had led him. Subconsciously he had already decided to do all in his power to protect Miss Hetta Stanton from the Honorable Jonathan Markham, even if that meant sitting in her pocket. Wryly he thought that such a development would certainly please Lady Pelborne's matchmaking heart. His last adventure threatened to involve him more deeply than he would ever have believed. He devoutly hoped that Miss Stanton would receive an acceptable offer for her hand before the Season was done, or his unofficial guardianship could prove awkward.

"My lord, is there something wrong?"

Lord Anthony roused himself from his thoughts to find Sedgewick regarding him with some anxiety. "Forgive me, Sedgewick. I was but reflecting on the twists of fate in one's fortune." He smiled suddenly at the solicitor. "I wish to acquire a small cottage."

His man of business was startled. "My lord?"

"I am a whimsical creature, Sedgewick," said the earl gravely. "I have a sudden compulsion to own a small cottage. An occupant will naturally need to be found. I suspect an elderly spinster would suit the purpose nicely."

He saw the dawning of understanding in his solicitor's eyes and said gently, "I am certain that you will know best how to fulfill my requirements."

"I will attend to the matter immediately, my lord," said Sedgewick, permitting himself a broad smile.

The earl rose from behind the mahogany desk. "Then I shall leave you to it. My afternoon ride is long overdue." Sedgewick bowed as the earl crossed the room. Lord Anthony paused at the door, his hand on the brass knob. "And, Sedgewick, I trust that my eccentricity will go unheralded."

"I shall be discretion itself, my lord," said Sedgewick gravely.

Lord Anthony nodded and left the study.

8

The week of the dinner party sped past in a flurry of activity. Lady Pelborne was determined that she and Hetta make the rounds of the various shops they had missed on their first shopping expedition. Hetta quickly came to acquire all of the necessary articles to a lady's wardrobe—hats and gloves, satin slippers, chemises made from sheerest silk and muslin, and the daintiest of corsets. Maggie stoically eyed the multiplying additions to her mistress's wardrobe and, without a word, set about enlisting the aid of an eager young housemaid who had aspirations of becoming a lady's dresser to bring order to Hetta's burgeoning possessions.

Besides the countless shopping excursions in the company of either Lady Pelborne or Lady Anthony, Hetta found herself put into the capable hands of a well-known coiffeur who ruthlessly cropped her heavy hair. When he had finished, he dressed it up on her head, leaving soft tendrils to waft free and becomingly frame her face. The halo of curls had the effect of emphasizing her wide hazel eyes. Hetta blinked at the transformation in her appearance, uncertain whether she cared for the change. The stoic Maggie was moved to observe that her ladyship's eyes had taken on the appearance of saucers.

After each day's excursion Hetta would return to the town house exhausted, and she could only marvel at her godmother's continued energy and cheerfulness. She began to wonder if she dared to disgrace herself by begging off from the seemingly unending trips, but at last Lady

Pelborne expressed herself satisfied that the appalling state
of her goddaughter's wardrobe was in a fair way to being
remedied and regretted only the necessity of waiting on the
orders from Lebonnier and the bootier, who had promised
to ready two pairs of kid half-boots by the following week.
Relieved, Hetta devoutly hoped that Lady Pelborne would
not suddenly think of another item she considered essential
for a lady's toilet.

Hetta was kept informed in a haphazard way by Lady
Anthony of the various details of the dinner party for that
Friday evening. That lady was determined that her new
friend's first London dinner party be a memorable one,
and she set about making the preparations with a zest just
short of incredible. Lady Pelborne granted her a free hand
with the ordering of the household, and the domestic staff
quickly took on a frenzied air as they went about their
tasks with Lady Anthony flitting close behind. It was not
long before the smell of silver polish and beeswax filled
the town house.

Lady Anthony deferred to her aunt on the composition
of the dinner guests, but Lady Pelborne found nothing to
criticize in the guest list or in the menu proposed by her
chef. Lady Pelborne did take issue, however, with Lady
Anthony's more whimsical notions and stated that to have
musicians strumming over one's plate was certain to give
one indigestion, and that she personally would firmly decline the nuts and fruit if the bowl were to be passed by a
monkey, however cunningly it was got up in a tiny footman's costume. Though Lady Anthony assured her that it
was a very well-behaved simian, having only once bitten
Maria Quayle, who quite deserved it because she had
sorely provoked the poor creature, her aunt stood firm.
Reluctantly Lady Anthony was forced to give up on the
monkey, but she did not stay long downcast as a new
inspiration for the entertainment of her guests soon struck
her. She refused to impart what treat was in store for them,
saying only with a mysterious air that everyone would
remember it as the most rollicking dinner party, and then
she bustled away to order that the piano be tuned and the
salon furniture arranged in an odd fashion.

Observing these preparations with a faintly jaundiced eye, Lady Pelborne said dryly, "One can only hope that it is not the monkey who is to play."

Hetta begged her godmother not to mention such an absurdity to Lady Anthony. "For it is just the sort of nonsensical notion to find favor with Loraine," she said with amusement.

Lady Anthony had sent out less than a half-dozen gilt-edged invitations, remarking that it was to be an intimate gathering only. "It will not be a particularly large party, dearest Hetta, but I promise you that it will be a merry one," she said. At that moment the arrival of the florists was announced and she jumped up to supervise the placing of the specially created flower baskets she had gone to such lengths to order.

With nothing more to occupy her and aware of the late hour, Hetta made her way upstairs to put herself in Maggie's hands to begin her toilet for that evening. Madame Lebonnier could not in all fairness be expected to deliver a new evening gown so speedily and her godmother had seen to it that one of the more acceptable gowns Hetta had brought with her to London was altered and refurbished with tuckings of lace at the neckline and cuffs for the occasion. When Hetta had tried the refurbished gown on earlier in the week, she had been well-satisfied with the result. She thought the sprigged muslin had never appeared brighter, nor more fashionable, and she was confident her appearance at the dinner party would be all that could be wished.

When she entered the bedroom, she was surprised to discover Maggie unpacking the first of two boxes that had arrived from Lebonnier only moments before. The maid lifted free a gown of a soft leaf green, long-sleeved and trimmed with lace at the neckline and in rows above the hem.

"Oh! How very pretty," exclaimed Hetta, coming forward to examine it. She held it up against her and glanced in the mirror.

"Aye, it is that," Maggie said approvingly as she lifted the top of the other box. Her surprised exclamation caused Hetta to turn in inquiry, and then she too was staring at the second gown Maggie had freed from its tissues. The puff-sleeved gown was made from a subdued mustard-yellow crepe trimmed with sable-brown ribbons.

"It is rather an unusual shade of yellow," Hetta said hesitantly. She wondered what could possibly have possessed Madame Lebonnier to choose such an odd color for her.

Maggie snorted expressively. "Unusual is scarcely the word, miss. Ye'll hardly be wishing to wear this one, I'm thinking."

Reluctantly Hetta agreed and, as she fingered the fine fabric of the gown, thought it was a pity that it should be this dress that was more suitable of the two for a private dinner party. The gown was elaborate and much more sophisticated than any she had ever worn. On impulse Hetta decided that she would see how it looked on her.

Despite a disparaging comment from Maggie, Hetta put on the yellow gown and turned to the mirror. Even the garrulous Maggie was silent as they digested her appearance. The gown's short bodice was scooped daringly low across Hetta's breast and filled with the sheerest lawn. The skirt, gathered high under the breasts, fell in clinging folds to her ankles. Hetta's eyes had taken on a gold light with the unusual mustard color, and her skin glowed soft as alabaster.

"Madame did not err in judgment after all, Maggie," she said quietly. She smoothed the tucked bodice and lawn. "I believe that I shall wear it this evening with the amber brooch that Papa left to me. It is just the same odd shade of gold."

"Aye, 'tis plain that it suits ye, though I canna but wonder how such a dirty yellow can look so fine on a body," Maggie said grudgingly, going to the wardrobe for her mistress's jewel box. She returned with a very old brooch set with an oddly shaped yellow stone. Before handing it to Hetta, she critically inspected the intricate design of the gold setting and shook her head. Her fingers touched the simple gold locket and chain lying against her breast. "Such an ugly piece, and so I have always thought."

"Perhaps I shall set a fashion for mustard yellow. What

do you think, Maggie? Shall I make it my trademark?''
Hetta asked flippantly. She seated herself at the dressing
table and fastened the brooch between the soft swell of her
breasts below the folds of fragile lawn.

The maid picked up a hairbrush and began to sweep it
through her hair. ''It may do very well for Lady Anthony's
dinner party, but I wouldna care to see ye making a
spectacle of yourself oot of doors,'' said Maggie dispas-
sionately. Skillfully she pinned up Hetta's dark chestnut
hair to leave only an artful fringe of curls around her face.

Hetta smoothed the soft fabric of her skirt. ''Have you
had occasion to peek in at the dining room? I think it
vastly pretty. Lady Anthony has positively transformed it
into a bower of spring flowers and greenery.''

''Aye, and a tangled wilderness it is,'' Maggie said
dourly. ''I couldna take my dinner for fear of wild beasties
leaping upon me.'' She gave a last pat to her mistress's
hair and set aside the brush.

Hetta turned from the mirror with the hint of a mischievous smile in the depths of her eyes. ''The wild beastie
would likely be naught but a small monkey, Maggie, for
Lady Anthony had set her heart on having one to scurry
over the table with the nut bowl.''

The maid's eyes gleamed in appreciation but she said
primly, '' 'Tis scandalous how these Londoners carry on.''

''Yes, isn't it delightful?'' exclaimed Hetta with a merry
laugh. ''I am forever in stitches, especially when I am
with Lady Anthony. She can be ever so droll and absurd
without once realizing it.'' She smiled reminiscently. ''I
had never before considered how dull we had become at
Meldingcourt after dear Papa died. Oh, Maggie, I *am* glad
that we came to London. When I think that I might have
accepted Cousin Jonathan and perhaps never have come to
know Lady Anthony, I positively bless my good sense.''

''He'll not be giving up on ye so easily,'' Maggie said.
She glanced at her mistress's face as she set a spray of
small white flowers in her hair. ''I'm thinking that it will
not be long before Master Markham shows his face in
Londontown. Ye ken that, chuck.''

''I fear that to be true,'' Hetta sighed. ''But I refuse to

waste more than a moment's reflection upon it this evening, for I intend to enjoy myself to the fullest while I may."

"Hetta! My dear Hetta, may I speak with you?" They turned as the door opened and Lady Pelborne put her head in. "Ah, you are dressed, and how marvelous you look too! Splendid, for I wish you to meet a very particular friend of mine." She widened the door to reveal a rotund figure in a gored coat and waistcoat and old-fashioned knee breeches. "Hetta, this is Sir Horace Meening, who will be joining us at dinner. I have asked him up as he is also my personal physician and I particularly wish him to examine that monstrous bruise of yours."

The gentleman made a leg and there was the ominous creak of a tightly laced corset. "Your servant, Miss Stanton."

"It is Hetta, sir, and I am very happy to make your acquaintance," said Hetta, putting out her hand.

Lady Pelborne turned her goddaughter's affability to advantage. "You will see, Horace. The bruise is simply spectacular. Hetta has assured me that she has not had a recurrence of the headaches from which she was suffering, but I naturally wished your professional opinion. One must be certain that no lasting harm was taken from the blow."

"Quite right, Bea." Sir Horace turned twinkling eyes on Hetta. "If you will but remain seated at your dressing table, young lady, we shall have this over in a trice." He nodded pleasantly to Maggie, who had stepped aside as he approached.

Hetta sighed in resignation. "Very well, sir. However, I must warn you that my dear godmother has unduly alarmed herself, and so I have told her."

Sir Horace tilted her head and gently felt around the bruised area of her brow, then peered intently into her eyes. "So it would seem, Miss Stanton," he said as he stepped back. He winked conspiratorially at her. "Your godmother mentioned the possible need for a prescription. It appears that it is not you who requires my attention, but Lady Pelborne. I should think a calming draft for the nerves will do nicely."

Lady Pelborne rapped his knuckles with her ivory fan. "How dare you to plot against me, you old quack! Pray recall who it is that pays your outrageous fees."

"Quite so," said Sir Horace, apparently much struck. "I must be certain to prescribe healthful potions for each member of your household so that I may assure myself of a handsome profit."

Lady Pelborne's retort was somewhat rude, but Sir Horace only laughed good-naturedly as he offered both ladies an arm so that he could escort them downstairs. By the time they had descended the stairs and entered the drawing room, Hetta was laughing at the easy flow of banter in which Sir Horace excelled, and had quite forgotten any nervousness she might have possessed.

As they entered the drawing room, the small group waiting turned inquiring glances toward them.

"Oh, there you are! Dear Hetta, do come greet our guests. I assure you that we will all soon be fast friends," Lady Anthony said, flitting to Hetta's side and drawing her forward. She made the introductions and Hetta exchanged civil words with an older gentleman with the most extraordinarily bushy eyebrows she had ever seen. Working his brows up and down, Lord Frobisher stared at her fiercely before giving an abrupt nod as Lady Anthony whisked her away to meet the only female guest.

Miss Maria Quayle, whom Hetta immediately recalled was reputed to be thoroughly disliked by a certain small monkey, was a plump lady of indeterminate age whose slightly protuberant eyes surveyed all around her with the liveliest curiosity. Her smile was friendly as she took Hetta's hand. "So nice to meet you at last, Miss Stanton! When I received Loraine's invitation, I simply knew that I must come, for one should always make a point of cultivating a new acquaintance whenever one can. I find people to be absolutely fascinating creatures, do you not?"

Somewhat disconcerted, Hetta began to murmur a polite agreement, but Miss Quayle had already turned her gaze on the small company around them. Sighing in contentment, she said, "It is such a charmingly intimate group, Loraine."

"I made sure that you would care for it," Lady Anthony said warmly. As Miss Quayle drifted off to join Lady Pelborne and Sir Horace, Loraine leaned close to Hetta's ear and confided, "She is the dearest, kindest of creatures, but never divulge a syllable you do not want known immediately throughout London!"

A fresh-faced young man approached them. Lady Anthony took his arm and drew him closer. "And this quite provoking creature is my own cousin, Edward Strappey. He has just come down from Oxford and already he is up to mischief. It is his first Season in London as well."

Edward grinned engagingly as he made his bows. "Honored, ma'am. I shan't say a word in my own defense except that one shouldn't put great stock in anything Cousin Loraine may say. I am the most honorable of fellows, 'pon my word."

Hetta laughed as she shook his hand. "I am utterly convinced of it, Mr. Strappey!"

"Well!" exclaimed Lady Anthony, outraged. "And to think that he has this very afternoon run a donkey down Bond Street too."

Hetta glanced at Edward to discover a half-shamed expression on his cherubic countenance and said promptly, "One must entertain oneself, after all."

Delighted, he grinned at her. "It was a wager, you see," he explained in a rush of boyish enthusiasm.

"I trust that you won, Edward?" asked Lady Pelborne, amused, as she extended her hand to him. She was rewarded with an abashed nod and an impudent grin.

While they spoke, Lady Anthony had turned to a quiet gentleman who leaned lightly on a smooth malacca cane in the background. She laid her small fingers on the sleeve of his coat, which was cut in the looser style favored by military gentlemen, and drew him forward. She now nipped at Hetta's arm for her attention. "Hetta, this is Captain Peter Trevor. He is a very dear, dear friend of mine," said Lady Anthony, glancing up at him with a smile that dazzled. "He was wounded in the same battle in which Edmond was killed and was good enough to tell me about it. So patient and comforting! I am sure that I positively drenched his coat with tears, but never a word of reproach did he utter.''

"One could never reproach so brave a lady,'' said Captain Trevor, his expression betraying him as he glanced down at Lady Anthony's ash-blond head, which hardly came up to his shoulder.

Oblivious to his look, Lady Anthony threw out expressive hands. ''You see!''

Captain Trevor took a halting step toward Hetta and bowed to her with seeming effortlessness. ''I am honored to make your acquaintance, Miss Stanton.''

She looked up into a pair of very blue candid eyes that held great good humor. Immediately she warmed to him, recognizing a potential friend. ''And I yours, sir,'' said Hetta, extending her hand to him. He smiled as he clasped her fingers for a brief moment.

''And now that we all know one another, we may all be comfortable,'' said Lady Anthony gaily. Espying a footman at the door, she suggested that the company retire to the dining room and the gentlemen offered their arms to the ladies.

Sir Horace turned to Lady Anthony and made her a quaint bow, his stays creaking. ''I would be most honored to secure the hand of one truly most fair to behold, Lady Anthony.''

Loraine accepted his arm and reached up to gently pat his cheek. ''You're such a dear sweet man, Sir Horace. Indeed, I wonder that you have not long since become an uncle, for I daresay you should make someone like myself a perfectly splendid one.''

Sir Horace cast a quick glance at Lady Pelborne's retreating back as she went into the dining room on Lord Frobisher's arm. ''My dear girl, we'll have none of your strange whimsy this evening, if you please. I beg you to leash your tongue.''

''Oh!'' Lady Anthony cast him an exaggerated look of innocence. ''My horrid tongue does run away with me at times. But pay it no attention, for I assure you that I do not.''

''Yes, my dear, I am well aware of it, and that is just

what I fear," said Sir Horace ruefully. Lady Anthony gave a trill of laughter and he chuckled in response as they entered the dining room.

Lady Pelborne smiled fondly on them from her place at the table as Sir Horace seated Lady Anthony. "It promises already to be a most congenial evening. One can only thank the hostess for her efforts to bring together the present delightful company."

"Oh, I say! I should think so," said Edward with barely suppressed enthusiasm as he surveyed the heavily laden table and sideboard. His hearty appetite informed him that a feast was in store and he was always willing to do full justice to a sumptuous dinner.

Dimpling at him, Lady Anthony shook her head. "You are a greedy boy, Edward," she said gaily. "I have asked Cook to specially prepare a plum pudding, for I knew that you would like me to."

"Famous! Thank you, cousin," said Edward, his eyes lighting up.

The guests sat down to a repast that soon met with unqualified approval and compliments. A clear barley soup and a respectable filet of veal were removed by baked quails served in a superb butter and herb sauce, accompanied by sauced chicken livers and such side dishes as French beans and tender new peas. Dressed lobsters appeared for the second course, and for dessert there were such tempting selections as the plum pudding, a tray of delicate pastries, and various cold jellies and creams.

Over the baked quail, Lord Frobisher took note of Hetta's brooch and inquired into its history with his characteristically abrupt manner. He remarked that as a young man when he had traveled a great deal, he had once come across just such a stone in the Holy Land.

Hetta touched the amber brooch lightly. "It is very likely, sir. This particular brooch has been handed down in my family for generations with the story attached to it that it once belonged to an ancestor who was fortunate enough to return from the Crusades. My father left it to me, but I have seldom worn it as it seems more like a man's cloak pin than a lady's brooch."

"Very rare piece, indeed," said Lord Frobisher gruffly.
"I have never before seen one with a bee entombed at its
center. I should hang on to it, Miss Stanton."

Edward, who had been listening with only polite interest, now stared closer at Hetta's brooch. "By Jove, there
is a tiny bee in it," he exclaimed, marveling. On his other
side Miss Quayle made an inquiry about the hunter he had
brought with him to London, and he turned to her, quickly
forgetting the amber brooch in the discussion of his con-
suming passion for hunting. The company were soon all
drawn onto the topic of horseflesh. Hetta, who had always
felt completely at home in the saddle and had participated
in the hunt from childhood, found to her surprise that the
craggy Lord Frobisher was regarding her with marked
approval. She learned later from Lady Pelborne that he
was an avid hunter and had little patience for anyone who
was mad enough to dislike hounds and horses.

The conversation turned to politics and the theater, becoming sparked by wit and warm camaraderie. When Lady
Pelborne rose as a signal to the ladies to repair to the salon
so that the gentlemen could enjoy their after-dinner wine,
it was thought a great deal too bad to interrupt the party
and the gentlemen were not long in joining them. A game
of charades was proposed by Edward Strappey and met
with indulgent approval. The game quickly took on the
proportions of an exercise in absurdities, and Captain Trevor
surprised them all with his inventive wit. The charades
eventually dissolved into laughter with even Lord Frobisher
lying back in his chair and giving way to great guffaws.

Lady Anthony skipped across the carpet to seat herself
at the piano and skillfully began to play a familiar country
dance. When Captain Trevor limped over to stand beside
the instrument to turn her music, she greeted him with a
shining smile before turning back once more to the other
guests and urging them to take to the floor.

Edward made an elaborate bow to Hetta. His eyes were
alight with mischief as he asked with mock formality,
"May I have the honor of this dance, ma'am?"

Hetta curtsied to him, her eyes laughing. "Certainly,

sir! I have reserved all my dances in hopes of just such an invitation.''

Edward swung her out into the area that had earlier been cleared of furniture and twirled Hetta about with energetic ease to the music. The other guests watched, enjoying the spectacle, but when the dance ended, Sir Horace immediately called for an old-fashioned minuet. Lady Anthony obliged and Sir Horace led Hetta out. The older man, for all his girth, proved to be an elegant partner and Hetta enjoyed his direction enormously. She saw that Edward was now skillfully leading Lady Pelborne around the floor. Lord Frobisher and Miss Quayle were urged to join in the exercise and presently succumbed to the general mood of jollity.

For the better part of an hour Lady Anthony played for the whirling couples who had quickly forgotten dignity in their plain enjoyment. The impromptu romp ended with a round dance that lady Anthony deliberately accelerated until the dancers were spinning ever faster in their circle. Lord Frobisher and Miss Quayle quickly dropped out, but a puffing and red-faced Sir Horace would not give up his hold on Lady Pelborne until she protested laughingly that she had grown too old for such strenuous activity. They turned to watch as Edward spun Hetta ever faster. Hetta became breathless and her lips parted on pealing laughter as their mad pace was encouraged by the amusement of the others.

Suddenly their clasped hands parted. They flew apart, Edward to fall back on Sir Horace while Hetta was sent spinning in the opposite direction, the laughter bubbling in her throat. She was flung upon a muscular chest to be caught fast in strong arms.

''Oh!'' she exclaimed breathlessly. She looked up with sparkling eyes, a merry apology on her lips, and met the enigmatic gaze of Lord Anthony. The laughter caught in her throat. She was stunned by his unexpected appearance. As she stared up at him, her mind played tricks, suspending the fleeting moment so that it seemed she had been forever standing in his arms.

There was an unreadable expression in his eyes as he

looked down into her questioning gaze. He watched as the bright animation in her face dimmed to consternation. He smiled, breaking entirely the spell between them. His voice was soft and for her ears alone. "Well met, my dear. It seems my fate to discover you in my arms wherever I turn."

She flushed bright pink, then she was freed. To those around them the brief encounter lasted but an instant, and her heightened color was taken as the natural reaction of a genteel young woman who was embarrassed by the unexpected position in which she found herself.

Lady Pelborne came up to Lord Anthony with outstretched hands, a welcoming smile on her face. "Michael! My dear! How happy I am to see you." She reached up to kiss him with affection.

Lord Anthony tucked her hand in his elbow while he turned to reply to Sir Horace, who had greeted him with the greatest good humor. Lord Frobisher and Miss Quayle chorused a general welcome, and he nodded pleasantly to them.

Lady Pelborne drew him over to introduce him to those of the company he did not know. Lord Anthony spoke a few civil words to Edward, gratifying that young gentleman as he had immediately recognized in Lord Anthony a downy one. Lord Anthony and Captain Trevor exchanged an easy greeting, apparently having met each other previously. Upon Lady Pelborne's inquiry, Lord Anthony said, "Trevor and I met at Waterloo, on the wing. He was good enough to lend me another horse when mine was shot out from under me. I was unfortunately unable to return it to him later as it, also, took a ball."

"What more could I do when his lordship chose to land on his head at my feet, hatless and with his laces torn, and swearing at me to be quick about it?" asked Captain Trevor humorously. There was general laughter at the picture he had conjured up.

Lord Anthony turned to his sister-in-law, who was still sitting at the piano. She looked at him with an expression of apprehension on her lovely face. He took her lifeless hand to carry it to his lips. "Loraine, I hope that I find you well?"

Lady Anthony turned white, then pinkened. She practically snatched her hand from his grasp. "Of course I am well. I am never out of sorts," she said, her voice unnaturally high.

Lord Anthony smiled slightly. Lady Pelborne laid firm claim to his arm and directed his attention to Hetta. "You have met my goddaughter Miss Stanton, of course," she said.

Lord Anthony bowed to Hetta. "Miss Stanton appears more charming than ever."

"Thank you, my lord," murmured Hetta with a faint tinge of color still in her cheeks. She lowered her lashes, unable to look directly into his mocking eyes.

"Pray tell us, my boy, to what do we owe this unexpected pleasure?" asked Sir Horace genially. "I had quite understood from Beatrice that you intended a rather lengthier stay at Davenchester."

"So I had. But as it was, I found the contractor readily agreeable to my suggestions for the needed repairs, and since I thought him a capable-enough fellow, I have left it entirely in his hands. The work is progressing smoothly and I saw no reason to prolong my absence from London."

"Ah, so your man of business has at last won his petition for repairs to the house. I recall that he was unsuccessful in urging both your father and then Edmond to agree to it. It was supposedly to cost a veritable fortune to renovate the main wing," Lady Pelborne said. "I had always considered it a great pity that the oldest wing of Davenchester was allowed to tumble into ruin."

"Oh, is Michael repairing Davenchester? Edmond always used to say that he should like to see it restored one day," Lady Anthony said. She gave a nervous titter. "It was such a great drafty place that one could not be expected to bear its discomforts for long."

Lord Anthony glanced enigmatically at his sister-in-law. "Unfortunately it is in astounding disrepair. It will take some time, but I hope to have it respectable again before the hunting season begins." He addressed himself to Lady

Anthony. "Perhaps you shall all come down for the Christmas season and give me the pleasure of showing you the improvements I have ordered made, Loraine. I feel sure that my brother would have been delighted. Edmond loved Davenchester as a boy."

Lady Anthony did not reply and the tension was marked between them. Captain Trevor glanced from one to the other, a faint frown forming between his sandy brows. Miss Quayle's interested gaze wavered only slightly as Lord Frobisher gave a discreet cough and leaned over to speak in her ear. Finally Lady Pelborne broke the uncomfortable silence and tucked her hand once more in Lord Anthony's elbow to gently draw him away with her. "I for one am glad you have come. Loraine's little dinner party has been an unqualified success and your unexpected appearance has crowned this evening for me."

Lady Anthony rose abruptly from the piano stool. She acknowledged Captain Trevor's quick assistance with a distracted smile. "Do pray excuse me. I have developed a headache. It has been a truly wonderful evening, but—" She brushed aside all exclamations of sympathy and with a wan smile allowed Captain Trevor to escort her solicitously from the room. Her exit was accompanied by an awkward silence, broken when Captain Trevor limped back to Lady Pelborne to make his bows. "I, too, feel the lateness of the hour, ma'am. I will regretfully take my leave of you and the present company." Lady Pelborne accepted his excuses graciously and he then turned to Edward. "If you care to accept a seat in my carriage, young Edward, I shall be glad to drop you off at your lodgings."

Edward thanked him for his obliging offer before turning to Lady Pelborne and Hetta. He confided ingenuously, "I feared it was to be a rather dull affair, you know. Cousin Loraine did not let on for a moment that it was to be such a bang-up party. I am awfully glad to have come, after all, for I was not at all sure that I wished to."

Hetta laughed at him, but Lady Pelborne managed to keep her composure admirably. Her eyes twinkling, she gravely assured Edward that he would certainly be added to any future guest list.

The gentlemen's exit was quickly followed by that of Lord Frobisher and Miss Quayle. Looking after them, Sir Horace sighed in regret. "Well, Bea, another lively evening has ended far too soon. I suppose that I also must take my leave." He planted a fond salute on Lady Pelborne's powdered cheek before turning to Hetta, who immediately held out her hand to him. Holding her slender fingers briefly between his palms, he said, "My dear, it has indeed been a rare pleasure to have met you. Davenchester, come visit with me one day at the club. I shall enjoy seeing you." He nodded at Lord Anthony, who had come up to stand beside Hetta.

Lady Pelborne walked with her old friend to the door and he addressed her in a lowered voice. "Terribly upsetting thing to have happen, you know, for the hostess to disappear in the midst of things. Put a damper on the entire company."

"Of course it did, and unfortunately my tactlessness did not help matters. But you are aware of how things stand, Horace," said Lady Pelborne.

"I find it small excuse to break up a perfectly good evening's entertainment," Sir Horace said in strong disapproval.

Lady Pelborne tapped his knuckles with her fan. "Pray be still, Horace, or I shall not wish to escort you to the front steps."

Sir Horace looked at her with warming eyes. "Why, Bea, I did not think you cared for my welfare."

"One is surely obliged by civility to provide safe-conduct to a guest, however obnoxious he may have proven himself to be," retorted Lady Pelborne with a show of primness.

Sir Horace chuckled and allowed himself to be propelled from the room.

Hetta watched them disappear with consternation. When Lord Anthony had come up beside her, she had given him only a polite smile and answered his civilities as shortly as she was able. She now glanced at him and discovered that he was regarding her with a certain lazy amusement. He said with polite courtesy, "You look admirably this evening, Miss Stanton."

"Thank you, my lord," said Hetta coolly.

"One hopes that you have contrived to amuse yourself during my absence?" he asked.

"Quite so, my lord," said Hetta, looking at him directly for the first time. She seized the opportunity to prove to him that she had not spared him a thought. "Dear Godmamma and Lady Anthony have kept me in such a whirl of activity that I have not had a moment to draw breath. Indeed, I have been unable to give even a passing thought to exploring the sights of London! However, I assure you that I have become intimately acquainted with the interior of every shop."

His voice came soft to her ear. "I could wish that you had not allowed your hair to be cropped." His gaze dropped from her face to linger on the sheer lawn cut low across her breast. "I remember it as a glorious cascade with the moonlight entrapped in its silken strands."

Hetta blushed furiously. She put her hands to her hot cheeks. "My lord! You should not—must not—address me in such a fashion." She trembled with the breathless feeling kindled by his words. Though he did not touch her, his low voice was as intimate as a caress on her skin and recalled emotions that she had hoped would remain buried.

"You think not? I am at least honest, Miss Stanton," said Lord Anthony quietly.

"What ever do you mean?" asked Hetta sharply, feeling unaccountably defensive. The implicit warmth in his green eyes stilled her, causing her heart to beat faster, and her blush deepened.

Lady Pelborne reentered the salon. "Sir Horace is off at last. He disliked intensely for our little gathering to end. The man would surely rise from his deathbed merely to attend what appeared to be a promising affair." She suddenly became aware of the tension between her nephew and goddaughter. Lady Pelborne glanced sharply from one to the other, but did not allow her voice to betray her acute curiosity. "And what may I have missed, dear ones?"

Upon her godmother's entrance Hetta had torn her eyes free of Lord Anthony's mesmerizing gaze and turned away, her hands once more against her face. He looked thoughtfully at her back before responding to his aunt. "I have succeeded in putting Miss Stanton out of countenance, ma'am," he said with a lurking smile.

Lady Pelborne relaxed. "You have always been an abominable tease, Michael. I only hope that you may one day attempt to curb your odd sense of humor. It is bad enough that you make game of myself and poor Hetta, but one hesitates to contemplate your reception by the *ton*."

"I imagine that my lofty position shall carry me through any disgrace," said Lord Anthony indifferently.

Hetta choked an incoherent word. She turned to her godmother, once more mistress of herself. "I shall say good night now, Godmamma. It was truly a lovely party."

Lady Pelborne looked at her in some surprise. "Hetta, you are surely not abandoning us as well?"

"I beg the excitement of the evening, dear Godmamma. Indeed, this last week has entirely overwhelmed me," said Hetta with some truth.

"Pray do not feel that you must leave on my account, Miss Stanton," Lord Anthony said, a mocking expression in his eyes.

"You flatter yourself unduly, sir," retorted Hetta. She saw the quick laughter in his eyes and closed her lips firmly, thinking better of her next words. She kissed Lady Pelborne with true affection. "I had a wonderful time. I do hope that poor Loraine is recovered in the morning. I thought that she appeared unusually strained toward the last."

"Fear not, child. Loraine will undoubtedly waken much refreshed. These abrupt headaches of hers tend to pass off fairly quickly," said Lady Pelborne with a swift glance toward her nephew. His face expressed only mild interest. She smiled at her goddaughter. "One hopes that you thought to bring your riding habit, child, for I have arranged for a lively mount to be put at your disposal. She will be ready to fly with you tomorrow in the park."

"Oh, how marvelous," exclaimed Hetta. Her eyes shone with anticipation. "I do thank you, Godmamma."

"I take it Miss Stanton rides?" Lord Anthony asked his aunt.

Lady Pelborne chuckled. "Indeed she does, and is quite an accomplished equestrienne. She had little choice in the matter, I fear. Her father loved the hunt and insisted that Hetta learn to take a jump at a very early age. Fortunately, Hetta inherited his love of horses and got along splendidly with him. I never saw his equal on a hunter. Hetta takes after him in that she rarely misses an opportunity for a gallop."

It suddenly occurred to Lord Anthony that a public park could provide the perfect opportunity for an abduction if that was truly Markham's scheme. But if he established himself from the first as a casual riding companion for Miss Stanton, his presence would surely complicate matters. "Then we must certainly ride together one day," he said with his pleasantest smile as he looked at Hetta.

"One day perhaps," said Hetta with a deliberately dismissive tone. She had the satisfaction of seeing a darkening of expression in his eyes and bestowed upon him a sweet smile. She then dropped a curtsy as she murmured her excuses and left them.

His good intentions thwarted, Lord Anthony stared frowningly at the closed door. "She wants manners, ma'am."

"Indeed, and in what way? One would not have believed you to be so sensitive, Michael," said Lady Pelborne. "She is, after all, only a pert chit like any other."

Her nephew looked at her with the beginnings of a reluctant grin. "Perhaps my vanity is pricked, ma'am. I am generally the deliverer of the gentle set-down!"

"One cannot help but applaud my goddaughter. She possesses an unerring sense for the appropriate," Lady Pelborne observed, laughter in her eyes.

"And one does not have to look far to find her example," retorted Lord Anthony.

"I admit that her company has been vastly entertaining," said Lady Pelborne. She had seated herself on a sofa and now indicated the space beside her. "Come, tell me of the improvements at Davenchester."

"You shall see them at the proper time and no hints shall you have beforehand," said Lord Anthony teasingly.

His smile faded. "Have you heard aught of the Honorable Jonathan Markham?"

Immediately Lady Pelborne was sober. "Not a word. I have asked Horace to make discreet inquiries among his cronies. He possesses a motley group of acquaintances, and if there's anything to be heard, he will learn of it."

Lord Anthony nodded. "I had occasion to mention Markham to my man of business. To my surprise, the gentleman was quite well-known to him in a roundabout fashion. It seems he is acquainted with the family solicitor. At any rate, from the few details I could glean, it appears that our friend Markham may have dealt somewhat shadily in securing his uncle's fortune. The elderly gentleman was known to have been easily influenced. He willed everything to Markham, though there was another branch of the family considered to be as deserving. I gathered that some sort of dust was kicked up over the settlement of the estate, but the will could not be proven false."

"One cannot help but feel a certain prejudice against the man," murmured Lady Pelborne.

"He seems to be more and more a thoroughly unsavory character," agreed Lord Anthony. "If he does appear to request the privilege of your goddaughter's company, I would suggest that you give him short shrift, ma'am."

"Never fear, Anthony. I reserve a touch of cold steel for those whom I have reason to distrust," said Lady Pelborne, a glint in her eyes.

"Then I shall take my leave with confidence, ma'am." Lord Anthony took up her hand and gave her fingers an affectionate squeeze.

"I suppose that is my cue to wish you a good night," said Lady Pelborne resignedly. "I do wish that you would settle down, Michael. I know full well that you now intend to spend the remainder of the evening in a club. Your display of energy fatigues me, dear boy."

He only laughed as he left her.

9

When Hetta went to her room, she found that Maggie was waiting up for her. "Whatever are you doing awake, Maggie? I am perfectly capable of undressing myself," Hetta said.

"Aye, and how was a body to sleep with that loud din downstairs?" asked Maggie tartly as she unbuttoned her mistress's creased dinner gown. The dress slid to the floor, followed by a sheer chemise. Hetta stepped out of the folds of the gown and allowed Maggie to throw a fine lawn nightgown over her head. "Ye must be fagged to death with the riotous partying ye have done this night," Maggie commented.

Hetta shook her head, happiness lighting her eyes. "Oh no. I could not possibly sleep yet." She circled about the room, her gown wafting gently about her waltzing figure. "Oh, Maggie, it was so delightful and I did so enjoy the dancing."

Maggie eyed her askance as she folded the discarded gown and chemise over her arm. "Ye need a sleeping potion, I'm thinking. Och, I ken the very thing." She left through the door connecting her mistress's room to her own. When she returned, Hetta was slipping into bed. Maggie carried a thin volume. "Tis a frippery novel, but a fair tale for all that," she said, giving the book to her mistress.

Hetta looked at her in astonishment. "Maggie, do not tell me that you have renounced your principles and have succumbed to romances."

Her companion's cheeks reddened. "I have not," said
Maggie with dignity. "I am still of the same opinion, but I
am that fair-minded, too. Some novels canna be as trashy
as the rest." Hetta could not hold back a splutter of
laughter. Maggie sniffed. "Good-night, miss!" She sailed
from the room, her back stiff with outrage at Hetta's
amusement.

Hetta settled herself against the pillows, still chuckling
over Maggie's discomfiture. She opened the book's cover,
curious to see what tale had so captivated her starchy
companion. A bold scrawl on the flyleaf leapt out at her.

Hetta's heart skipped a beat. She had forgotten the novel
Lord Anthony had given to Lady Pelborne, and why he
had done so. The fire of his kiss, the feel of his powerful
arms holding her close, came rushing back. Hetta shook
her head sharply. She must be mad to have such feelings,
she thought, staring angrily at the apology written in Lord
Anthony's bold hand.

Her eyes widened in fresh comprehension. She had
supposed that Lord Anthony's purpose in sending the novel
to her was to further her embarrassment. She saw now that
he was attempting to express his regret in a private manner
that would not excite undue curiosity from Lady Pelborne.
Hetta was shamed that she had so obviously misjudged
Lord Anthony's motives. She brushed aside the thought
that it was inexperience with such situations that had mis-
guided her. Hetta felt the least she could do now was to
acknowledge his overture of peace by showing him a more
gracious manner in future.

However, her noble intentions were to be frustrated, for
Hetta saw little of Lord Anthony in the next few weeks.
On the brief occasions when they chanced to meet it was
only to exchange the most commonplace of civilities. Hetta
came to harbor a perverse pique against him. She was not
only unable to demonstrate her generous spirit to him, but
she discovered that she had enjoyed the sparring of wits
between them and she now missed it.

Hetta was given little time to reflect upon her grievances. Lady Pelborne had announced her intention of giving her goddaughter a come-out ball at the beginning of

April and set in motion a train of preparations. Seeing Lady Pelborne immersed in such details as the engagement of musicians and dealing with her temperamental French chef on the question of refreshments, Hetta offered to address the gilt-edged invitations. It was an impulse she swiftly came to regret, for the length of the guest list was staggering. The unaccustomed exercise soon gave her fingers a painful cramp. When she appealed to Lady Anthony for assistance, that lady only gave a merry laugh and continued to pull on her lavender kid gloves. "Now, you know why I was so quick to offer to see to the ballroom decorations. Dearest Hetta, you do have my sympathy but I really must be off to the shops." Hetta's retort was unmaidenly but Lady Anthony paid not the slightest heed as she set off to lighten Lady Pelborne's ample purse.

To her dismay, Hetta discovered that her major duty in preparation for her come-out was to stand for several long fittings while her godmother critically assessed Madame Lebonnier's creations. At last Lady Pelborne expressed her approval of an evening dress of watered gold gauze over a satin slip. "For the insipid pale pink or blue prefered by most of our debutantes would not become you at all. This soft gold will be much more the thing," said Lady Pelborne with satisfaction. She noticed the tired look on her goddaughter's face and said gently, "Go to bed, child."

Hetta tumbled into bed that night utterly exhausted, but she rose with the early-morning sun, as was her usual custom, and donned her riding habit to take the mare, Firefly, for a gallop in the park. Her solitary morning rides had come to be the times she could relax and renew her energies from the rigors of the London Season. Afterward when she returned to the town house and turned Firefly over to the waiting groom, she crept upstairs to fall asleep again until Maggie wakened her for breakfast with Lady Pelborne.

Lady Pelborne glanced approvingly across the table at her. "I am given to understand that you ride each morning before breakfast. It is obvious that you and the mare suit each other admirably. I have never seen Firefly look fitter, while you positively glow with healthy color."

"I have truly enjoyed riding her, Godmamma. Thank you so much for providing Firey for me. I shall regret relinquishing her when I return to Meldingcourt," Hetta said, pouring a second cup of tea.

"Perhaps I shall present her to you as a wedding gift," said Lady Pelborne, half in earnest.

Hetta laughed, raising her well-arched brows at her. "Dear ma'am, are you not anticipating matters a trifle? I have not even become acquainted with an eligible suitor, much less reached an understanding."

"Odder things than an engagement have occurred during a young lady's first Season, my dear," said Lady Pelborne serenely. "I made certain to invite several eligible young gentlemen to your ball this evening. We shall see how you take."

"One hopes for the best, of course," said Hetta flippantly.

She was remembering the conversation as she stood before the cheval glass that evening. Her simple gold evening gown clung softly to the slender curves of her figure and from beneath its hem peeped the toes of her gold satin slippers. Her hair was dressed high on her head but for the soft tendrils around her face. Despite her undeniably charming appearance, Hetta could not help feeling a certain degree of anxiety. Tucking back a curl from her brow with nervous fingers, she asked, "Maggie, shall I pass?"

The maid was kneeling beside her taking a last quick stitch in the hem, which had been discovered to be a shade too long. Glancing up at her mistress's query, she smiled slightly. "Aye, miss, ye look bonnie. The young gentlemen will be flocking about ye this night."

Hetta gave a nervous laugh. "Pray do not attempt to terrify me, Maggie. Godmamma was saying only this morning that she had invited scores of eligible gentlemen to meet me and that we would then see how I would 'take.' I have the most lowering scene pictured in my mind in which I am standing at the head of the receiving line and every gentleman shakes his head because I will not do. Oh, Maggie, I almost wish that I had never come to London."

Maggie snorted at her. "What foolishness is this? Can it be that your father's daughter is balking at a wee fence? Shame on ye, miss."

Hetta straightened and raised her chin at a defiant angle. "Certainly I am not. I never have, and never shall."

"Och, I am that relieved," said Maggie gravely, hiding a smile. She gave a last twitch to Hetta's skirt and stood up.

The door opened and Lady Pelborne swept in, the demitrain of her sapphire-blue gown rustling behind her. "My dear, you look lovely. I hope that you are quite ready? Our guests are due to arrive at any moment."

Despite the fluttering in her stomach, Hetta managed a brave smile for her godmother's benefit. "Yes, of course. I am compelled to admit, however, that I am in a veritable shake at thought of meeting all of London."

"Never mind it, child. We all have a touch of stage fright now and then. You shall soon feel more at ease. Believe me, it will not be many weeks before you become thoroughly bored with meeting everywhere the same personages," Lady Pelborne said cheerfully. "Now do come along! Loraine awaits us with the greatest impatience downstairs. I have yet to behold a more excitable young female. One would think it were her own come-out!"

Together Lady Pelborne and Hetta descended the stairs and made their way to the ballroom to station themselves with Lady Anthony in the archway. Scarcely had they joined her when the first guests began to arrive. As Hetta extended her hand, Lady Pelborne or Lady Anthony made the introductions. The gentlemen bowed, saying all that was civil, while the ladies bestowed upon her inquisitive smiles as they extended courteous invitations or assurances of welcome. Hetta quickly felt herself to be floundering in a vast sea of faces. Half of London seemed to have accepted Lady Pelborne's invitation. She was therefore delighted to greet one or two old cronies and her new acquaintances from the dinner party.

Upon his arrival, Sir Horace squeezed her fingers in a friendly manner and said, "Quite a crush, ain't it?" There was a lull in the line and Hetta seized the chance to glance into the ballroom. She was staggered by the size of the milling company and thought she surely could not have met so many people in such a short time. Something of her feelings must have shown in her expression, for Sir Horace pulled her hand through his crooked elbow. "Bea, I am taking this delightful chit off with me to discover the refreshments. She has done her duty, heh?"

Lady Pelborne chuckled. "Even if I disagreed with you, Horace, you would not pay me the least heed. But, yes, I shall relinquish Hetta to your care. Most of those who are coming have already made an appearance. I think it high time to mingle with our guests. Indeed, Loraine deserted me some ten minutes ago when young Edward Strappey and Captain Trevor arrived."

"We have been granted official permission, Miss Stanton. Let us be off," said Sir Horace jovially.

As he guided her to the crowded ballroom, Hetta said gratefully, "Thank you, sir. I was beginning to wonder if I had taken root."

"I daresay! Monstrous, these functions. I hardly know why I bother to attend them," Sir Horace said, waving to one acquaintance and bowing to another. Their progress was necessarily slow, interrupted by hails from his many acquaintances and the exchange of civil greetings with several society matrons.

Hetta swiftly realized that Sir Horace was extremely well-liked, and because she was in his company, she came to immediate notice. Sir Horace's large circle of friends and acquaintances responded to her with a warmer interest than they had given upon introduction to an unknown debutante. Hetta managed to respond with grace and an apparent lack of awe to their curiosity even though she recognized some of their names from perusal of the newspapers.

When they at last reached the refreshments, twenty minutes had passed and Sir Horace was chuckling with satisfaction. "You have a cool head on your shoulders, my dear. Most of the young chits I have had occasion to observe would have pokered up or else tittered inanely were old Chislehurst to practice his acid tongue on them.

But you gave him tit for tat and it was plain he liked you for it. You'll become the rage before the month is out, mark me.''

Hetta accepted the glass of punch he offered her, shaking her head and laughing. "Come, sir! You much exaggerate the case. One must first be an acclaimed beauty or command a fabulous fortune. I have neither to recommend me.''

Her older companion shook his head. "One sees that you do not truly understand society, Hetta. Novelty is the rage and you, dear girl, are an unusual young woman. Your unconscious wit and fresh unspoiled charm have already made a mark on this jaded assembly, believe me.''

A deep voice spoke near Hetta's shoulder. "The lovely Miss Stanton does indeed inspire admiration of a sort, Sir Horace.''

Hetta looked around, startled. Upon meeting a familiar gleaming gaze she felt herself color warmly.

"Davenchester, my boy! Most happy to see you here," said Sir Horace genially. He suddenly noticed Hetta's blush and lowered lashes. Pursing his mouth thoughtfully, he said, "Tell you what, Davenchester. They have just struck up a quadrille. I'm an old man and I should know better than to be among the first to claim the hand of a lively young lady. Lead her out, won't you?''

"An excellent suggestion, Sir Horace," said Lord Anthony imperturbably.

Hetta uttered an incoherent protest but neither gentleman paid her the least heed. With excellent presence of mind, Sir Horace plucked the glass from her hand as Lord Anthony took her arm. A moment later Hetta found herself standing up with Lord Anthony in the midst of the French square dance. He did not address her but guided her with consummate ease, his hand warmly clasping hers. She did not know where to look and fastened her eyes on the sparkling emerald jewel in the folds of his snow-white cravat. Whenever the intricacies of the set brought them together, his proximity played havoc with her senses, leaving a weak sensation in her knees.

The silence between them had grown painfully awkward

and Hetta said, without raising her eyes, "Sir Horace seems inordinately fond of Lady Pelborne."

"Indeed. For several years they have been reputed to be lovers," said Lord Anthony casually.

With a gasp Hetta raised a startled face. "Sir!"

"I was not mistaken. Your eyes do possess the most enchanting gray-green flecks in their depths," said Lord Anthony with satisfaction.

Hetta felt her face flame and was thankful when the movement of the dance separated them. When next they came together, she had realized that it had been his intention to put her out of countenance. She met his gaze with the faintest challenge in her smile. "You are ridiculous, my lord."

"That is much better. One can hardly feel confident when his partner preserves a stoic silence," said Lord Anthony. "I had begun to question my prowess in the ballroom."

"One could never fault my lord's accomplished skill on the dance floor," said Hetta with unintended honesty.

Lord Anthony glanced down at her, a flash of surprise in his eyes. "You are kind, ma'am."

"I promise you that I shan't make a habit of it," said Hetta, half-annoyed that she had betrayed her enjoyment of his skill.

Lord Anthony laughed. "No, I don't expect you shall."

She looked up to encounter a friendly warmth in his eyes and responded with a smile of her own. She felt quite in charity with him at that moment and gave herself up to the joys of the music. Hetta knew herself to be an accomplished dancer and had quickly sensed an equal skill in Lord Anthony. He guided her effortlessly so that they appeared to move almost as one through the steps of the quadrille.

Onlookers were quick to note that Miss Stanton and the Earl of Davenchester were remarkably well-matched and there was a stir of speculation. Lady Pelborne was one of those watching and she pinched Sir Horace on the sleeve. "Do but look, Horace. One cannot help but wonder . . ."

He immediately guessed what was in her thoughts and

said hastily, "Come, Bea, do not let your romantic fancy run away with you." He espied a crony on the edge of the crowd. "Ah, there is old Spratling. We must go speak with him, Bea. I hear he has been up north recently. He may be able to tell us of the conditions there."

"Very well, Horace," said Lady Pelborne, throwing a last glance backward at her nephew and goddaughter as Sir Horace led her off.

The quadrille marked the end of the set, and Lord Anthony escorted Hetta from the crowded floor. "Have you enjoyed your visit to the metropolis?" he asked politely.

"Of course! It is all so very new and exciting to me," Hetta said with quick enthusiasm. "Yet at the oddest moments I experience an overwhelming desire to be again at Meldingcourt."

"Is it the place itself or those whom you have left behind that call to you?" asked Lord Anthony with curiosity.

"Naturally I miss dear Cheton and the rest, but I think it is Meldingcourt itself. It has always been my home, you see," A fleeting sadness crossed Hetta's expression. "But it has not been the same since dear Papa died."

"One's memories of a loved one can often be bitter-sweet," said Lord Anthony.

Hetta looked up swiftly. "Oh, I was not thinking of Papa! He was all that was dear and kind. It is my cousin who—" She suddenly caught herself.

Lord Anthony waited a moment for her to continue, then prompted her. "You were saying something about your cousin, Miss Stanton?"

Hetta dismissed his query with a forced laugh. "One can hardly choose one's relations, can one? Do you hunt, my Lord?"

Lord Anthony graciously accepted her abrupt change of subject, perceiving that she would not willingly confide in him. They spoke amiably for a few moments as he escorted her to Lady Pelborne's side. Handing her over to his aunt's care with a few civil words, Lord Anthony bowed and strolled off.

Lady Pelborne narrowly scrutinized her goddaughter's face for any sign of distress at Lord Anthony's departure and was disappointed to find none. "Are you enjoying yourself, my dear?" she asked hopefully.

Hetta gave her a wide smile. "Indeed yes, ma'am! Sir Horace was good enough to draw me into his conversation with several exalted personages and I became not the least awed by anyone, for they were all very kind." She suddenly laughed, her eyes dancing. "Sir Horace is such a complete hand. In an attempt to puff me up, he prophesied that I shall become all the rage in a month's time. Isn't that the most absurd thing you have ever heard?"

"Of course it is, my dear," said Lady Pelborne with a note of surprise in her voice.

A young gentleman came up to ask permission for Hetta's hand in the country dance that was forming, and Lady Pelborne graciously gave her assent. She looked thoughtfully after her goddaughter and wondered why Sir Horace would have made such an outrageous statement. It was very unlike him to pay fulsome compliments.

Much later in the evening Hetta stood in the midst of a small group of admirers. Flushed and laughing in protest as the gentlemen vied for her favors, she was about to accept the plea of one young gentleman for the remainder of the set when a mellow voice intruded. "Do give way, Chesterfield. I believe the lady has promised this particular cotillion to me." Sir Rupert Sikes smiled down at Hetta, a full head taller than any other gentleman in the group. Feeling butterflies in her middle, Hetta thought dazedly that he was easily the most handsome as well. He had a fascinating world-weary look about him that drew her to him. "Am I not correct, Miss Stanton?" asked Sir Rupert gently.

Though flustered, Hetta had yet the wit to make a tolerable pretense of reflection. "Oh, it is true! Pray do forgive me, Lord Chesterfield, I had quite forgotten."

With practiced ease Sir Rupert extricated her from her protesting admirers to lead her onto the floor. "That was very neatly done, sir," said Hetta, laughing up at him with a becoming sparkle in her eyes.

Sir Rupert looked down at her with a kindling of warmth in his bright-blue gaze. "I am certain that some one of your several admirers must surely have complimented you already this evening on your beauty, Lady Stanton. And if they have not, then I must conclude that they are all of them blind dolts.''

Hetta pinkened with surprised pleasure. "I thank you, Sir Rupert. From you that is a lavish compliment indeed, coming as it does from a truly elegant gentleman.''

Sir Rupert smiled faintly. "I perceive that we have established a mutual admiration society, Miss Stanton. How wise of us to do so.''

Hetta was laughing at this absurdity when the music ended. Sir Rupert brought her gloved hand to his lips in gentle salute. "This cotillion has ended entirely too soon for my taste, Miss Stanton. I shall of course return you to your circle of admirers, but first I must extract a promise from you for a future dance.''

"You have it, Sir Rupert," said Hetta, somewhat dazed that he should show so much interest in her. He escorted her back to her chair. One or two gentlemen still hovered nearby and greeted her arrival with pleasure. As she sat down, she saw Edward Strappey waving to her as he approached.

"Hullo! Isn't it a marvelous do?" asked Edward cheerfully. He gave a nod to the two young gentlemen, with whom he was already acquainted, and glanced curiously at Sir Rupert.

"Edward, how good to see you again," exclaimed Hetta, holding out both hands to him. She turned her head to address the tall man standing negligently at her side. "Sir Rupert, I do believe that you have not made the acquaintance of Lady Anthony's cousin, Edward Strappey, who is just down from Oxford this Season. Edward, this gentleman is Sir Rupert Sikes.''

At the tall gentleman's name, Edward's open grin faltered. He shot a quick look of surprise at Hetta, and when he looked again at Sikes, there was a certain measure of distaste in his candid brown eyes.

Sir Rupert was quick to note the young man's change of expression and gave a sardonic smile. He thought it amusing that the young puppy had heard of him. He put up his glass to inspect with an insulting pointedness Edward's carelessly tied cravat. "One would certainly never have guessed that you are just down from Oxford," he murmured with a superior air of amusement.

Edward's smile faded entirely and his jaw began to jut. The gentlemen who had been silent witnesses to the meeting shifted, coughing, before they faded discreetly from the scene. Completely oblivious to Sir Rupert's deliberate insult, Hetta stared with a frown at Edward. She was puzzled by the odd constraint in his manner and wondered at it, for surely he must be delighted to make the acquaintance of such a distinguished gentleman as Sir Rupert Sikes.

Lord Anthony, who had been observing Miss Stanton and her court from a distance, came up beside Edward and put a friendly hand on his shoulder. "How are you, Edward? I was speaking with your kindly mentor a moment ago. Captain Trevor tells me that you have a well-set-up jumper. I should like to see him one day," he said.

Edward flushed with pleasure. "I would be honored, sir!"

"I should like to see Rufus as well, Edward. When you described him at the dinner party, he sounded perfectly marvelous," Hetta said quickly.

Sir Rupert looked over at his cousin. "You surprise me, Davenchester. I confess that I somehow cannot quite conceive of a Corinthian such as yourself playing the role of doting uncle," he drawled.

Lord Anthony felt Edward stiffen beside him. He did not glance at the younger man as he casually flicked nonexistent lint from his coat sleeve. "Can you not, Rupert? But then our tastes have always run counter. As you may recall, friendship and the family name mean a great deal more to me." The expression in his eyes was hard even as he smiled gently at Sir Rupert. "I should tell you that as long as Miss Stanton is under my aunt's protection, I consider her to be a member of my own family. Pray remember that, Rupert."

Hetta gasped at the unmistakable warning in Lord Anthony's voice. "My lord!"

Sir Rupert's lips tightened. He was about to make a hasty retort when he encountered the appalled expression in Hetta's eyes. With an effort he bit back his anger and summoned up a strained smile of weary charm. "Forgive us, Miss Stanton. In the midst of our family squabbles we sometimes forget where we are."

Lord Anthony gave a crack of laughter and Hetta looked up at him angrily, baffled by the entire exchange.

With an aplomb of one older than his years, Edward bowed to her. "Will you give me the honor of this dance, Miss Stanton?"

"Thank you, Edward. I am obliged to you," said Hetta, rising to take his arm. She was only too happy to quit the disturbing company of the other two men. "Pray excuse us, gentlemen." She swept them a stiff curtsy before Edward led her away.

When the young couple were out of earshot, Lord Anthony once more addressed Sir Rupert. "Lady Pelborne would strongly disapprove of your familiarity with her goddaughter, Rupert. To spare her unnecessary anxiety, I suggest that you do not set up Miss Stanton as one of your usual flirts."

Sir Rupert bared his teeth in a disagreeable smile. "One is naturally reluctant to displease a lady, in particular one as redoubtable as Lady Pelborne. Pray convey my deepest regrets, Davenchester, but I please only myself."

Lord Anthony's eyes were cold points of green ice in his tanned face. His voice was unusually soft. "You will oblige me in this, Rupert. As my prospective heir, I believe that you will see the wisdom of agreeing to my wishes now and then."

Sir Rupert stared at him, his mouth tightly drawn. When he spoke, it was in a soft hiss. "God, how I detest you! Would that it had not been Edmond!"

Lord Anthony smiled with a flash of genuine humor. "Fate deals us all the odd hand on occasion. Thank your stars that it *was* I who returned, for I promise you that you would not now be enjoying your customary good health if Edmond had lived. His temper was shockingly violent."

Sir Rupert's knuckles whitened as his fingers clenched

around his quizzing glass. For a brief moment he considered smashing his fist into his cousin's arrogant face but suppressed the mad impulse. He had himself witnessed Lord Anthony's sparring prowess at Jackson's Saloon and he had little desire to be on the receiving end of his cousin's punishing fists. Breathing hard, he said, "Pray reassure Lady Pelborne that her goddaughter has nothing to fear from me. She is at any rate somewhat insipid for my tastes." He started to turn, then said tightly, "And be damned to you, Davenchester!" Sir Rupert swung on his heel and strode quickly away.

Smiling to himself, Lord Anthony went in search of an agreeable companion or two.

From the dance floor Hetta had caught sight of Sir Rupert's set expression as he left Lord Anthony's side, and her sympathies were immediately aroused. Her eyes flashed after Lord Anthony. She choked furiously, "How dare he!"

Startled, Edward looked at her with a slackened jaw. "What? Who, Hetta?"

Hetta recalled where she was and shook her head. "Forgive me, Edward. I fear Lord Anthony's manners have put me out of all patience. He had no right to establish himself as my warder and intimidate one of my acquaintances."

He realized immediately that she was referring to the confrontation between the Earl of Davenchester and Sir Rupert Sikes. Edward cleared his throat and said, "If you will pardon my saying so, Hetta, in this instance Lord Anthony may have been justified in his championing of your interests. Sir Rupert's reputation is hardly one of the best."

Hetta was diverted from leaping to Sir Rupert's defense. "What is his reputation, Edward?"

Her partner reddened. "One could never divulge it to a lady's ears. Very sorry that I mentioned it. Forget that anything was said."

"Pray do not treat me as though I were a mindless dolt. Really, Edward, how am I to know whom to trust if no one dares tell me anything to the purpose?" demanded Hetta indignantly. Despite his obvious reluctance to pursue the subject, Hetta persisted until finally he was guided into revealing a greatly laundered description of what he had heard concerning Sir Rupert Sikes.

Hetta stared at him. "But there must be dozens of gentlemen who share the same reputation for indulging in that sort of—of flirtation," she said, unwilling to admit that she was shaken. She found it difficult to doubt Sir Rupert's integrity when she found him to be so attractive and so like her imagined ideal of the perfect gentleman.

By this time they had gravitated to a settee against the wall. Edward snorted derisively. "If I had a sister, I would not trust her a minute in his company." Once he had taken the plunge, Edward forgot his reservations in repeating the particulars concerning the gentleman's reputation. "The man is reputed to be a loose screw, Hetta. It is whispered that his last flirtation ended with the lady being in the family way and her husband was forced to bundle her off to the country to save themselves the public humiliation."

Hetta was shocked to the core. She struggled to conceive how any gentleman could possibly commit such a dastardly breach of conduct, and failed. "I cannot believe that it is true, for it would be a terrible sin. Even if Sir Rupert was involved with the lady, I could not lay the entire blame for the incident at his door. The woman must have been extremely foolish and encouraged him outrageously in some manner," she said, explaining to herself as much as to her companion. "I truly cannot find it in my heart to judge him too harshly, for he must suffer agonies with his conscience. We cannot know the whole after all, Edward."

He agreed somewhat dubiously and the subject was allowed to drop when a mutual acquaintance came up to them.

Throughout the remainder of the evening Sir Rupert seethed with fury. He had come off badly from the encounter with Lord Anthony in his own eyes, and his pride was offended. Once out of Lord Anthony's proximity, Sir Rupert began to cast around in his mind for a suitably subtle way to revenge himself upon his cousin.

His eyes fell on Miss Hetta Stanton as she went down a

set with another admirer. He recalled suddenly that she
had been angered by Lord Anthony's declaration and had
seemed to view him with sympathy. Sir Rupert smiled
unpleasantly while he watched the couple turning about on
the dance floor. Perhaps there was a fitting weapon to suit
his purpose after all. His cousin had extracted his assur-
ance that he would not attach himself to Miss Stanton, and
he had every intention of keeping his word. However, he
could hardly be blamed if it were the lady herself who
desired the connection.

Though Sir Rupert was anxious to put his inspiration to
the test, he nevertheless waited until he had seen Lord
Anthony take leave of Lady Pelborne and depart from the
gathering before he approached Miss Stanton. She met
his smile with a troubled gaze and he was shrewd enough
to guess the probable cause of her hesitation. Immediately
he put on his most charming manner and said ruefully, "I
perceive that my lamentable reputation has at last gained
your lovely ear and was undoubtedly accompanied by a
well-intentioned warning against me! You have naturally
taken Lady Pelborne's words to heart. One can only be
sorry for it, for I had quite hoped we were to be friends. I
shall not embarrass you with my presence a moment longer,
ma'am." He bowed gracefully and made as though to
leave her.

Hetta quickly put out her hand. "Pray, what did you
mean by your reference to my godmother?"

Sir Rupert feigned lively surprise. "But surely you know!
It was she who sent Lord Anthony to warn me against
insinuating myself into your good graces. Indeed, Lord
Anthony made it painfully clear that my tarnished reputation makes me totally ineligible company for a well-bred
young lady." Sir Rupert paused with a weary smile, noting with satisfaction the gathering storm in her expressive
hazel eyes. He congratulated himself on nicely gauging her
reaction to Davenchester's interference. She was ripe for
running counter to what she perceived to be restrictions
upon her freedom. "I would have accepted his heavy-
handed suggestion without question but that I felt somehow you might perhaps have quite different wishes in the

matter. Indeed, I had hoped . . .'' He broke off and sighed as though in regret. "But, alas, it is not to be."

Hetta gazed up at him, suddenly breathless. "Pray, what is it you had hoped, Sir Rupert?"

He took her hand, turning it over to lightly trace the warm pulse in her slender wrist with his thumb. "One had cherished humble hopes, which are now best left unsaid. Perhaps if Lady Pelborne did not object so strongly, I would have requested permission to call upon you on the morrow. But that of course is now an impossibility."

"But I should be most happy to receive you, sir," said Hetta shyly. Her heart was beating fast at his thumb's intimate caress. She thought dizzily that it hinted at more than had been spoken between them. It must surely mean that Sir Rupert felt the same attraction for her as she did for him.

Sir Rupert threw a meaningful glance toward Lady Pelborne, who stood in conversation several paces away. Hetta followed his eyes and a frown formed between her prettily arched brows. He smiled gently at her. "My dear, you are very young. You cannot have considered the consequence of your rash words. Lady Pelborne would hardly approve—"

Hetta interrupted him, her eyes bright. "One assumes that you shall be calling on me, sir, and not my godmother. I hope that I am mistress enough of myself that I may choose whom I wish to receive. Shall I look for you perhaps around two o'clock, Sir Rupert?"

His laugh was soft as he bowed deferentially over her hand. "Rest assured that I shall not fail you, Miss Stanton." He lightly kissed the soft tips of her fingers before releasing her hand. His bright eyes caught hers in an intense gaze that sent the blood to her face and left her trembling. "Until tomorrow, fair lady," he murmured, and left her.

Hetta stared at him with shining eyes, oblivious to her surroundings. Sir Rupert was all that a fine gentleman should be. Despite the galling treatment given him by Lord Anthony, his sense of humor had remained intact. His gallant consideration of her position greatly impressed itself upon her as well. Surely a gentleman who possessed such elegance of mind did not deserve the horrid reputation Edward had imparted to her.

A touch on her elbow roused her and she turned to find Lady Anthony standing beside her with a faintly anxious air. "Dear Hetta, pray do not pay the least heed to whatever Sir Rupert may have said to you. He can positively crush one's feelings with but a look. Was he too frightfully rude?"

"On the contrary, I found him to be quite the gentleman," said Hetta, surprised. "Why should he have been uncivil?"

"Oh! Of course, why should he? Silly of me! It is just that, with certain people, one may never know when . . ." Lady Anthony broke off in confusion. "Oh, dear! Do come and speak with Lord Frobisher. He was but this minute loudly declaring that you were the only female worth talking to because you, at least, possess a particle of hunting sense."

Greatly amused, Hetta allowed herself to be led off.

As Sir Rupert made his way toward Lady Pelborne to make his excuses, he was unable to restrain a faint smile of triumph. He was well-satisfied with the way things had gone with Miss Stanton. She had reacted exactly as he had hoped. Even his cousin could hardly fault him for calling upon the lady in the proscribed manner when it was at her request. Indeed, it would seem odd if he did not pay his respects to Lady Pelborne and her goddaughter on the day after the latter's successful come-out.

The complacent smile was still on his lips when he came up to Lady Pelborne. She eyed him narrowly. "One must always suspect you of mischief, Rupert, for you have such a calculating look about you. It is one of the characteristics I find least objectionable in you, for one is then forewarned."

Sir Rupert laughed softly in ironic amusement. "I thank you, dear lady. You are among the few who have never underrated me."

Lady Pelborne smiled lightly, but there was the hint of steel in her eyes. "Indeed, Rupert, I am often beforehand where you are concerned. When you call on myself and

Hetta, pray keep your visit as brief as civility allows. I should be excessively displeased if it were more than a polite morning call.''

He was shaken but took care not to allow it to show. His smile twisted. "I am constantly amazed by your incredible perception, Lady Pelborne. Allow me to assure you that my visit shall be all that is gentlemanly and proper.''

''But of course it shall be, Rupert,'' said Lady Pelborne gently. She smiled, dismissing him with a look as she moved off to speak to another departing guest.

Sir Rupert stood where she had left him with the feeling that he had been subtly outplayed. He shrugged a shoulder in irritation and left the ballroom.

The last guest finally departed in the early-morning hours. Hetta stumbled up to her bedroom to find that Maggie had waited up for her. Gratefully she accepted the maid's assistance in shedding her dress before tumbling into bed. Her eyes closed almost immediately despite her certainty that she would lie awake recalling each moment of her come-out. She slept more deeply than she ever had since arriving in London, her dreams filled with Sir Rupert's intense blue eyes.

10

Hetta did not waken until late the following day when Maggie, despairing of her mistress, pulled back the drapes to allow the sun to fall across the bed. Hetta yawned, stretching languorously in the warmth. She suddenly sat bolt upright. "Maggie! What o'clock is it?"

The Scotswoman sniffed in disgust. "Well may ye ask, Mistress Slugabed! M'lady Pelborne insisted that ye be allowed to sleep as long as ye liked, but here it is after noon and ye are still under the covers."

With a horrified cry, Hetta scrambled from the bed and flung off her lacy nightcap. Maggie stood with open mouth as her mistress hurried to the wardrobe and threw it open to begin searching through it with a frantic air. The maid found her voice. "Miss, whatever are ye doing?"

Hetta did not heed the amazement in her companion's voice, but demanded impatiently, "Maggie, where is the leaf-green gown Madame Lebonnier made up for me? I cannot and will not receive Sir Rupert in one of my old gowns."

Maggie joined her mistress at the wardrobe and nudged her out of the way. "And who might this Sir Rupert be?" she asked as she unerringly laid hold of the gown.

Hetta took a turn about the room, her eyes shining with excitement. "Oh, he is the most wonderful gentleman I have ever had occasion to meet. And so handsome, Maggie! His eyes are so blue that his gaze is positively unnerving."

The maid pursed her lips in astonishment. " 'Tis an attractive gentleman, then."

"Yes, and he is to be here at two o'clock," said Hetta, suddenly recalling the lateness of the hour. "Maggie, I must be ready to receive him."

"Do not fret so, miss. Ye'll soon be properly got up," said Maggie soothingly, turning her attention to the details of her mistress's toilet.

In a surprisingly short time Hetta was seated on a sofa in the sitting room pretending an interest in the latest fashion plates in a ladies' magazine. Impatience was in the glance she sent toward the mantel clock whose hands moved with maddening slowness. For the hundredth time she stood up to check her appearance in the gilt mirror above the occasional table. Critically she examined her gown and twitched an errant fold into place. Despite her own misgivings to the contrary, she presented an attractive picture in the soft leaf-green muslin. The gown came high at the throat and its long sleeves buttoned tightly at her wrists. The skirt was cut in the wider style that was becoming fashionable and the soft color brought a vibrant glow to her face, though the sparkle of anticipation in her fine hazel eyes was due to something other than her attire.

Quite unnecessarily Hetta began to rearrange the blooms in the bowl of cut flowers set beneath the mirror. While she was engaged in this task, a footman announced her expected visitor. Hetta turned quickly, a long-stemmed rose still in her hand. She was quite unconscious of the femininity of her pose.

Sir Rupert paused for a moment, his appreciative eyes taking in her slim figure and the contrast of the red rose against her breast. "My dear Miss Stanton, you are stunning," he said with a velvet smile.

Blushing furiously, Hetta hastily returned the rose to the bowl and held out her hand in welcome. "Sir Rupert! It is a pleasure, sir." She thought irreverently if anyone were to be described as stunning, it should be he. His gold hair was brushed carefully into a semblance of disorder. His coat was of fawn and his snow-white cravat was intricately tied with a topaz pin nestled among its exquisite folds. Superfine breeches molded tight to his long limbs, and the Hessians he wore gleamed with a mirrorlike finish.

Sir Rupert took her hand and carried it to his lips, lingering over her fingers a moment longer than civility demanded. "Would it be forward of me to say that I count myself fortunate to find you alone, Miss Stanton?"

Confusion made Hetta stammer. "Pray—pray won't you be seated, sir?" She disengaged her hand and sat down on the sofa.

Sir Rupert's smile broadened. He seated himself beside her, completely at his ease. "I am surprised that my Lady Pelborne consented to this delightful tête-à-tête. One would have expected her to take every precaution to protect you against such a degenerate character as myself."

"My godmother is in general of a very liberal nature, as you must well know, Sir Rupert. I cannot imagine why she should object to your visit," said Hetta.

His chuckle held a note of irony. "My dear child, you are so young. Do you not yet know how the world regards me? I assure you that it is most unusual, indeed even improper, for a young female to receive a gentleman without a chaperone. Lady Pelborne will undoubtedly rake me over the coals for endangering your unblemished reputation and ring a thundering scold over you as well."

"Am I to be considered very fast, then?" asked Hetta, almost pleased by the suggestion. Her lashes dipped low to hide her eyes.

He took her hand and clasped it comfortably between both of his. "Outrageously so, my dear! However, I must confess that your lack of pretension over the matter is quite refreshing."

"Alas, you are saying, though in a very kind way, that I lack town bronze," said Hetta mournfully, peeping up at him through her lashes.

Sir Rupert smiled, recognizing the flirtatious gleam in her eyes. He bent his head close to her ear, preparing to whisper a sweet phrase.

Lady Pelborne entered the sitting room and took in the tableau at a glance. "A vastly pretty picture, upon my honor! How are you, Rupert? Somehow one did not expect you to call so soon, nor to find you making love to my goddaughter."

Hetta snatched her hand from Sir Rupert's grasp, ready color flooding her face.

Sir Rupert rose gracefully to his feet to greet the older woman. "But as you see, dear lady, I am here. Your delightful goddaughter persuaded me last night that it would be the height of bad *ton* to neglect my social duties," said Sir Rupert easily.

Lady Pelborne shot a glance at her silent goddaughter. "Indeed? I have never known you to be so amenable to your conscience, Rupert."

"How could one do otherwise when bid by such a charming party?" asked Sir Rupert with a slight bow in Hetta's direction. He was aware of her discomfiture and was satisfied that his suspicions were correct. She had not informed Lady Pelborne that he was to call at her invitation.

Lady Pelborne did not react to his lavish praise of her goddaughter but instead inquired if he had heard anything of the new play at the theater. Sir Rupert replied readily enough and a half-hour of agreeable conversation was passed before he bethought himself of another call he wished to make that afternoon. He was taking his leave of the ladies when a second visitor was shown into the sitting room. Sir Rupert was quick to note a curious altering in Miss Stanton's expression and he delayed his leavetaking to examine the new visitor.

The Honorable Jonathan Markham raked Sir Rupert's exquisite person with a cold eye. His expression could not have been said to be friendly, though his manners were easy enough when Hetta, with a noticeable restraint, made the two gentlemen known to each other. Markham acknowledged the introduction with a nod, saying that they had met once before, though very briefly, at a social function.

Sir Rupert was well-versed in the signs of a possessive nature and he smiled faintly at Markham's challenging gaze. Deliberately he infused his attractive voice with an unmistakable warmth as he once more took his leave of Hetta. He lingered over her hand when she gave it to him, relinquishing her fingers with seeming reluctance. Through half-hooded eyes he watched the stiffening of Markham's expression. His curiosity now thoroughly aroused, Sir Rupert determined to discover the exact nature of the relationship between Miss Stanton and her churlish cousin. "I shall look forward to meeting with you again, Miss Stanton. Lady Pelborne, your servant as always." Lady Pelborne acknowledged his bow with an amused smile, well-aware of the game he had just played. He nodded briefly to Markham and left them.

Lady Pelborne cordially invited Markham to make himself comfortable, saying that she would not stand on ceremony with him. "For my goddaughter has told me a great deal about you, sir. One gathers that you spend much of your time in London. Queer, is it not, that we have not previously met?"

Markham showed his large square teeth in an ingratiating smile. "I fear that I do not move in the exalted circles in which you do, Lady Pelborne."

"Quite so." Lady Pelborne turned her shoulder on him to gently request Hetta to pour the tea that the butler was that moment bringing into the sitting room. Markham's ruddy face darkened at her casual set-down. But nothing could have been more gracious than Lady Pelborne's manner when she then inquired if he wished for refreshment. He assented, eyeing her somewhat warily. Lady Pelborne did not appear to notice, but instead made a polite observation on the latest *on-dit*. Hetta stared at her godmother in astonished perplexity, for she had never before heard Lady Pelborne engage in common gossip. She glanced at her cousin as he replied to Lady Pelborne's conversational gambit and saw that Markham's rather cold eyes had brightened.

Markham mentioned a certain name and the conversation warmed between him and Lady Pelborne. Hetta listened quietly, murmuring an appropriate comment only when directly addressed. Markham glanced at her once, his lip curling, with the passing thought that she was still the gauche nonentity he had always believed her to be.

From talk of London society, Lady Pelborne adroitly led Markham to reveal more about himself than he realized as he replied to her inquiries of his family.

An hour passed and Lady Pelborne judged it time to bring Markham's visit to an end. "Your visit to us this afternoon has proven most enlightening, sir. I look forward to your next visit when perhaps we may further our acquaintance," said Lady Pelborne.

The hint was plain, and Markham rose immediately. "Of course, ma'am. It has been delightful to have made your acquaintance at last. My cousin often spoke of you with such fond affection. And it is extremely pleasant to find my dear cousin in such admirable looks," he said, directing an intimate smile in Hetta's direction. Her fingers curled in her lap, but otherwise she did not react and merely gazed at him with a cool air.

Lady Pelborne raised her brows and made a quick decision. She detained Markham with a gesture. "A word with you if you please, Mr. Markham."

"I hold myself entirely at your service, Lady Pelborne," said Markham with a ready smile, a confident gleam in his eyes.

Lady Pelborne returned the smile, but it did not quite reach her eyes. "Though it is most unusual to breach such a topic in this manner, I know Hetta shall not mind that I speak my mind. I am of course aware of your longstanding devotion to my dear goddaughter. Indeed, I believe you have engaged to win her hand on a number of occasions, and quite properly, she has refused you." Lady Pelborne caught and held Markham's eyes. "This Season is Hetta's first exposure to polite society, and not unnaturally, I feel it my duty to discourage any sort of understanding at this time. You are no closer than any other gentleman to winning Hetta's hand. Therefore, it would be most unwise to consider yourself her suitor, for as her guardian I shall not countenance it."

Markham stared at the older woman, somewhat disconcerted by her blunt speech. A choking laugh caught his ear and his gaze traveled swiftly to his cousin's face. Her expression betrayed an obvious delight, which infuriated him. Despite his annoyance, Markham managed to address Lady Pelborne with a respectful air. "I understand your concern well enough, my lady. My disappointment is naturally great to learn that these are your feelings. Yet I shall continue to cherish the hope that once I have become better known to you, my suit may be seen in a more favorable light.''

"One must of course always hope for the best. I am certain we shall see more of you in future, Mr. Markham,'' said Lady Pelborne cordially, holding out her hand to him.

"Indeed you shall, ma'am.'' Markham bowed over her hand, then turned to Hetta. His smile was thin. "Cousin, I give you my compliments,'' he said meaningfully, and bowed to her before he strode from the room.

Hetta jumped up. "Oh, ma'am, you were superb! I thought I should laugh in his face! But I had hoped you would squelch his pretensions for good. Instead, he has left much encouraged and I expect that now he shall be forever dogging my steps. I shall not be able to turn around without tripping over him.''

"Pray do not be absurd, my dear,'' said Lady Pelborne bracingly. "I have placed him now. His breeding is well enough, but it lacks true distinction and therefore he has but few connections with the *haut ton*. He aspires to establish such connections, of course. That is easily seen. Indeed, one must wonder how he has managed to ingratiate himself so well as he has done. I was certainly astonished to learn that Lady Sinton receives him, for as a rule she is inordinately discriminating.'' Lady Pelborne paused thoughtfully. "Your cousin strikes me as an extremely ambitious and resourceful young man, Hetta. I should not care for you to be in his company more than is necessary, and certainly not alone. I mistrust a gentleman with such a carnivorous look.''

"And I, ma'am. You need not fear that I mean to keep him dangling after me, for I don't,'' Hetta said firmly. "And I am grateful to you, Godmamma, for denying him permission to make his addresses. I trust it is now plainer to him that a match between us is improbable.''

"As indeed I mean it to be. I saw instantly that he hoped to turn me up sweet, but I am not so easily persuaded,'' said Lady Pelborne. "He is determined to have you, but until you come of age or undergo a violent reversal of feeling toward him, I shall continue to refuse my consent.''

"Thank you, dear ma'am. You do not know how you have relieved my mind," said Hetta. Impulsively she hugged Lady Pelborne. "I have the best of guardians.''

Lady Pelborne emerged from her embrace somewhat disheveled. "Nonsense! I would be negligent in my duties if I did not look higher for you," she said, feeling an absurd pleasure in her goddaughter's display of affection. She cleared her throat. "There is something I must discuss with you, Hetta, and I suspect that you know already what I am about to say.''

Hetta eased back from her with a nod. Her chin was firmly set and a stubborn light appeared in her eyes. "It is about Sir Rupert, is it not?''

Lady Pelborne was disconcerted by an uncanny resemblance to the late Lord Stanton in her goddaughter's expression. Recalling his lamentable obstinance, she prudently modified the scold she had planned to deliver. "I shall not forbid you to receive him, Hetta, for I do myself. However, it is not quite the thing for a young female to be unchaperoned when a gentleman calls. And one doubts you would have been so happy to receive Mr. Markham without my presence. Am I not correct, my dear?''

Hetta was forcibly struck by her observation. "Indeed, ma'am, I had not given it thought, but you are quite right.''

Lady Pelborne nodded, satisfied that she had made her point. "I should much dislike it if my goddaughter were to earn the reputation of a heedless baggage. And I should be insulted if you took refuge behind my skirts only as it suited you to do so, Hetta. One should cultivate a consistency of manner.''

Hetta smiled at her. "I shall remember, Godmamma. In future I shan't receive a gentleman without either you or Loraine at my side.''

Lady Pelborne drew a sigh. "Thank you, my dear. By the by, I must tell you that you have done remarkably well in acquiring a polished manner in so short a time. Loraine's example has contributed to it, I know, but it is your own determination that has truly made the difference. At times I have even thought that you appeared positively driven about it.''

"Perhaps I am," said Hetta frankly. "I think I told you that my cousin once made it quite plain that I could never appear particularly pleasing to the eye of any gentleman. I fear I possess a rather wretched temper when patronized.''

Lady Pelborne chuckled. "You mean to put his nose out of joint, then. A commendable ambition indeed! From your confidences these past weeks I had developed an extraordinary dislike for the fellow, which has not been allayed upon meeting him. His impertinence begs to be taken down a peg or two.''

"I hope to accomplish more than that, ma'am," Hetta said with a laugh. "But, as I have cause to know, he is not a man to be easily swayed from his intentions.''

"Never mind that, my dear. You shall soon be in such a mad whirl that he may find it much more difficult to approach you than he would like," said Lady Pelborne. "Now be off with you and find that frippery niece of mine. She will be ecstatic to learn she is to accompany you shopping.''

On the quiver of a laugh, Hetta asked, "Are we going out, ma'am?''

"One hopes so. An aged woman like myself requires a bit of peace now and then," Lady Pelborne snapped crossly.

Hetta merely laughed and dutifully went in search of Lady Anthony.

In the weeks following her come-out Hetta found herself enjoying a certain measure of popularity, and Sir Horace's fantastic prediction came to have a degree of truth in it. Her easy grace of manner and pleasing appearance, coupled with a respectable inheritance, gained her quick acceptance into the inner social world of which her godmother was a part and which her cousin hoped to enter.

Lady Pelborne was well acquainted with the patronesses of Almack's and she had no difficulty in procuring vouchers for her goddaughter. Even the stiff Mrs. Drummond unbent enough to compliment her on Miss Stanton's circumspect manners. Therefore she had no qualms in accepting an invitation from Sir Horace to attend the theater while Lady Anthony chaperoned Hetta to Almack's on Thursday evening.

Lady Anthony proved to be the most lenient of chaperones, disappearing almost at once onto the dance floor with a succession of partners and leaving Hetta to her own devices. Hetta herself did not lack for dancing partners, and prominent among their number was Sir Rupert Sikes. Without realizing that she was doing so, Hetta created a stir among the gathering when she accepted an invitation to dance with Sir Rupert for the third time.

When Lord Anthony made his appearance at Almack's that evening he was greeted by Lady Cowper, the best-liked patroness at Almack's and a friend of Lady Pelborne's. She immediately gave him to understand that Miss Stanton was in a fair way to creating a scandal.

"It will be fatal to her, Davenchester. The girl must be given a gentle hint," said Lady Cowper.

Lord Anthony quirked a brow at her. "Surely my aunt is more than capable of curbing Miss Stanton's exuberance, Emily. I am hardly in the position to interfere."

"Beatrice did not accompany Miss Stanton. She is chaperoned by Lady Anthony," Lady Cowper said succinctly. She saw the quick comprehension flash in his eyes and the tightening of his firm lips. Tapping him with her fan as she left him, she said, "I wish you luck, Davenchester."

Lord Anthony entered the assembly room and leisurely made his way through the company as he greeted various acquaintances. It did not take many minutes for him to realize that Lady Cowper's concern had not been exaggerated. Miss Stanton had already incurred the wrath of the starchiest of the society dames, and their glacial stares as she danced past warned the initiated that Miss Stanton was in grave danger of losing the social position she enjoyed.

When Lord Anthony appeared before Hetta, she did not attempt to disguise the quick smile that warmed her eyes. With pleasure she accepted his request for the next dance and did not notice the rather stern cast of his features. As he swept her away, his hand warmly clasping her, she said gaily, "We have not seen much of you of late, my lord. Indeed, Lady Pelborne has quite given you up."

"Am I then such a sore trial to my aunt, Lady Hetta?" asked Lord Anthony shortly.

She was disconcerted that he should have taken her remark to be censorious. Delicate color rose in her face. "I should not make so bold to tell you such a thing, my lord."

"Yet one would gather from your growing reputation that you have become just so bold, ma'am," said Lord Anthony.

Hetta searched his expression with dawning wariness. She had forgotten the capricious nature of his character, which led him to derive a certain enjoyment out of baiting her. "What can you possibly mean? I am certain that my reputation is most respectable."

"On the contrary, Hetta, from the moment I entered Almack's sacred portals, I have heard rumblings of disapproval on every side for your irresponsible behavior. You have successfully alientated a number of our more formidable society dames by showing a certain partiality for a particular gentleman. In short, you have become known as a desperate flirt," said Lord Anthony.

Hetta gasped at the injustice of his unexpected attack. "How dare you!" She started to pull out of his embrace, but he had felt her stiffening and kept a firm hold on her.

He glanced down at her furious expression with a humorous light in his eyes. "Pray do not compound your sins, sweet lady! It has not gone unnoticed that I have condescended to lead you out, and as a consequence, your tottering respectability has been given a much-needed boost. But you will ruin all by initiating a public quarrel with the Earl of Davenchester, who, as you must be aware, is one of the most eligible bachelors in England."

"Your arrogance is only exceeded by your outrageous effrontery, sir. Unhand me at once," hissed Hetta, aware of the curious glances being thrown in their direction. She had found that the arm about her waist, which she had before thought so comfortably placed, now bound her to him. Virtually a prisoner she was forced to follow his lead.

"Undoubtedly arrogance numbers high among my few known faults," said Lord Anthony blandly. "However, in my aunt's absence I am compelled to fill her role and drop a quiet warning in your lovely ear. You are courting headlong disaster with your behavior this evening."

"Lady Anthony is my chaperone and she has not breathed a syllable to me of indiscretion," snapped Hetta, her eyes flashing. She brushed aside the thought that she had seen but little of that lady since their arrival at Almack's.

"My sister-in-law's sense of duty obviously leaves much to be desired," said Lord Anthony grimly.

Hetta opened her eyes very wide. "Forgive me, but I must confess that I find you preposterous, my lord. Your pompous niceties have led you to commit a far more abominable solecism than the one for which you have condemned me. But doubtless the impropriety of a single gentleman interesting himself so nearly in the affairs of an unattached lady escapes you." She had the satisfaction of seeing a hardening of his expression.

"You deserve a paddling, my girl," said Lord Anthony in clipped accents. His green eyes had narrowed perceptively. "Believe me, I would that I was not placed in the role of nursemaid to a bumptious baggage. If it were only yourself, Miss Stanton, I should not lift a finger to guide you through the shoals, but I have too high a regard for my aunt to allow her to be upset by the heedless actions of a thoroughly selfish miss."

Hetta found that she was trembling. "Pray allow me to return to my chair, sir. I find that I do not care for this particular dance," she said in a stifled voice, feeling the sting of angry tears in her eyes.

"With the greatest of pleasure," said Lord Anthony. He promptly led her off the floor. As they passed a curious group of bystanders, he made an amiable observation to her on a neutral topic.

Without realizing that he spoke for the benefit of those within hearing, Hetta thought furiously that he behaved as though he had not that moment deliberately insulted her.

The tears threatened to choke her and she was hardly able to make a civil reply, but she was determined not to allow her feelings to be known to him.

Lady Anthony stood beside their empty chairs. An expression of relief flashed through her eyes when she saw Hetta. The tension was palpable in her voice when she spoke. "Hetta! I was just coming to search for you. I have called for our carriage." She cast a distracted glance around the crowded assembly room and it seemed to her fancy that a score of disapproving stares were directed at her. She shuddered at an unwelcome memory.

"Good evening, Loraine. One sees that you enjoy your customary good looks," said Lord Anthony. "What is this about your carriage? Is it not early in the evening for one of your gay disposition to be thinking of leaving a party?"

Lady Anthony seemed to notice him for the first time. She flushed delicately. "Oh! Are you here, Michael?" She played with the sticks of her fan, a hunted look in her eyes.

Hetta was astonished by Lady Anthony's obvious distress and it drove her own concerns from her mind. She laid a gentle hand on her friend's arm. "Loraine, what has happened to upset you? Have you the headache?"

"Yes—no. The headache . . . yes, yes, I have the headache! Oh, pray let us go at once," said Lady Anthony, pouncing gratefully on the excuse.

"I shall be happy to escort you to your carriage if you wish, Loraine," said Lord Anthony. Hetta flashed him a look of loathing, but she had perforce to take his arm when Lady Anthony hastily assented. He escorted them from the assembly room outside to their waiting carriage. After handing them up into it and making certain that the carriage door was latched, he signaled to the driver and stepped back up onto the pavement.

As the carriage began to rumble over the cobbles, Lady Anthony burst into tears. Hetta leaned toward her in concern. "My dear ma'am, what could possibly have overset you so?"

Sniffing pathetically, Lady Anthony made a valiant effort to dry her eyes with the scrap of lace she called a handkerchief. "Oh, it is too bad of me! I am sure if I had but known I would have done my best to . . . but there! I did not have the slightest inkling and it is so beastly unfair that I should be held to blame for your indiscretion," exclaimed Lady Anthony somewhat incoherently.

Hetta leapt to an unwelcome suspicion, and her anger rekindled. "Has Lord Anthony anything to do with your distress?"

Lady Anthony cast her a look of astonishment. "Michael! No, why should he? It was that horrid Lady Jersey, whom I cannot bear even if she is a patroness of Almack's. She inquired in that sepulchral voice of hers—*just* what one would expect to arise from a grave, I assure you!—if I was aware of your blatant flirtations. Of course I saw at once how it was, for her bony nose positively quivered with relish as she made known her disapproval. My chaperonage was little better than a grant of permission, if you please! She shall lose no time in hinting to Aunt Beatrice in the most obnoxious manner that I positively encouraged you. And I did not!" Her voice was indignant and then her face crumpled and she wailed, "Oh, Hetta, how could you allow any gentleman to lead you out more than twice in an evening, and at Almack's of all places! I never dreamed that you would do anything so indiscreet." She sought refuge once more in her damp handkerchief.

Hetta was nonplussed and stammered in dismay, "I did not realize! No one ever told me that more than two dances were unacceptable, and I cannot conceive how—" She suddenly broke off as an uncomfortable heat mounted her face. She recalled with horrified clarity how she had reacted toward Lord Anthony. He had attempted to warn her out of a sense of responsibility to his aunt and she had repaid him by behaving much like a spoiled miss fresh out of the schoolroom.

"Oh, that was not the worst of it," said Lady Anthony tragically, dabbing at her flooding eyes. "By morning all London shall be linking your name with Sir Rupert Sikes. With all the gentlemen to choose from, Hetta, it was he whom you chose to dance with *four* times. One can scarcely believe it to be possible. Sir Rupert!"

Hetta shrugged, feeling a sudden burst of impatience. "It quite escapes me why it should be any more scandalous to dance with Sir Rupert than with any other. I find him to be charming company."

"Certainly he is, and that is why he is considered so fatal to one's reputation," said Lady Anthony tartly. An errant thought occurred to her. "Though I do not understand why he should have singled you out for his attentions, for as a rule Rupert does not care for debutantes. Married women are much more his style. It is far more comfortable for him, you see."

Somewhat stiffly, Hetta said, "Perhaps Sir Rupert has simply taken a liking to my company."

Lady Anthony stared at her in the passing light of a streetlamp. "Dear Hetta, you cannot be serious! Why, Rupert has been on the town for ages. It isn't likely that he shall retire now. He is too much the rake for that."

There was a short silence until Hetta asked softly, "You do not care for him overly much, do you?"

Lady Anthony was thrown into a flutter. "Oh, as to that, I am sure I liked him very well once. But Rupert possesses a perfectly horrid streak in his nature that catches one unaware at the worst possible moment. Indeed, it would not amaze me in the least to discover that he has a hidden purpose in dancing attendance on you."

"But how ridiculous! What dark motive could he possibly have? We have simply grown to be friends, and that is all."

"I have the oddest notion that his flirtation with you is simply to annoy Aunt Beatrice," said Lady Anthony, cocking her head thoughtfully. "Indeed, it would be like Rupert to do such a thing, for he quite detests her. She has never succumbed to his charm and it would be just his way to needle her in such a twisted manner."

Hetta's sense of the ridiculous was aroused and she laughed in protest. "Really, Loraine! Sir Rupert hardly strikes me as so devious or melodramatic a character!"

Lady Anthony took affront at what she perceived to be her companion's ridicule. "That is all very well, but I wish you will stop throwing yourself at the man. It is highly unbecoming.''

Hetta gasped. "I have not thrown myself at any gentleman.''

Lady Anthony gave a superior sniff. "Pray see that you don't, for it is extremely bad *ton*, and vulgar besides.''

The carriage stopped before Hetta could make a suitable retort. The ladies were handed out and they walked up the steps of the town house, neither much in charity with the other. When they entered the front hall, it was to find Lady Pelborne waiting for them. She requested their presence in the sitting room. Exchanging puzzled glances, her niece and goddaughter followed her into the room. Within a few minutes Lady Pelborne had informed them that she had chanced to meet an acquaintance upon her return from the theater who had just left Almack's. At the end of a pungent fifteen minutes she had reduced the two younger women to trembling mortification. Lady Anthony emerged from the sitting room in tears and immediately fled upstairs. Hetta was no less white-faced as she retired to her own room. She no longer doubted the gravity of her position. Lady Pelborne had made it abundantly clear that she had all but ruined herself socially in a single disasterous evening at Almack's. Yet her dominant thought was how she was to face Lord Anthony, and she came to the conclusion that her disgrace was such that he would in all probability never cross her path again.

11

Hetta had still not resolved the dilemma of how to apologize to Lord Anthony when she was out for her customary ride the following morning. She saw a tall gentleman on a handsome chestnut gelding in the distance and paused in her own progress to admire the gentleman's horsemanship. Rider and mount moved as though wedded, in perfect harmony. As they trotted nearer Hetta recognized the rider with a feeling close to dismay. Her fingers tighted on her reins and her mare was sidestepping nervously when Lord Anthony reined in beside her.

"A fine morning, is it not, Miss Stanton?" he asked with a distant civility.

"Yes, it is," she said. She met his eyes, half-expecting to discover contempt reflected in their green depths. But his expression was merely a degree cooler than she was used to from him. Bravely she plunged into the subject that most troubled her thoughts. "I owe you an apology, my lord. My ignorance led me into behavior that was abominably ill-bred. I would be grateful if you could overlook my unbecoming conduct toward you last evening."

Lord Anthony was both surprised and pleased by her forthright manner. "Handsomely done, my lady," he said quietly. He smiled at her and indicated with his crop the long green before them. "I would deem it an honor if you would choose to join me in a short gallop."

Hetta flashed him a warm smile that lighted her face. "Indeed, sir, I would like it above all things."

Together they urged their mounts to a gallop near the

verge of trees. Hetta spoke softly in her mare's ear as she sensed worthy competition in the gelding. The mare stretched her neck and her stride lengthened until Lord Anthony was forced to urge his mount to greater speed. The riders flew over the dewy grass. Suddenly the mare streaked ahead, and when at last Hetta pulled her up, there was a considerable distance between her and Lord Anthony.

She was laughing breathlessly when he reined in beside her. He looked appreciatively at the glowing color in her cheeks and her brilliant eyes. "You are an exceptionally fine horsewoman, Hetta. My compliments!"

Hetta pushed back a stray lock that had fallen across her brow. "Forgive me! I could not resist making it a race, my lord. Firefly and I like nothing better than a headlong flight, and it is seldom that we may pit ourselves against so worthy an opponent."

Lord Anthony bowed from the saddle. "My mount and I are flattered, ma'am. You are obviously much practiced on horseback." They had turned their mounts and were retracing their course at a more decorous pace.

"I cannot recall a time when I was not in the saddle. As Lady Pelborne told you, dear Papa was an ardent sportsman and brought me up in his own passion for good horseflesh. For generations the Stantons have all been chronicled as bruising riders." She shot a mischievous glance toward him. "Indeed, it is Maggie's dark opinion that somewhere in the dim mists of the pagan past one of my ancestors must surely have loved a centaur."

"By all accounts our ancestors were a singular lot," said Lord Anthony, only by the slightest quiver of his lips giving away his amusement. "I myself have been told on innumerable occasions by my old nurse that I was a changeling left in the cradle as a penance to my unlucky family." Hetta spluttered into laughter. He shook his head and sighed, his solemn expression belied by the wicked points of light in his green eyes. "I enjoy a confirmed reputation for bold mischief, I am afraid."

"As I am all too aware," retorted Hetta warmly, the smile still curving her soft lips. "I don't suppose you have ever considered putting the lie to such a belief in your character?"

"Should I?" He appeared to give it serious consideration, then shook his head with a mournful sigh. "Alas, I fear I am too far gone, my lady. My friends and acquaintances should only regard me with the gravest suspicion if I were to make the attempt, thinking it were but a plan of particularly devious quality."

Hetta managed to preserve a serious demeanor. "Such injustice must wound one deeply. You have my profound sympathies, sir."

Lord Anthony inclined his head. "Your sensitivity touches me, ma'am."

Their ridiculous banter had carried them back to their meeting point and Hetta slowed the mare. She held out her gloved hand to Lord Anthony. "I must return Firefly to my godmother's stables, my lord. It is quite the nicest excursion I have experienced since my arrival in London."

Lord Anthony retained her fingers in his warm clasp a moment longer than was necessary. He was surprised by the depth of his own pleasure. "And I also have enjoyed myself, Miss Stanton." Blushing, Hetta gently withdrew her hand. He did not appear to notice her confusion, but asked, "Do you often exercise the mare in the mornings?"

"As often as I may, but I do not publicize it. I fear that my custom of dispensing with groom or chaperone would be thought indecorous by the sticklers. I have told only Edward Strappey because he is such an ardent horseman himself that I knew he would not care," said Hetta. She chuckled suddenly. "He is at times able to roll himself out of bed early enough to join me, but I have noticed never after an evening spent at one of the gaming clubs. I suspect that he has little head for wine."

"If I would not be intruding on your privacy, I would like to join you later this week for a good gallop," said Lord Anthony. He smiled at her with a warm expression in his eyes. "I will endeavor to be the most unobtrusive of chaperons."

Hetta's soft color heightened. "I should like that very much, my lord," she said with a touch of shyness. She heard her name called and turned her head.

A trio of horsemen was approaching them. Hetta recognized her cousin on the outside hack and her lips tightened. Lord Anthony, after a cursory glance at the horsemen, had turned to his companion with an idle remark and saw her expression stiffen. Curiously he looked again at the approaching group, guessing that one of the riders was Miss Stanton's bothersome cousin.

Markham was accompanied by Sir Rupert Sikes and another gentleman whom Hetta did not know. Brief surprise touched her that her cousin should be on such friendly terms with Sir Rupert, but she recalled Lady Pelborne's opinion that he was desirous of establishing social connections and thought that would explain it.

"Well met, cousin," said Markham as he came up. He acknowledged Lord Anthony's presence with the briefest of nods and a narrow look. "I see that you have already been taking the air. We are fortunate to be able to join you."

"Actually I am this moment on my way back, Jonathan," Hetta said shortly as she turned to greet the other two gentlemen. She held out a gloved hand to Sir Rupert, giving him a friendly smile. "It is nice to see you again, sir."

Lord Anthony, who was quietly observing Markham's darkened face, was surprised by the warmth of Hetta's greeting for Sir Rupert. He caught his cousin's wary and faintly malicious sidelong glance. Lord Anthony's smile was thin. Rupert acknowledged, then, that he should tread lightly where Miss Stanton was concerned.

"The pleasure is definitely mine, dear lady," Sir Rupert said, bowing conventionally over her hand before he addressed his cousin. "I hope I see you well, Davenchester?"

Hetta was swiftly reminded of the animosity between the two men at their last meeting. She shot an anxious look at the earl.

Lord Anthony glanced down at her, aware of her sudden tension. He said blandly, "I am as always, Rupert."

Sir Rupert smiled, relaxing almost imperceptibly in the saddle.

Relieved that the gentlemen had left off their hostilities, Hetta said, ''My lord, I do not believe that you have met my cousin, Mr. Jonathan Markham. Jonathan, this is Lord Anthony, the Earl of Davenchester.''

Markham's eyes betrayed his astonishment at discovering her in such exalted company. His arrogant expression altered to become deferential. ''A pleasure, my lord,'' he said, bowing from the saddle.

The earl nodded to him and said pleasantly, ''I have heard of you, sir. Indeed, Miss Stanton has mentioned you in the same breath as Meldingcourt.'' He was gratified by Markham's visible start.

Markham quickly looked to Miss Stanton for explanation, but she had turned to Sir Rupert with a wish to be made known to his silent companion.

''Forgive me, ma'am. I have quite forgotten my manners,'' said Sir Rupert smoothly. Introductions were made among those of the group who were not acquainted and a few minutes passed in general conversation.

Hetta was soon able to make her excuses and, lifting her crop in farewell, touched a light spur to her mount.

Markham looked after her with a calculating expression, tugging thoughtfully at his full underlip. When he turned his attention back to the other gentlemen, he was disconcerted to discover Lord Anthony's eyes upon him. The earl addressed a desultory remark to the third gentleman, dispelling the impression of interest, and Markham shrugged it off as coincidence.

Lord Anthony soon took his leave of the other gentlemen and rode back to his town house. After giving his mount into the care of the groom, he went inside. His valet, Gregors, was waiting for him with fresh attire. When Lord Anthony descended to the breakfast room several minutes later, he had changed his dusty riding coat and breeches for a pale superfine coat, starched cravat, lawn shirt, and buff pantaloons that smoothed without a crease into gleaming top boots.

While Lord Anthony was engaged in his morning repast of coffee, steak, and kidneys, a visitor was shown in. He looked up from cutting his steak to greet Captain Trevor. "I am glad to see you, Trevor. Pray join me."

"Thank you, my lord," said Captain Trevor, taking him at his word. He seated himself opposite and began to fill a plate.

"To what do I owe this unexpected pleasure?" asked Lord Anthony.

"I'm on my way to Tattersall's this morning and I would be honored if you would accompany me," said Captain Trevor. "I am commissioned with choosing a team of cattle suitable for a lady's carriage and I would value your opinion."

The earl looked at him in quizzical surprise. "My opinion, Trevor? Surely that is between you and the lady."

Captain Trevor shot him a challenging look from under sandy brows. "The team is for Lady Anthony, my lord. As her nearest relative, I thought you would be best qualified in pointing me to a team certain to please her."

As Lord Anthony met the steady regard of his visitor's eyes, he realized that Captain Trevor was aware of his animosity toward his flighty sister-in-law. Yet the man was openly making known his interest in Lady Anthony. The earl could not deny an admiration for the fellow's forthrightness. He thought fleetingly that Lady Anthony could do worse than to have this man as her champion. Lord Anthony said, "I will naturally be happy to lend you whatever assistance I may."

Captain Trevor imperceptibly relaxed. "I am obliged to you, my lord."

The breakfast-room door swung open and a bluff voice said, "In here, you say? Good, I shall just pop in for a moment." Sir Horace entered, silver-knobbed malacca cane firmly in hand. "What, Trevor, you here as well? Davenchester, my boy! Thought I would stop in on my way to White's and drop a word in your ear about that fellow Markham."

Lord Anthony straightened in his chair, an alert expression entering his keen eyes. "Have you, by God?"

Captain Trevor recognized the clipped note of attention in the earl's voice and immediately rose from the table. "I apprehend that this is a private matter, so I shall take my leave. I shall meet your lordship later at Tattersall's."

Sir Horace made a shooing motion with his broad hand. "Nonsense, Trevor. Nothing so private here that you need to fly. Indeed, as a friend of Miss Stanton's, it may be just as well that you are here."

Captain Trevor sank back into his chair, his curiosity stirred.

"Pray what have you learned of Markham?" asked Lord Anthony.

Sir Horace sat down at the table and pulled the pot of coffee to him. As he poured a cup, he shook his head. "He's a scurvy-enough fellow, as we had suspected. Pleasant and all that on the surface, of course. Nothing to complain about in the fellow's manners. However, I have gathered quite a different picture of the man when he is not in society. As you are aware, Davenchester, I have cultivated over the years certain personages one would hesitate to make known to one's better acquaintances. Some of these shady acquaintances of mine tell me that Markham is quite active in the political arena."

Sir Horace paused to sip carefully at his hot coffee, then shrugged. "Nothing against that; I am myself involved in politics. However, Markham has a certain reputation for ruthlessness and he is not above breaking a few heads here and there to attain his ends. He has little power behind him, but he is a wily manipulator and I don't doubt that in time he may gain a few ears. Without lands, however, he can never be in the foreground as much as he might wish."

Lord Anthony leaned back in his chair, playing negligently with his knife. His green eyes suddenly glittered. "I find this intelligence highly interesting, Sir Horace."

The older man gave him a shrewd glance. "No doubt you will enlighten us in your own good time as to what has piqued your interest."

The earl smiled slightly. He thought he knew now why

Markham was so persistent in his pursuit of Miss Stanton. But until he hit on a way to force Markham into the open, he was reluctant to voice his suspicions. "As you say, Sir Horace. Was there any other useful information on our man?"

Sir Horace pursed his mouth in an expression of distaste. He nodded at Captain Trevor. "This is the bit that may be of interest to you as well, Trevor. My friends have reported rumors of ravishment, in particular of a young girl from a respectable family. The incident was naturally hushed up, but these things do get nosed abroad eventually. If it is as Bea says and this fellow is barking at Miss Stanton's heels, I should keep a close eye out for her. Her cousin is not the pleasantest of fellows."

The implication was not lost on his audience. Lord Anthony's eyes narrowed and his fingers slowly curled about the haft of his steak knife.

"Good God!" exclaimed Captain Trevor blankly.

"I assume that you have spoken to my aunt regarding this?" asked Lord Anthony, his voice sharp.

"I shall when next I see her. Thought you would wish to know as well, since you appear to have taken a friendly interest in the chit," said Sir Horace mildly. Prudently he said no more, though he guessed that Davenchester's interest in Miss Stanton was warmer than anyone knew. He began to lever himself up from the chair, his whalebone stays creaking alarm. "Well, I must be off. I daresay old Forbes will be looking for me." Lord Anthony rose to accompany him to the door, but the older man waved him back. "Pray don't trouble yourself on my account, Davenchester. I can find my own way. I ain't in my dotage yet."

"I know it, sir," Lord Anthony said with a smile.

Sir Horace grunted acknowledgment of the compliment. He waved his cane in salute as he left the room.

Captain Trevor looked across the table at the earl, his expression appalled. "My lord, if what Sir Horace says is true concerning Miss Stanton's cousin, then . . ." He halted, uncertain how best to phrase his thoughts.

Lord Anthony threw him a glance as he picked up the coffeepot and freshened his cup. "Yes, Trevor. It means that Miss Stanton may need her friends about her. I think that between the two of us, and my aunt, we may prevent any rash impulses Markham may harbor."

"Yes, of course," agreed Captain Trevor, frowning at Lord Anthony's indifferent air. His observant eyes took sudden note of the unusually hard look about the earl's mouth. He said gently, "Forgive me, my lord, but I believe that you feel more concern for Miss Stanton's welfare than you care to admit."

Lord Anthony looked at him with a hint of surprise in his eyes. Then he smiled faintly. "Perhaps I do, Trevor." He casually turned the conversation to Tattersall's, ending any further discussion of Miss Stanton.

Captain Trevor was left to his own conjectures.

Rain fell for the next two mornings, making it impossible for Hetta to indulge in her solitary rides. When the third day dawned bright and clear, within an hour of wakening she had donned her olive-green riding habit and was riding in the park. From afar she espied a gentleman on a chestnut mount and she reined in, a welcoming smile lifting the corners of her generous mouth. But she quickly realized the chestnut's gait was too rough to be that of Lord Anthony's mount, and as the rider drew closer, she was able to recognize her cousin. The pleasure in her eyes disappeared entirely and she touched the mare to movement once more.

Markham swung his hack in beside the mare. "A delightful meeting, cousin."

"Surely that is a matter of opinion," said Hetta shortly, presenting her profile to him.

Markham laughed good-naturedly. "You disappoint me, Hetta. I had thought to find you sweet-tempered thus early in the morning and taking your favorite exercise."

"How did you know where to find me?" asked Hetta, wondering if one of Lady Pelborne's grooms could possibly have been bribed.

"Having once discovered you in the park was enough for me to deduce it, cousin. You forget that your unladylike habits are well-known to me. I only wonder that it did not occur to me sooner. You are too countrified to have given up riding even in the metropolis," Markham said amiably, pleased with himself.

Hetta did not bother to mask the unfriendliness in her glance. "What do you want, Jonathan?" she asked. She felt sick anger that he had discovered her morning excursions with Firefly, for she knew full well it meant that she could never be certain when he might not grasp the opportunity to intrude on her. The beauty of the morning seemed to pall with her thoughts.

"Could I desire more than the simple pleasure of your company?" Markham asked softly as he reached across the short distance separating them. The mare danced to the side at the hidden touch of a spur and carried Hetta out of reach. His lips thinned and he dropped his hand to rest on his thigh. He said sharply, "I have something of import to say to you, cousin, and I would be gratified if you would condescend to control your mount."

Hetta leaned down to give the mare an affectionate pat, her mood suddenly lightened. "She is particularly restive this morning, I fear," she murmured.

Markham reached over to catch her reins in his fist and drew both mounts to a standstill.

Quick fury sparked in Hetta's eyes. Her voice was icy. "Oblige me, cousin. Unhand my reins on the instant."

"In a moment, dear cousin." Markham narrowed his eyes suddenly as he gave her a measuring look of surprise. There was a fine color in her face and her dark sparkling eyes appeared enormous. The froth of lace at her throat that served for a cravat fell low over the front of her well-cut habit and emphasized the quick rise and fall of her breast. "Surely my compliments are in order. Lady Pelborne has worked wonders with your appearance. One may even describe you as an attractive little piece," said Markham in congratulatory accents.

"Vastly pretty, cousin. You have always a way with a compliment," said Hetta with swift contempt.

Markham's ruddy face darkened. "You have still—"
He controlled himself with an effort and managed to conjure up a smile that did not quite reach his hard eyes.
"Dear Hetta, I only speak so boldly through a true admiration for you. Many times in the past I have offered for
your hand and been spurned—"

"And I shall continue to do so," said Hetta quickly.

Markham inclined his head. "Your maidenly scruples
did you honor, dear cousin. I came to understand your shy
reluctance, but you have now had an opportunity to become better acquainted with the world. You have seen
your absurd romantic fancies for what they are. Dearest
Hetta, could we not at last put an end to the unnecessary
distance between us?" He ended on a cajoling note and let
go her reins to gently caress her cheek.

Hetta recoiled sharply from his touch. "You mistake the
matter greatly, cousin. I have indeed seen more of the
world and it has convinced me that my determination
against your suit was the wisest decision I could have
made." She gathered up her reins and turned the mare's
head.

Markham grasped her shoulder. She turned on him with
an indignant gasp, her eyes blazing. "You would try the
patience of a saint, Hetta. I am but a man. Do not goad me
too far," Markham said tautly. As he looked down into
her lovely flushed face, a certain angry excitement flared
to life in his eyes.

"Unhand me at once," said Hetta through gritted teeth.

"Hetta, we could deal better together than this," said
Markham, tightening his fingers on her shoulder. His eyes
fell to her softly parted lips, then dropped to the lace at her
breast rising swift as a cresting wave. He drew closer.

Revulsion shook her and she choked out, "Do not dare
to touch me." She tried to shake off his hand and under
her the mare shifted uneasily.

"By God, I have withstood your arrogance for too
long," exclaimed Markham. He let go her shoulder to
ungently force up her chin. Savagely he brought his mouth
down on hers, crushing her lips against her teeth. Hetta

tasted blood as she struggled against him. Markham dropped his reins and attempted to drag her from her saddle, but he underestimated the strength she had acquired through years on horseback. Their mounts shifted restively, snorting alarm. Markham's punishing fingers suddenly freed her chin and Hetta tore her mouth from his. There was the sound of ripping lace and she felt the cool morning air on her bare breast. Then his heavy breath was hot against the frantic pulse in her throat.

"Dear God," she gasped, her thoughts churning with revulsion and fear. Blindly she struck out with her leather crop, again and again.

With a profane exclamation Markham jerked back, a red welt rising across his square jaw. Desperately Hetta dug her spurs into the mare's sides, and with a squeal Firefly bolted into a dead run. Hetta only just managed to keep her seat. Regaining her balance instinctively, she leaned far over the mare's neck to urge her on. The mare took the bit between her teeth and Hetta let her have her head. Tears blinded her and she could not see the direction of her desperate flight, but she dared not slacken the mare's headlong flight. The pounding of hooves in swift pursuit drummed loud in her ears.

Lord Anthony, hoping to meet Miss Stanton again, entered the park at a slow canter on his chestnut gelding. The sound of furious hoofbeats on his left made him glance around in curiosity for it was unusual that a rider would give such a strenuous workout to his mount so near the trees. The horse was a runaway stretched out at full gallop, the rider's green habit flapping wildly from its back. Another rider on a hack rode in hot pursuit, but his mount was hopelessly outdistanced. Lord Anthony spurred the gelding to a gallop, angling to intercept the runaway.

When he was close enough, he reached far out of the saddle to catch the runaway's bridle in his gloved fist. Forcibly he hauled the mare to a standstill until it stood trembling, blowing hard through flared red nostrils. The rider turned on him, striking out wildly at his face with her crop. Tears had streaked her face and her eyes were dark with fear. With shock Lord Anthony recognized Miss

Stanton. He deflected the crop, then caught her close to his side.

An inarticulate cry broke from her lips and she pulled frantically against him.

"Miss Stanton! My dear, look at me!"

His commanding voice at last penetrated her unreasoning fear. She blinked as though wakening, and Lord Anthony's face swam into focus. His expression was frowning, almost stern, but she recognized the concern in his eyes. "My lord!" she choked. A fresh rush of tears started to her eyes and she drooped against him as shuddering sobs shook her.

He was appalled by the abandon of her weeping and held her as close as he was able on horseback. "You're safe, sweetheart," he murmured comfortingly. Over her bowed head he saw the gentleman on the hack turn his mount and ride swiftly in the opposite direction, and his eyes narrowed. It seemed odd that the rider should not wish to assure himself of the runaway's well-being. His quick mind flashed to an abhorrent conclusion. Rage exploded hot within him. With difficulty he mastered it, for the sake of the frightened young woman burrowed against his shoulder.

For several minutes the horses stood quietly, recognizing the strong grip of a master on their reins. Lord Anthony waited until Hetta's sobs had subsided to hiccoughs, and then gently eased her away from his shoulder. "I had thought that the mare was a runaway, but that was not the case, was it?" he asked her quietly.

She shook her head mutely, dashing away the remainder of her tears with the back of her gloved hand. "It—it was my cousin," she said in a low voice. An eddy of cool air caressed the sensitive skin of her throat and breast. Hetta suddenly recalled the sound of ripping lace, and a tide of color swept her cheeks. She fumbled at the torn front of her bodice. "It is very difficult to—to explain. My cousin—"

Lord Anthony's glance had followed her clumsy attempt to repair the ragged edges of her cravat, and his lips tightened. There was a hard look about his mouth that made Hetta shrink inside. "I understand perfectly. May I suggest that in future your riding be done in the company of known acquaintances?" She avoided his gaze, acknowledging his suggestion with a tiny nod. Satisfied, Lord Anthony said, "I shall escort you myself on your return to the town house if I may."

"I thank you, my lord," said Hetta, her face averted. Shame stained her cheeks and she felt almost physically ill that he had discovered her in such straits. He could not possibly be expected to understand what had transpired, and surely he suspected her of the most improper behavior. Hetta did not think that she could ever look him in the face again.

The ride to Lady Pelborne's was accomplished quickly and in silence.

Immediately upon their arrival, Hetta murmured a low excuse and, to the astonishment of the footman, ran up the stairs. Lord Anthony stood in the hall looking after her with a forbidding frown on his face. The footman somewhat hesitantly addressed him. "May I be of further assistance, my lord?"

Lord Anthony turned to him with a cold look in his eyes. His voice was harsh. "Pray convey my compliments and inform my aunt that I desire an interview with her at once."

"But, my lord, Lady Pelborne has not yet risen," faltered the footman. Something flickered in his lordship's eyes and the footman hastily backed away. "Very good, my lord." He exited smartly on his errand, glad to escape the earl's dangerous presence.

When the Honorable Jonathan Markham presented himself at Lady Pelborne's some days later, he was informed that Miss Stanton was not available but Lady Pelborne would be happy to receive him. He stood irresolute only a moment, then allowed himself to be shown into the morning room, where Lady Pelborne awaited him. She inclined her head in greeting and graciously invited him to be seated. "We have seen little of you of late, Mr. Markham,

and just when we had grown accustomed to your visits,"
she said pleasantly.

Markham relaxed and a smile came to his lips. "Not
through choice, I assure you, dear lady. I have unfortunately had other obligations of late that became rather
pressing."

"One assumes that your rather tawdry disagreement
with my goddaughter had nothing to do with the discharge
of those obligations," said Lady Pelborne mildly.

Markham reddened at her insinuation. "Hardly, ma'am!
I do not know what Hetta—Miss Stanton—may have told
you, but I fear that her maidenly imagination sometimes
leads her to misconstrue what was meant."

"Indeed? But you interest me, sir." Lady Pelborne's
expression was one of polite inquiry. "Perhaps then you
would be so good as to relate the true particulars of the
incident. I must confess my goddaughter was a good deal
upset and incoherent."

Markham considered his position quickly, a look of
calculation in his hard blue eyes. He made slow to answer,
as though reluctant to breach etiquette. "Before your kind
invitation to Miss Stanton, my lady, I was almost constantly in her company. I am therefore perhaps better
acquainted with her character than most. Forgive me if my
blunt speech offends you, ma'am, but I have often thought
Miss Stanton to be of a rather volatile nature. As for our
meeting in the park, I can assure you that it was not my
intention to overset her. Quite the contrary! I simply conveyed the wish that she honor me with her hand in marriage." He threw up his palm in a well-timed gesture of
acknowledgment. "I realize now that in doing so I went
against your express wish to restrain my ardor. I humbly
beg your pardon. However, Miss Stanton's initial reaction
gave me hope that my feelings were at last to be recipro-
cated. But, alas, I was chagrined to discover that the
depth of my passion was a startling revelation to Lady
Stanton's high-strung disposition. In short, Lady Stanton
became somewhat hysterical in manner and fled before I
had the opportunity to reassure her." Markham spoke with
apparent sincerity, but his sharp eyes did not waver from

Lady Pelborne's face. He was alert for any altering of her serene expression, well aware that he could be treading on thin ice. Lady Pelborne's hostility would be all that was needed to close certain social avenues to him.

"The odd mark on your face, Mr. Markham. One could almost mistake it for the half-healed weal from a crop," Lady Pelborne said softly. "I suspect that your ardent declaration met with a sort of treatment you hardly foresaw."

Markham said quickly, "Miss Stanton, as I said, was overwrought and but misunderstood me. She reacted thoughtlessly and without malice."

"One can only applaud the gallantry with which you dismiss so lightly the punishment inflicted upon your person," said Lady Pelborne with inescapable irony.

"Believe me, my lady—" protested Markham.

"No, Mr. Markham, I cannot." Her quiet authority overrode his attempt to recover. He saw that her eyes had turned to frost. "Your manners and actions can hardly be called those of a gentleman, Mr. Markham, nor are they worthy of a man who aspires to public life." He appeared startled and she smiled pityingly. "I have access to certain channels of information that keep me alerted to ripples in the political arena, Mr. Markham. Your ambitions are hardly as secret as you might wish to believe." He was frowning and she was satisfied that she had shaken his confidence. "As to my goddaughter, you would have me believe that she is forward and a liar. Allow me to inform you, sir, that I know her to be neither. I have maintained a regular correspondence through the years with both my goddaughter and Mr. Cheton. I am therefore quite familiar with the history of your extraordinary harassment of my goddaughter. The incident that occurred but days ago merely confirms my opinion of your lack of character, Mr. Markham. Your visits to this house will no longer be permitted, nor will I tolerate advances toward my goddaughter in society. I trust that I make myself perfectly clear?"

"Perfectly, ma'am," said Markham. His face and neck were an alarming shade of red, except for a thin line of white etching his tight mouth. The rage he felt threatened to choke him.

Lady Pelborne rang a silver hand bell and the sitting-room door was immediately flung open by a footman. She said quietly, "I do not think that we have anything further to discuss, Mr. Markham. I wish you good day."

Markham had no choice but to rise from his seat. He executed a somewhat jerky bow in her direction and turned to the door.

She watched in silence as he beat an ignominious retreat from her chilly presence.

12

The announcement of the Earl of Davenchester's ball sent a wave of anticipation rippling through the *ton*. Lord Anthony, whom a few vaguely recalled to have been a merry young gentleman ripe for mischief before he purchased a pair of colors and went to war, was an object of curiosity during the course of the Season. He had made several appearances at select functions and proved himself to be an affable if somewhat aloof guest. It was generally agreed that he carried himself well, that his person was handsome and his manners exquisite. His only fault lay in an obvious preference for the card room, where he was often able to exchange civilities with his sister-in-law and her favored escort, Captain Trevor. There was not a hostess worthy of the name who, once honored by his attendance at her party, did not make a decided effort to introduce him to the suitable young ladies of her acquaintance. None voiced the opinion openly, but it was felt to be a disappointment that the highly eligible earl did no more than his polite duty in escorting the young ladies in to dinner or honoring them with a turn once or twice about the ballroom floor. Though the sharp-eyed tattlers whispered, none could discover that the earl had a preference for any particular young lady over another, and attempts to pump Lady Pelborne concerning the matter met with cool rebuff. Lady Pelborne did not appear to be making an effort to bring her own goddaughter to his notice, and she was thought to be positively shortsighted not to give Miss Stanton a push in the Earl of Davenchester's direction.

When Lord Anthony was informed by his secretary that every invitation to his ball had been accepted, he laughed, for he was well aware of the buzz of speculation surrounding his person. He asked Lady Pelborne and Lady Anthony to act as joint hostesses for him while Hetta found herself in the position of a favored guest.

Fearing Lord Anthony's contempt, Hetta was uncertain how to act toward him after he had discovered her in such a compromising situation. He realized her discomfort because he at once inquired if she still rode in the mornings. "Yes, though not alone. Edward Strappey and occasionally Captain Trevor join me now. We make quite an amiable party. I would be most happy to include you among our number," said Hetta shyly.

"I shall hold you to that invitation," Lord Anthony said. "Have you met Markham on your excursions?"

A flush rose to her face. "We have met him two or three times, but he is oddly out of sorts and does not tarry long." She smiled faintly. "Edward has a low opinion of Cousin Jonathan's taste in horseflesh. He refers to his hackney as a rough-gaited brute of mean intelligence."

"Trust young Edward to instantly size up a piece of horseflesh," said Lord Anthony with a grin. "I understand that he has won several bets of late by identifying a rider from a distance simply by observing the action of his mount."

Laughing with him, Hetta discovered that she felt quite at ease again, and she was grateful to him for his unspoken reassurance.

Lord Anthony provided well for the entertainment of his guests. Music and dancing were to be enjoyed in the huge ballroom while adjoining card rooms were available to those who preferred to pursue a less energetic pastime. The refreshments seemed unending in supply. The night was exceedingly warm for mid-May and the doors entering the ballroom from the garden were left invitingly open for those who wished to cool their heated brows. Colored lights had been strung in the trees and in the splashing fountains to give a fairy-tale appearance to the garden that won admiring acclaim from all who saw it.

Lady Pelborne and Lady Anthony stood dutifully at the head of the receiving line to greet newcomers while Lord Anthony divided his time among his several guests. Hetta was taken aback when Lord Anthony called on her to exert herself on his behalf, but she quickly adjusted to the role of minor hostess. She thought his request was simply further proof of his sensitivity toward her shaken confidence. Her face lighted with a warm glow whenever Lord Anthony approached her to introduce an acquaintance, and she blossomed under his attentiveness.

Onlookers began to raise their brows, for it seemed that the Earl of Davenchester was making much more of Miss Stanton than he had in the past. It was quickly noted that Miss Stanton appeared in exceptionally fine looks. Her large hazel eyes sparkled; her conversation was laced with gracious wit. The jade-green satin gown she wore, set off by a string of pearls, clung flatteringly to her slim figure, and it was the general opinion of the company that she had never appeared lovelier. A swell of curiosity rose among the *ton* and whispers of an engagement announcement made the rounds.

Lady Pelborne heard the speculation with gathering concern and finally sought out her nephew. She tapped him on the arm with her fan. "What are you about, Michael? I realize you are attempting to restore some measure of my goddaughter's credibility, and for that I am grateful, but I must warn you that you are in a fair way of making Hetta and yourself an item."

"That is precisely my intention, ma'am," said Lord Anthony with a quiet smile. "I intend that Markham shall hear from a dozen separate sources before the week is out that I am fixing my interest on Miss Stanton. I hope to incite him to an action that will enable me to finally deal with him as he deserves."

Lady Pelborne frowned as she gazed across the room at her goddaughter's vivid laughing face. "One wishes you success, of course. Michael, I have never seen Hetta so vivacious or lovely as she appears tonight, and I fear that it is in large part due to your attentiveness. Do not hurt her, Michael."

He looked down at her in astonishment. "Ma'am! Surely you know me better!"

"Yes, I know you," said Lady Pelborne, her eyes still on her goddaughter. She thought she knew Hetta as well, and she feared for her goddaughter's vulnerability.

Sir Rupert Sikes arrived at the ball late in the evening. Almost at once he became aware of the excited speculation surrounding the Earl of Davenchester and Miss Stanton, and observed Lord Anthony's deliberate devotion to the lady for himself. The thought crossed his mind that his cousin might be contemplating making an offer for Miss Stanton's hand. With a sinking feeling close to nausea he wondered how that would leave him fixed, for he realized that he would no longer be able to trade on his expectations as Lord Anthony's sole heir with his creditors.

Lady Pelborne noticed his dour expression as he watched Lord Anthony leading her goddaughter onto the dance floor and she could not resist a gentle dig. "They make a handsome pair, do they not, Rupert?" she asked casually. "One could almost say that they have an instinctive understanding of each other, so well do they move together. It is as though they were meant for each other."

Sir Rupert's frown deepened. He shrugged dismissively. "A happy coincidence. Miss Stanton has always danced well." Lady Pelborne hid a smile and with a murmured excuse passed on. Sir Rupert did not see her go, but brooded on the dancing couple, who were seemingly oblivious of the stir they were creating. Almost before his eyes, Lord Anthony turned Hetta close in to him. She was laughing in delight, and as she looked up at Lord Anthony, her eyes sparkled with an emotion Sir Rupert had no difficulty interpreting. He cursed softly under his breath.

A few moments later Lord Anthony returned Hetta to her seat and Sir Rupert seized the opportunity to request a dance of her. Hetta accepted with a quick smile, her eyes glowing still with pleasure. As they turned about the floor, Hetta mentioned she was to be presented to the Prince Regent at Carlton House on the following evening. Filing away the information in his mind, Sir Rupert led the conversation around to the heat and suggested that they take a turn about the gardens. Hetta hesitated a moment. She had carefully kept her distance from Sir Rupert in the days since the disastrous evening at Almack's in an attempt to retrieve her shaken reputation, but she saw no harm in a sedate walk in the gardens when several other couples had already set the example. Assenting, she allowed herself to be led through one of the open doors. Sir Rupert and Hetta strolled slowly down a peaceful walkway to a stone bench set under a leafy tree and seated themselves.

Sir Rupert took her hand and his demeanor became serious. "Dear Miss Stanton, it has long been my intention to admit to a great admiration for you."

"Why, that is exceedingly kind of you. I am flattered," said Hetta, surprised.

"Surely my devotion has not gone unnoticed?" he asked, gentle reproof in his voice. "Alas, I see that I have stood too long silent. But there was never the appropriate time or place to declare my heart. And too, I am somewhat of a coward, for I hardly dared to contemplate your reaction. In short, my dearest lady, I throw myself at your exquisite feet and humbly beg the honor of your hand."

Hetta had listened to his passionate speech in growing astonishment. She discovered that her fingers were still clasped in Sir Rupert's hand and gently extricated herself. She stammered, "You do me a singular honor, Sir Rupert, truly. But I am all in a whirl. I never suspected—"

Sir Rupert placed a silencing finger against her warm lips. Hetta looked up at him, her eyes wide. "Pray do not utter a single word of discouragement, my fair one. I should be utterly devastated. I ask only for your gentle consideration, for you must know that all I have and am is at your beckoning. But give me the answer I most desire, sweet Hetta, and I shall be the most fortunate of men."

"I—I do not know quite what to say, Sir Rupert," said Hetta, shaken.

"I perceive that my impetuosity has taken you unaware." Sir Rupert raised her hand to his lips and pressed
a lingering kiss to her soft palm. He felt her shiver.
Looking deeply into her wide eyes, he said softly, "If you
but knew how I burn to call you mine."

"Oh!" Hetta felt her face flame at the intimate suggestion in his velvet voice. She snatched away her hand to lay
it against her hot cheek. "Oh, you must not! Pray do not
say such things."

Sir Rupert leaned closer to her, his long fingers sliding
warmly up her bare arm. "Dearest Hetta—"

"Ah, here you are, Hetta!"

With a gasp Hetta leapt up from the bench, her face
expressing embarrassment as Lady Pelborne appeared out
of the shadows. Sir Rupert rose with nonchalant ease in
courtesy to the older woman. Lady Pelborne did not appear to notice her goddaughter's stricken expression. "I
was just coming to find you, my dear. There is a particularly dear friend of Loraine's whom she insists you must
meet. The gardens are absolutely fascinating in this light,
are they not? Quite like a fairyland. Rupert has likely
shown you the prettiest spots, but one can hardly wander
forever in the walkways, can one?"

"Of course not, Godmamma," said Hetta, a faint note
of relief in her voice. "I shall go to Loraine at once." She
did not look at Sir Rupert.

"Then run along, child. Loraine is all impatience. You
will find her near one of the card rooms, I expect," said
Lady Pelborne. She glanced at Sir Rupert with a certain
glint in her eyes. "I shall follow directly with Sir Rupert,
who I feel certain will be kind enough to offer an arm to
an old woman."

Sir Rupert sketched a leisurely bow, a faintly amused
expression on his face. "But naturally, dear Lady Pelborne."

With a quick glance and murmured word to Sir Rupert,
Hetta sped quickly toward the ballroom.

Sir Rupert and Lady Pelborne made their way more
slowly. "Well, Rupert, have you nothing to say to the
purpose? I own that it surprised me to discover you mak-

ing pretty love to my goddaughter," said Lady Pelborne amiably.

"A mild flirtation only, dear lady. As you well know, Miss Stanton does not conform to my usual bill of fare," said Sir Rupert.

"One hopes that is meant as reassurance, Rupert," said Lady Pelborne, so softly that he had to bend his head to hear her. She looked up at him suddenly and the arctic expression in her eyes startled him. "I should dislike it excessively if I were obliged to drop a well-placed word here and there concerning one of my relations. One would feel such distaste for the necessity, you understand."

There was a tense silence until Sir Rupert said curtly, "I understand you all too well, I think. Never fear, Miss Stanton is safe enough with me. I am in fact fast developing an aversion for the young lady. But I feel it my duty to point out that our flirtation is not one-sided. Miss Stanton, I believe, is somewhat enamored of me."

They had reached the ballroom and Lady Pelborne paused a moment before entering the brightly lighted ballroom. She laughed softly in derision. "Your overwhelming conceit is boundless, Rupert. I assure you that, given room, my goddaughter would soon perceive your true colors. For you cannot, and never shall be able to, keep them hidden for long. In a month, she herself would give you the roundabout." Lady Pelborne's contemptuous glance raked him as she passed through the door to be swallowed at once by the milling crowd.

Sir Rupert stood staring after her, white-faced with anger and shock. That the old woman would dare to speak with such disdain to him! He swore thickly, almost choking on his own rage. "We shall see, dear Lady Pelborne," he muttered viciously. "We shall see who has the last laugh." He swung on his heel and left the scene.

The carriage set them down at Carlton House in Regent Street, and Hetta, accompanied by Lady Anthony, Lady Pelborne, and Lord Anthony, entered the Prince Regent's residence. Immediately upon crossing the threshold Hetta was struck by the heat and heavily scented air. Lord Anthony noticed her expression and flashed a grin at her. "The Prince Regent believes strongly in the evil effects of the night air and an open window will never be found in any of his residences."

"How extraordinary," Hetta said faintly, feeling the perspiration begin to break out on her brow as Lord Anthony escorted them through the crowd. Hetta gazed at the interior of Carlton House and was impressed with the elegant gilt furniture and the masterpieces mounted on the walls. Dozens of mirrors reflected the rich colors of velvet draperies and the ladies' gowns. Scores of scented candles set the rooms and archways ablaze with light.

Lady Pelborne presented her goddaughter to the Prince Regent, a corpulent figure in gorgeous evening clothes. His rather prominent blue eyes inspected Hetta with approval and he patted her hand between his fat palms, saying that he liked pretty young women. Blushing in confusion, Hetta thanked him and he laughed jovially before turning his attention to another guest.

In the crowd Hetta somehow found herself separated from her companions. While she sought in vain for sight of Lord Anthony's tall figure, she felt a touch on her elbow.

Sir Rupert stood at her side and smiled down at her. "Are you suitably impressed with our Prince Regent and his abode?" he asked with a hint of superiority as he waved his hand at the noisy scene.

"Oh, yes! It is quite extraordinary, and not in the least as I expected it to be," said Hetta, thinking that the Prince Regent and his party were not as formal as one might expect.

Sir Rupert's smile broadened and he lowered his voice to a conspiratorial whisper. "It is, perhaps, a bit vulgar?"

Hetta laughed outright. "I am not so easily trapped, Sir Rupert."

"I shall not attempt to do so, then. Would you care to tour an area rather less crowded than this circus?" he asked.

Hetta nodded her acquiescence since she did not care for

the idea of being unescorted. Sir Rupert led her to a display of portraits that others before them had already discovered in a hall off the ballroom. He kept up a running commentary of nonsense that so thoroughly entertained Hetta that she did not realize they had gradually progressed farther away from the other guests. Sir Rupert showed her into what appeared to be a small sitting room, gracefully appointed with a cheerful fire around which were grouped two wing chairs and a settee. Hetta glanced around in curiosity and realized that they were alone. She turned to Sir Rupert to discover he was quietly closing the door.

Hetta gave him a straight look from under her fine arched brows and said with a smile, "I think that we should return to the gathering, Sir Rupert. My reputation will not stand for long if it is discovered that I am gone off with a gentleman to a private room."

Sir Rupert came away from the door to take her gloved fingers in his. "Forgive me for my subterfuge, Miss Stanton. I desired to have a private word with you when there would be no inopportune interruptions as there were yesterday evening. We had left so much unsaid that I felt it necessary to risk a possible scandal."

Hetta dropped her eyes. Gently she withdrew her fingers from his clasp, half-turning from him. "Pray say no more, Sir Rupert."

"Surely you have not forgotten?" asked Sir Rupert, stepping up so close behind her that his coat brushed her muslin gown.

His warm breath stirred her hair and Hetta's own breath came a little quicker. She wondered what it would be like if he were to kiss her. She looked up at him, a frank openness in her hazel eyes. "I have not forgotten. But I cannot give you yet the answer you desire, Sir Rupert. I am not certain of myself or of my feelings for you."

"But I am certain of my own feelings, dear Miss Stanton," said Sir Rupert softly. With his eyes fixed on her face, he slid his hands up her bare arms to her shoulders and turned her to face him. Slowly he drew her close until he encircled her within his arms. His other hand cupped her chin and tilted up her head. He gazed deeply into her eyes, then his lips sought hers. He kissed her thoroughly and her soft lips yielded to the expert pressure. His tongue darted to explore her sweet mouth and his hold tightened around her unresisting body as his kiss grew more demanding. He let his fingers trail caressingly down the smooth column of her slender throat, then his palm was pressed possessively against her firm breast. Gently his thumb played back and forth until the point of her breast pressed erect beneath the thin material of her gown.

It was a long moment before Sir Rupert raised his head. His eyes were half-hooded with desire and a confident smile played about his mouth as he studied Hetta's face. Her color rose against the warmth of his gaze. He laughed softly in satisfaction and with his forefinger traced her full lips. "You will not give me your answer now, my little ladylove, but remember that I am not a patient man," he said in a voice of velvet. "I have shown you why I must have you. I shall await your decision with eager anticipation." He bent his head suddenly and his teeth met delicately in her underlip.

Hetta gasped in shock, drawing back so sharply that he released her. Sir Rupert was not at all perturbed by her reaction. He looked down at her still with the half-hooded expression of desire in his eyes and murmured, "A remembrance of me, my dear." He bowed and left her alone in the sitting room.

Hetta stood where he had left her. She lifted both hands to her scarlet face, feeling utter confusion. She had known Sir Rupert meant to kiss her, and out of curiosity she had allowed him to do so. She had not expected her own bewildering reaction. The tumult of raging emotions she had experienced with Lord Anthony had not recurred in Sir Rupert's embrace. Hetta was aware of a vague disappointment. What she had felt with Lord Anthony, and what she felt now, were totally incomparable.

Absently she touched her tongue to her throbbing lip and tasted blood. Her eyes widened. She went swiftly to the elaborately framed mirror above the settee to anxiously inspect her mouth. Her underlip was beginning to swell in an alarming manner. Hetta thought hopefully that it was only if one looked closely enough that the cut could be seen.

"Hetta, I—"

She whirled with a startled gasp, her hands clutching at the settee. Hetta's heart was pounding as she looked into Lady Anthony's astonished eyes. "Oh, I did not mean to come up behind you all unawares, dearest Hetta. I had seen Sir Rupert leave with you and thought perhaps I should . . ." Lady Anthony broke off, looking more closely at Hetta's face. "Oh, Hetta, what has that fiend done? Your poor mouth!"

Hetta gave a shaky laugh and touched a tentative finger to her swollen lip. "I had not thought it so obvious."

Lady Anthony shook her head at her naiveté. "Positively everyone will notice and guess at the cause, Hetta. The old tabbies who delight in such things will be simply puffed with joy to catch you out at last. You simply cannot return to the Prince Regent's party sporting a bee's sting where there are no bees. At least, there are none of the winged sort. The best course is to make your excuses and to leave immediately."

"But how am I to do so without bringing on just the sort of notice I wish to avoid?" asked Hetta, rapidly becoming appalled at her own foolhardiness in going off with Sir Rupert. Her imagination painted a scene of the curious eyes and whispers that were sure to attend her reappearance, and she knew that her reputation could not survive this last blow. Fleetingly she wondered why Sir Rupert had not realized the consequences of his action.

"I shall say that you have been overcome by the heat and have the headache, and indeed, there is nothing unusual in that, for it is excessively hot. Already Maria Quayle and two others have fainted dead away. One of the ladies was so inconsiderate as to do so before Prinny's very eyes. It was positively scandalous," said Lady Anthony cheerfully as she glided across the sitting room to a draped window.

Hetta laughed, somewhat cheered by her artless nonsense. "At least I have not been so inconsiderate as that. What ever are you doing, Loraine?"

Lady Anthony turned back to Hetta, dusting her hands daintily. Cool air eddied through the draperies, soothing their warm faces and bare arms. Her voice was matter-of-fact. "Aunt Beatrice has always maintained that one must set the stage properly to be believed. Now you are to lie interestingly arranged on the settee while I go to make your excuses. I shall return in a trice." Despite Hetta's protest that she would feel ridiculous to lie down when she did not feel in the least faint, Lady Anthony was insistent. When Lady Anthony finally left her, she found herself lying comfortably on the sofa cushions.

In the few moments before Lady Anthony's return Hetta had the leisure to reflect upon Sir Rupert's surprising declaration the evening before and his subsequent actions. She thought it strange that he should so forget himself that he had run the risk of creating a scandal, but she thought her own reaction even odder. She suspected that if he had declared himself but a few weeks earlier, she would have gladly accepted his offer without hesitation. She knew now that her feelings toward him had undergone a profound change, but for what reason she could not fathom.

Lady Anthony reentered the sitting room and expressed herself immensely satisfied with the picture Hetta presented to any who might discover them. "For we must fool simply everyone, you see. Michael will soon come to let us know that the carriage has been brought around. He will turn up at the most inopportune times. It was not my idea to involve him in the least, but he was already looking for you. He offered to call the carriage for me while I was making your excuses, and what was I to say? But no one thought it the least odd in you to be suffering the headache."

"I am such a poor creature, after all," said Hetta humorously.

Lady Anthony gave a trill of laughter as she sat down on the settee beside her. She proffered a small cut-glass bottle and a delicate lawn handkerchief. "I have brought my eau de cologne. A cool compress may reduce the swelling."

Hetta looked at her with surprised gratitude as she took the handkerchief. The eau de cologne stung as she placed it against her lip and she winced. "You have thought of everything, Loraine."

Lady Anthony shrugged her slim shoulders. There was a trace of uncharacteristic bitterness in her melodious voice. "Oh, as to that, I have been on the town long enough to know how best to defend myself against the tattlers. Believe me, dear Hetta, it is *not* by going off alone with a gentleman for a private tour of Carlton House even if it were Prinny himself." She cocked her head. "Especially if it were Prinny! He is a terrible flirt."

Hetta made a face. "I realize I have been extremely foolish. But I did not think Sir Rupert would be so ungallant as to compromise me in such a way. Indeed, he has done me the honor of asking for my hand. I cannot imagine how he could then act so foolishly."

Lady Anthony stared at her and the blood slowly drained from her face. She laid a hand on Hetta's arm. "Hetta, you are my dearest friend. Before Michael appears, I wish to reveal a secret to you that is known only to two others. I would not tell you but that I must, even if it were to mean that you would turn from me in disgust."

Hetta reached out for Lady Anthony's hand to feel it trembling. "Loraine! What are you saying? I shall always be your friend."

Lady Anthony shook her head. Her lips trembled and she spoke with obvious distress. "When Edmond was gone in that horrid Spanish campaign, I was very lonely. I threw myself into every imaginable amusement so that I would not think about it. On his last leave to England I begged him not to return to the war. He became furious with me. He said that his honor was involved. Oh, he was so very angry! But so was I. I swore to him that if he left me alone once more, I should not wait for him, but that I would petition for a divorce." Lady Anthony shuddered, caught up in her own memories. Yet she heard Hetta's gasp of disbelief. She smiled waveringly, her eyes filled with tears. "Dear Hetta, can you not understand? I loved him so passionately and so furiously that I wanted all of him. I did not understand then that a man . . . At all events, I tried to force him to return to me. I wrote him of an admirer who was particularly encroaching and who had urged me to run away with him. Edmond returned my letter with his blessings and his permission. I hated him then. It was that same day that I told Sir Rupert Sikes that I had changed my mind and that I would elope with him.''

''With Sir Rupert? But you were married to his cousin.'' Hetta stared at Lady Anthony with fascinated eyes. She could not conceive of her friend involved in such a disastrous tangle.

Lady Anthony avoided her gaze and stared instead at her own hands, which were clenched tightly in her lap. Her voice was shaking as she continued. ''Michael somehow discovered our plans and came after us. When he caught up with us, he—he tore into Rupert like—like a madman with his crop. I truly thought that he meant to kill him. And then he looked at me in such a way. He said such—such hateful things! I still cannot bear to think of it. It is why he frightens me so even now.'' She threw a beseeching look at Hetta's frozen face and tears spilled over onto her pale cheeks. ''Oh, Hetta, you must feel such disgust for me. But I could not allow you to marry Rupert when you did not know the kind of man he is. He would not be faithful to you. He cares nothing for wedding vows. Hetta, pray, pray do not look at me like that. I shall not be able to bear it if you turn from me. Oh, I shall not!''

''Oh, my dear! How could you think that I ever would?'' Hetta put her arms around Lady Anthony's bowed shoulders and murmured to her comfortingly. She chanced to glance past her and saw the Earl of Davenchester's still figure standing inside the door. Their eyes met and Hetta realized he had heard most, if not all, of his sister-in-law's confession. He came forward and there was nothing in his expression to betray he had been a silent witness. ''Loraine, I have arranged for the carriage to convey both you and Miss Stanton home. If you will endeavor to close the Prince Regent's window, I will assist Miss Stanton to her feet.''

At the sound of his voice Lady Anthony had given a violent start and gasped in fear. Hetta tightened her arms in reassurance and then let her go. "I thank you for your kind attentions, Lady Anthony. I am certain that with Lord Anthony's able assistance I shall be fine."

"Of—of course," said Lady Anthony. She rose and without a glance at Lord Anthony crossed to the window. Surreptitiously she wiped her eyes.

Lord Anthony turned away his gaze out of respect for her privacy and held out his hand to Hetta. His green eyes narrowed on her mouth with instant perception. Hetta had forgotten Sir Rupert's parting gift, but Lord Anthony's sudden quirk of a brow swiftly reminded her. She put Lady Anthony's handkerchief up to her lips as though she felt ill.

A spark of humor lit Lord Anthony's eyes. "Do not be alarmed, Hetta. I am hardly the one to cry shame and that ludicrous scrap of lace hides it nicely. You appear suitably vaporish to satisfy anyone who were to question your untimely retreat."

"You are insufferably rude, my lord," snapped Hetta.

He only laughed and suggested to Lady Anthony that it was time they made their exit. She acquiesced quietly with no sign of her former distress appearing on her face, though she did not once lift her eyes to her brother-in-law's countenance. Lord Anthony regarded her frowningly for a moment before he offered his arm to her.

Rather than escort the ladies back through the crowded ballroom, Lord Anthony led them to a side entrance of Carlton House. The carriage awaited them and he handed them up into it. "I would escort you back myself except that Lady Pelborne will wish to remain for some time yet."

"Oh, no! Pray do not disturb Aunt Beatrice's jollity on our account. I shall take good care of dear Hetta myself, I promise you," said Lady Anthony quickly.

"I know that you shall, Loraine," Lord Anthony said gently. He closed the door and lifted his hand to the driver as he stepped back onto the curb.

As the carriage moved down Regent Street, Lady Anthony sat back in astonishment. "Well! That is positively the first time that Anthony has ever spoken civilly to me. Oh, I don't mean that exactly, for he is always civil. But he has a nasty habit of sticking one with a barb when one least expects it."

Hetta was reluctant to reveal to her that Lord Anthony had heard her emotional confession. "Perhaps Lord Anthony has mellowed since his return from the war. I believe that war can drastically alter one's opinions."

Lady Anthony appeared much struck and she did not volunteer another word until they had reached the town house. Once inside the hall, she kissed Hetta on the cheek and wished her good night. Hetta followed Lady Anthony's swift diminutive figure up the stairs. Maggie was waiting for her and she was grateful for the maid's ministrations. The Scotswoman, after a single look at her preoccupied expression and the wound on her underlip, did not offer her usual running commentary but put her mistress quickly under the bedclothes.

Once alone, Hetta found her thoughts turning again to Sir Rupert Sikes. She had once believed him to be the embodiment of her romantic dreams, but no longer. She thought now that she understood her passionless reaction to his kiss. Lady Anthony's story had merely confirmed what she had begun to realize instinctively of the man. He was totally deserving of his reprehensible reputation. As for Lady Anthony, Hetta could not find it in her heart to condemn her for her past indiscretion. She herself had been taken in by Sir Rupert's charm. What must he have seemed to a young, lonely girl who was hardly a wife before her husband left her side to go to war? Hetta was too well-acquainted with Lady Anthony's nature to have difficulty guessing how Sir Rupert's attentions could have been comforting to her bruised spirit.

However, Sir Rupert was a different matter altogether. He had behaved with the most ignoble intentions imaginable in persuading a married woman to elope with him. Hetta wondered if he had given a thought to Lady Anthony's reputation afterward. She rather thought Sir Rupert had probably not cared, and she understood at last Lord Anthony's and her godmother's distaste for him.

Hetta fluffed her pillow and settled herself more comfortably. Her mind drifted to Sir Rupert's passionate love-making, and a smile touched her lips. If Sir Rupert had been privy to her thoughts then, he would have been shaken to discover how inconsequential his exquisite kisses were rated.

13

Hetta had made her decision to reject Sir Rupert's offer, but as the days passed, she gradually came to realize that she would have difficulty conveying her answer to him. Sir Rupert did not put in an appearance at Lady Asquith's card party, nor did he call at the town house. Hetta learned from an acquaintance that he had gone out of town for an unspecified time. Some conjectured that his unusual absence from society's drawing rooms was due to the recent arrival in London of a certain couple who had newly become parents.

Hetta shook her head in wonder at the gossip. Despite his scoundrelly conduct, she thought that she should temper her rejection of his suit with gentle friendliness, for he had made an honorable offer to her.

She had yet to hear from Sir Rupert on the evening she accompanied Lady Anthony and the Earl of Davenchester to an assembly. The ladies did not lack for admirers and quickly had each dance spoken for. Late in the evening Hetta chanced to glance toward the ballroom entrance in time to witness Sir Rupert's arrival. He did not immediately perceive her and she did not bring herself to his attention because she felt it was more properly his place to approach her. She turned her attention to the names written on her dance card and with a warm smile allowed herself to be led out for another set.

It was during the country dance that her partner trod heavily on her hem and tore a ruffle of lace. "Oh, I say! Awfully sorry, miss," he exclaimed in dismay. He apologized profusely even as Hetta laughingly forgave him and said that she would have it pinned up again in a trice. She excused herself to duck into a small curtained room adjacent to the dance floor.

A few minutes later she had successfully made her repairs and was preparing to return to the ballroom when she heard a familiar voice outside the velvet curtains. She remained still in hopes that her cousin would soon move on. Markham was speaking to someone and her interest quickened at mention of her own name.

". . . appear well acquainted with Miss Stanton. Indeed, one could almost mistake your attentions toward her as being loverlike," said Markham.

An indulgent laugh came in reply. Hetta's eyes widened, for she recognized it as Sir Rupert's. Cautiously she edged nearer to the curtain.

"One could indeed have that impression, I suppose," said Sir Rupert suavely.

"Allow me to offer a suggestion, my friend," said Markham. "You would be wise to maintain your distance from Miss Stanton. I intend her for my future wife."

"Strangely enough, Markham, I have the distinct feeling that Hetta dislikes you enormously. That hardly smells of a prospering romance," said Sir Rupert musingly.

Markham shrugged irritably. "Your impressions are hardly of moment to me, sir. Remember only that you are to keep your distance."

Sir Rupert's voice came softly to Hetta's ears. "And if I should become affianced to the lady?"

There was a moment of silence during which Hetta waited with bated breath for her cousin's reaction. "It would be extremely . . . unhealthy, sir," said Markham in a curiously flat tone.

Hetta gasped audibly but neither gentleman appeared to hear her.

"One feels certain that your poorly veiled threat is meant to be disturbing, but somehow—yes, somehow, I fail to feel it. I must in all honor inform you that at this very moment I await with high hopes for Miss Stanton's acquiescence to my suit," said Sir Rupert silkily. He watched Markham's expression with a faintly malicious smile on his face.

He was not disappointed. Markham turned an alarming brick color and his naturally cold eyes narrowed to pinpoints of blue ice. "You jest, of course!"

"Of course," agreed Sir Rupert easily. Unbeknown to him, Hetta drew her hand back from the curtain and waited curiously to hear what else he might say. Sir Rupert gave a twitch to his sleeve, enjoying Markham's frown. There was a great deal of amusement in his voice. "My dear Markham, I wish you joy of the skinny wench. Upon first meeting I would have described her as a nondescript female with great hungry eyes like a starving cat's. I knew instantly she but wanted a tumble, and my opinion has not greatly altered. She has been nothing more to me than an amusing toy with which to bait Davenchester and Lady Pelborne. The former has, for some inexplicable reason I fail to comprehend, appointed himself as her champion. I have of late found it necessary to redirect Miss Stanton's obvious hero-worship of him, but as for serious contemplation of the married state, pray do not think it."

A slow smile played about Markham's mouth. "I, too, have noticed his lordship's singular interest in Miss Stanton, and she naturally cherishes high ambitions in that direction. I readily understand your concern, for it would hardly suit you if the earl should set up his own establishment and beget himself an heir."

"As you say," said Sir Rupert shortly, disliking his companion's blunt assessment. "However, once Davenchester learns that the object of his gallantry is entertaining a suit from me, I have every reason to believe that his ardor will abruptly cool."

"He'll not want your leavings, you mean." Markham laughed in a way that made Hetta's hands clench at her sides. "I must give credit where it is due, Sir Rupert. I would not have thought a gentleman like you possessed such subtlety of purpose."

Hetta swept back the curtain and confronted the two startled men. Her eyes glittered dangerously. "Nor I, Sir Rupert. It may interest you to know that this precious scheme of yours merely underscores a most enlightening conversation that I held with Lady Anthony some days ago. I decided then that I would reject your suit, though I meant to do so with proper civility because I believed you were at least sincere. That consideration no longer exists. Allow me to tell you that I possess far too much common sense to ever ally myself with such a poor creature as yourself. Indeed, I find you pathetic, sir.'' With a last scathing look, she swept away with her head held high.

The gentlemen stood mute in shared astonishment. Markham was the first to recover. His smile was malicious. ''Tut tut, sir! Your lamentable tongue. Your careful strategy is now fallen to ruin, and all due to a touch of indiscretion.''

Sir Rupert eyed him in acute dislike. ''You forget, Markham. With the discovery of my motives, your loss is as great as mine. She'll have Davenchester now if only to spite us both.''

''I would not wager on the odds just yet,'' said Markham as his eyes followed Hetta's retreating figure. ''Pray excuse me, sir. I believe it may now be my moment.'' He strode off, leaving Sir Rupert staring after him in extreme annoyance.

When Hetta rushed away from her cousin and Sir Rupert, she had no clear thought but to put as much distance as possible between herself and those two gentlemen. She was still shaking with rage and humiliation when she realized she was in the midst of the ballroom. She caught herself as it occurred to her that it would be the height of folly to join the assembly without first schooling herself to at least a semblance of calm. She was unaware that Lord Anthony had witnessed her reckless entrance, and prompted by her furious expression, he was already making his way toward her. As Hetta stood irresolute, Miss Maria Quayle approached her. ''My dear!'' As her smiling eyes met Hetta's feverish glance, her expression changed swiftly to one of concern. ''Miss Stanton, are you quite well? I should not wish to pry, my dear, but truly you do not look at all the thing.''

Hetta laughed on an edge of anger. ''Do I not? Perhaps

it is because I have suddenly come to realize how stifling it is."

Miss Quayle's prominent eyes widened in comprehension. "Of a certainty, dear Hetta, I quite agree. I know just the thing, for I, too, suffer dreadfully from the close air. Lady Valen has thoughtfully informed me of a small sitting room, quite deserted, where one may retire for a moment or two in just such a circumstance. Do pray come with me, for I am persuaded a few moments alone will work wonders for you." As she spoke she urged Hetta away from the crowd and down a short hallway. She opened a door and beckoned Hetta after her. "Here we are. Lady Valen showed me in particularly, and you may see that it is charmingly appointed. She has provived for every comfort, even to the cozy fire in the grate and a smelling salt. You shall be quite comfortable, I am sure."

Hetta glanced around the sitting room and felt some of her tension ease. She smiled gratefully at the other woman. "I am truly in your debt, ma'am."

"Think nothing of it, my dear," said Miss Quayle, already preparing to close the door. "I am so often in such straits myself that I recognized immediately the cause of your distress. If anyone were to realize that it is the closeness of the crowds that unnerve me, rather than the heat, I should be thought quite mad. It is much more comfortable to be thought of as weak, do you not think so?" She waggled her plump fingers and closed the door, leaving Hetta alone. Hetta could not help the smile hovering about her lips as she turned to the small fire in the grate.

As Miss Quayle made her way back to the assembly, she glanced only briefly at the gentleman who passed her in the hall. She thought vaguely that he was a rather well-set-up young man but perhaps a bit too stocky for her taste.

For his part, Markham barely glanced at the lady. His attention was trained on the door through which he had seen her leave.

Hetta was sitting in a wing chair contemplating the crackling fire when she heard the door open. She did not immediately look around, taking a moment to wipe the tears from her face.

"Well, cousin, it appears that I am come in good time."

She swung around in her seat, her expression far from welcoming. "Jonathan! What are you doing here? Did Maria . . . ? No, of course she did not. I have no wish to speak with you, ever. Pray leave me."

Markham walked languidly to the mantel and laid his arm along it. His sharp eyes took note of her damp lashes and reddened nose. He smiled gently. "My dear cousin, I feel for you. It is difficult when one's eyes are opened in such a painful fashion. If you had only applied to me for guidance, I could have endeavored to spare you this foolish heartbreak over Sikes."

Hetta's eyes flashed brilliantly. "Do not be a prosy bore, Jonathan. I am not languishing for love of Sir Rupert Sikes."

Markham shook his head. "You were always inordinately proud, Hetta. However, I flatter myself that I understand you somewhat better than you understand yourself at this moment, and I will not be put off by such a pitiful attempt at bravery. Sir Rupert has proven himself completely unworthy of the warmer feelings of a naive young woman's tender heart. Naturally you feel abominably low and oppressed, but pray rest assured you still enjoy my unaltering devotion, my dear cousin."

"Insufferable!" Hetta raked him with a glance of disgust. "You are so bound up in your own conceit and arrogance that you have never attended a word I have ever said. Pray attempt to understand this, Jonathan. My pride suffered at Sir Rupert's hands, not my heart. I had thought him an honorable gentleman and my friend, but instead he is but a scoundrel. I have never seriously considered his suit and I would have told him so privately days ago if he had but called on me. But he did not and tonight . . . Oh, why ever am I explaining it all to you?" She leapt to her feet and turned toward the door.

Markham stayed her with a hand on her wrist. "Come, cousin, do not desert me so soon. I have not yet told you why I have followed you."

"It cannot signify in the least," said Hetta impatiently. "We have nothing to say to each other."

His fingers tightened on her wrist. Temper cracked his voice. "You want taming, my girl."

Hetta rounded on him and threw back her head with a challenge bright in her eyes. Furiously she shook off his hand. "And I suppose that you consider yourself the proper person to discipline me, cousin? I shall not be so easily frightened this time, Jonathan."

His lip curled unpleasantly. "Your short time in society has improved your appearance beyond recognition, Hetta. As I noted on a previous occasion, you appear magnificent when you are in a temper. But mark me, no one will have you as long as you possess that damnable tongue. Only I am willing to offer you an honorable marriage, and I promise you that once wed to me, you shall learn proper womanly submission."

Hetta opened her eyes very wide. "How truly noble of you, to be sure! Your sacrifice on the altar of duty shall not be called for, however, for you are quite out. I have already accepted a most obliging offer."

"Indeed! From whom, if I may make so bold to inquire?" asked Markham, patently disbelieving.

"From the Earl of Davenchester, of course," said Hetta, driven to recklessness. She stared straightly at him, daring him to dispute her word.

Markham laughed harshly. "You must do better than that, cousin. Davenchester would sooner have his chambermaid to warm his bed than he would a pale frigid miss such as yourself."

"You are disgustingly vulgar, Jonathan," Hetta said, trembling. She made to brush past him and he caught her arm to stop her once again. She rounded on him and flashed, "Let me go!" Her hazel eyes were so angry in expression that Markham involuntarily loosened his grasp.

"There you are, my love," said a suave voice. Hetta and Markham pivoted. Lord Anthony was standing in the doorway, one hand still on the knob. He closed the door and approached them in a leisurely fashion until he stood beside Hetta. He took up her quaking hand and clasped it lightly in his. "I apprehend that you have been giving Markham the happy news. Very proper, I am sure. However, he may perhaps be entitled to his doubt, for we have hardly been aboveboard with the world, have we, my love?"

"No—no, we haven't," said Hetta, stammering a little in surprise and sinking embarrassment. She could not believe her ill luck that he had overheard her rash declaration.

"Allow me to allay your doubts, Markham," said Lord Anthony. Before Hetta could guess his intention, he had taken her in his arms and proceeded to thoroughly kiss her. She went rigid but almost immediately realized she could not struggle without giving the lie to their pretended engagement to their startled audience. Feeling outrageously used, Hetta forced herself to remain quiet in Lord Anthony's arms. His lips were gentle, teasing, and slowly her cousin was forgotten in the wonder of Lord Anthony's kiss. Hesitantly her arms went around his neck.

When Lord Anthony at last released her pulsing lips, Hetta came back to earth with a vengeance. She started to draw away from his arms but he held her firmly against his side. His arm remained securely about her waist as he looked across the short distance that separated them from her cousin. Markham stood rigidly, his hands bunched into fists.

Lord Anthony said softly, "You may offer us your felicitations, Markham."

Markham's expression was stony. "My congratulations, cousin! You have done well for yourself." He jerked a bow before turning abruptly on his heel and stalking from the sitting room.

When she was certain that her cousin was gone, Hetta whirled out of Lord Anthony's embrace and slapped him with all of her strength. She backed away, dashing a hand across her mouth. Her breast heaving from emotions she dared not name, Hetta told him in pithy terms what she thought of his methods.

"Strangely enough, I thought you would be grateful for my inspired performance," said Lord Anthony, enjoying himself.

"Grateful!" exclaimed Hetta. "You used me shamefully, my lord. You knew that I could not protest and so took unfair advantage of me."

"My sweet vixen, when a lady proclaims herself engaged to me, it would be incredibly rude to deny it," said Lord Anthony. There was a wicked gleam in his eyes. "Especially when the lady in question has by far the most delectably soft lips in England."

Hetta took a hasty step backward and a suddenly wary expression came into her eyes. "I thank you for your gallantry, Lord Anthony. Fortunately our engagement is to be of the shortest duration, for I do not think that I could endure it longer. Pray excuse me, my lord." She swept him a curtsy and without a backward glance flounced out of the room. She hardly saw Miss Quayle standing just inside the doorway. That lady hastily moved out of her path, a startled expression on her round face. When Hetta was gone, Miss Quayle turned to the earl with her hands fluttering in embarrassment. "My lord! Forgive me, but I did not realize that you and Miss Stanton . . . That is, I came to peep in on her to see if she had quite recovered, but I would never have dreamed of intruding if I had but known."

Lord Anthony smiled down at her as he offered her his arm. "There is no harm done, Maria. Miss Stanton and I were merely indulging in an amiable spat of sorts." She accepted his escort, keeping to herself the opinion that their disagreement had sounded much more akin to a lover's quarrel. It was a thought that sent her mind racing.

Lord Anthony glanced down at her in amusement, aware of the bursting curiosity that consumed the lady. In the ballroom he found a vacant chair for her at the edge of the crowd. He bowed, preparing to take his leave of her. She detained him with a gloved hand on his sleeve and very daringly breathed, "My lord! Pray forgive me, my lord, but did I not hear something about an engagement existing between you and Miss Stanton?"

Lord Anthony hesitated, his eyes searching for the source of a certain delightful gurgle of laughter that came to his ears. Across the floor Hetta was holding court among a trio of gentlemen, and if her eyes appeared to possess an unusually feverish sparkle, she was considered never to have been in more admirable spirits. The earl's gaze rested on her in consideration a moment longer, then he looked down at Miss Quayle. "Certainly you did not overhear an official announcement, Maria." He saw her mouth round in an O of amazement as he bowed once more over her hand. "I know that I may rely upon your discretion," he murmured.

"Oh, certainly you may, my lord. With the utmost confidence, I assure you," said Miss Quayle, her eyes almost starting from their sockets with excitement.

"I knew I could," said Lord Anthony with dry amusement. He treated her to his most engaging smile before he took himself off.

From across the crowded room Hetta saw Lord Anthony begin to make his way toward her, stopping only to exchange civilities with a few acquaintances. She turned to one of her gallants and, pleading a ruinous headache, requested that he escort her to Lady Anthony's side. She smiled around at the generally voiced concern. "Pray do forgive me, gentlemen! No, Sir Lawrence, I fear a lemonade will not serve the purpose, but I thank you for the kind thought."

Within five minutes Hetta was able to notify Lady Anthony of her malaise, and the ladies made their excuses to Lady Valen and departed. Several minutes after their departure the assembly room was buzzing with the latest *on-dit*. Outwardly the Earl of Davenchester did not appear to notice the sudden lag in conversation whenever he approached a group of his acquaintances or the curious glances that were thrown in his direction, but it was only a half-hour later before he too took leave of his hostess. With his exit, the speculation concerning the Earl of Davenchester and Miss Stanton was openly discussed.

The news of the engagement did not reach the ladies at the town house until the following day. By midafternoon Lady Pelborne had sustained no less than half a dozen visits from curious acquaintances. One of the callers actually had the audacity to inquire of Lady Pelborne into the particulars of the marriage settlement. Lady Pelborne gave short shrift to the lady and made her feel certain that she had committed a grave faux pas. Lady Pelborne saw the lady out and then immediately went in search of her goddaughter.

Hetta was soon found in the sitting room, composing a letter to her friend and mentor, Cheton. Lady Pelborne wasted no time in coming to point. "Well, puss, and what do you have to say for yourself? I have learned today from more than one source that you and Michael have plighted your troth."

"What?" exclaimed Hetta, disconcerted, dropping her pen.

"I was assured by a very sensible acquaintance of mine that it is well-known around London, even though there is no official notice yet in the *Gazette*," said Lady Pelborne calmly. "One of my callers went so far as to inquire what the settlement was, if you please! Naturally I played down the whole as well as I was able without giving it the flat denial, for I did not know if there were any truth in the rumor or not. Pray give me the round tale, and quickly, Hetta. I am not unnaturally all agog to hear it."

"But of course it is not true! I cannot think how such a tale came about," said Hetta in bewilderment.

Lady Anthony ran into the room. Her eyes were sparkling with excitement. "Oh, my dears! You positively will not believe the tale I have had from Maria Quayle. Why, I could scarcely believe it myself. Michael and our own dear Hetta! There is not, surely not, any truth to it!"

At mention of Miss Quayle's name, Hetta suddenly recalled a minor detail from the evening before. Her expression stricken, she exclaimed, "Oh, dear!"

Lady Pelborne noted the dawning of horrified comprehension in her goddaughter's eyes and sighed. "We have but just heard it ourselves, Loraine, and if I am not mistaken, Hetta has realized how such a rumor could have come about. Well, child?"

"I very much fear it is my fault," confessed Hetta. "My cousin was pressing me again for my hand, and to be rid of him I unwisely declared myself already affianced to

Lord Anthony. He did not believe me, of course, but Lord Anthony chanced to overhear at least part of our exchange and corroborated my declaration.'' For some unaccountable reason her cheeks became rose-colored. ''Jonathan was forced to believe in the engagement then and he left in a towering rage. I informed Lord Anthony that our engagement was likely to be of the shortest duration, and when I turned to go, I vaguely recall that Maria Quayle was standing behind me. She must have heard enough of our conversation to mistake what was meant. I thought nothing of it until this moment. I was too rattled, I suppose, by the circumstances to realize the consequences of her presence.''

''And so we now have an exceedingly difficult coil, and it may be impossible to extricate ourselves from it,'' said Lady Pelborne with a certain grimness.

''There is nothing for it, Hetta. You shall have to marry Anthony,'' said Lady Anthony gaily.

''Loraine!'' exclaimed Hetta, flushing deeply.

''Loraine, you denied it to Maria of course?'' asked Lady Pelborne.

''Certainly I did! I am not such a scatterbrain not to see at once that it was one of her hums,'' said Lady Anthony indignantly. She nibbled at the tip of her forefinger. ''It is the oddest thing. She swore that she had it from Michael himself. I could not believe that, of course. Oh, shan't Michael be livid when he hears of it! I shudder to think what he will say.''

''My nephew's feelings are of little moment to me. I am far more concerned with the scandal,'' said Lady Pelborne.

''Can I not simply deny the story? For it is quite preposterous when one thinks on it,'' said Hetta. ''Surely no one could possibly take it seriously.''

Lady Pelborne looked at her with exasperation. ''My dear Hetta, it is a sublimely believable tale. I will have been cast as the shrewdest of matchmakers while you are the clever miss who saw her golden opportunity and seized it without hesitation. You shall be congratulated for snaring the catch of the Season, I assure you.''

Lady Anthony untied the ribbons on her chip-straw hat and tossed it carelessly to the sofa. Seating herself, she nodded agreement. "Every breast shall be filled with envy for you. They will smile at your face, but beware the tongues behind your back! But you are not to let their little darts wound you, dear Hetta. I daresay that cattiness shan't last more than a month at the outside."

Hetta stared blankly at her companions. "Good God."

"One cannot deny that it will be extremely uncomfortable for you, but only think of poor Michael. I dare not think of what his reaction will be to find that he is positively obligated to marry," said Lady Anthony, lacing her fingers around her knees. She rocked a little and gave a trill of laughter. "It is almost worth the scandal simply to see his face."

Hetta shaded her eyes with her hand.

Lady Pelborne said dampeningly, "You have let your good sense go begging, Loraine!"

The sitting-room door opened and the footman bowed in the Earl of Davenchester. Lady Anthony's laughter broke off and the three ladies stared at him with varying degrees of dismay.

Lord Anthony raised a quizzical brow. "I am naturally gratified that my presence generates such unalloyed pleasure," he said ironically.

Lady Pelborne held out her hand to him. "Michael, my dear. We did not expect you this afternoon."

He took her hand and bent to give her a fond salute on one powdered cheek. "No? Not even when my name has become inexplicably linked with that of Miss Stanton's?" He glanced at Hetta with an inscrutable expression and her face drained of color. She averted her gaze, suddenly finding it difficult to breathe.

"He has heard," squeaked Lady Anthony.

Lord Anthony's gaze flickered briefly in her direction. "I have heard, yes. It appears that I must accept your undoubted felicitations on my upcoming nuptials when you at last think to offer them." He was again watching Hetta's face. She rose abruptly from her chair and went to stand at the window with her back to the occupants of the sitting room.

Lady Pelborne regarded him frowningly, wondering at

his cool acceptance of the situation. "You are mightily calm, Michael. One can only suppose that you have a scheme to scuttle this pretty tale?"

"Not a thought, ma'am," said Lord Anthony cheerfully. "I propose to let the rumor stand."

Hetta whirled around from the window, her fingers clutched in the drapery. She stared across at him in mute shock as an audible gasp came from Lady Anthony.

"My dear! Surely you must realize the consequences of such a course," exclaimed Lady Pelborne. "In the eyes of the world you are honor-bound to marry Hetta. I cannot believe the marital state is a particularly welcome prospect for either of you at this point."

"I am fully aware of the obligation laid upon me, Aunt," said Lord Anthony. "However, a vehement denial could only fan just such interest as we wish to avoid. I believe our best course will be to behave much as usual and to laugh off any inquiries as may come our way. When it is seen that we do not respond and that there is no notice placed in the *Gazette*, then I have every confidence that the rumor will die a natural death."

Lady Pelborne's expression was thoughtful. "Maria is known as an inveterate gossip. There is every likelihood that such a source will in itself lend doubt to the tale. You may possibly be right, Michael. An amused indifference will go farther to resolve the matter than an open denial."

"Surely you cannot expect me to behave as though it were of no account, Godmamma. I would far rather deny the story at the outset," exclaimed Hetta.

"Would you indeed, Hetta? I assure you that there will be those who would have no qualms in using that information against you," said Lord Anthony.

Meeting his eyes, Hetta realized that he spoke of her cousin. She knew that he was right. Her cousin would be certain to renew his importunities if she were to publicly deny that she was engaged to Lord Anthony. The false engagement had been created for the Honorable Jonathan Markham's benefit and it had become a cage for her.

"Do listen to Michael, dear Hetta. I for one can vouch for the power of poisonous tongues on one's reputation.

Believe me, you will be positively crucified if it is thought that you jilted Michael out of hand. A lady is not easily forgiven so casual an affair,'' said Lady Anthony earnestly.

"It is hardly an affair, Loraine,'' said Hetta quickly. "The earl and I are scarcely acquainted.''

Lord Anthony laughed, his eyes suddenly gleaming at her with a wicked light, and to her annoyance she felt herself coloring.

"If you spoke just so to anyone else, my dear, it would fuel exactly the opposite impression,'' said Lady Pelborne. "Michael is quite right. You must behave as though the gossip has never reached your ears and preserve an unparalleled serenity. It will be difficult, for you shall be under the sharpest scrutiny. But you must remain seemingly indifferent to it all, Hetta, if you and Anthony are to come off with your reputations intact.''

"Very well! But I wish it known that I do not find it all amusing,'' Hetta said shortly.

"Do you not, Miss Stanton? I must confess that I find a certain piquant charm to the irony of the situation,'' drawled Lord Anthony.

Hetta met his eyes and drew in her breath. "Intolerable!'' she said in a shaking voice. Her color high, she flounced out of the sitting room.

"Michael, must you tease the poor girl at every turn?'' asked Lady Pelborne reprovingly.

Lord Anthony gave a soft laugh. "I very much fear that I must, Aunt.''

"You are an insensitive beast, Michael,'' said Lady Anthony fiercely as she followed in Hetta's wake.

The Earl of Davenchester only laughed.

14

Hetta found that Lady Anthony's prediction of the *ton*'s reaction to the news of her supposed engagement was accurate. She was met at every turn with fulsome congratulations that were nearly always accompanied by dagger glances. With a smile just touching her lips, she managed to turn the inquisitive questions with an amused calm that defeated even the most persistent of gossips. It seemed an eternity that she endured the public eye. However, it was but a fortnight before interest in Miss Stanton and the Earl of Davenchester began to give way under the flurry of actual announcements to be found in the *Gazette* that June. By the third week the gossip had waned to such an extent that Hetta had ceased to be the center of attention and she could once again feel at ease among company. When the ladies accepted an invitation to the Countess Lieven's summer masquerade, Hetta was thus able to look forward to the entertainment with unalloyed pleasure.

Lady Anthony had appealed to Captain Trevor and Edward Strappey to act as their escorts the evening of the masquerade. "For they are certain to enter into the spirit of the thing, just as they did at your first dinner party," she said happily.

Hetta said teasingly, "I have noticed that you seem to have a particular fondness for Captain Trevor's company, Loraine."

Lady Anthony blushed prettily and tossed her head. "Oh, as to that, I like him well enough. He is my dearest friend, after all. Certainly I am fond of him. Peter is sweet and kind and—and everything a woman could possibly ask for in a gentleman. But I could never—I could not possibly . . .'' With an unusual flash of irritation, she snatched up a ladies' magazine and urged Hetta to glance at the newest fashion plates.

Surprised, Hetta gave her a thoughtful look but said nothing as she turned her attention to the fashion illustrations.

Lady Pelborne was engaged to attend the theater with Sir Horace and so did not make up one of the congenial party that set out for Countess Lieven's establishment. The night was very warm and the ladies dressed accordingly in the sheerest of muslins under their silk dominoes. They had donned loo masks and through the eye slits their eyes sparkled with anticipation. Captain Trevor and Edward Strappey were similarly attired in dominoes and masks.

Their party entered the countess's ballroom, which was ablaze with light and laughter. A sea of colored dominoes mingled on the dance floor and from behind a painted screen rose merry music. Hetta sensed immediately that manners were freer and the flirtations bolder among the company.

Lady Anthony leaned close to her ear. ''How delightfully wicked it all is. I know that I shall enjoy it above all things.''

Hetta laughed but said, ''I should not like to come unescorted, however. I suspect that we shall be only too glad to have Captain Trevor's and Edward's protection at such a party.''

While they stood surveying the scene, a tall angular woman in a pale-yellow robe glided up to address Lady Anthony in a heavily accented voice. ''My dear Lady Anthony! One would recognize you whatever the disguise. And of course this must be Miss Stanton. What an extraordinary domino, my dear. I do not believe I have ever seen such a rich gold silk. I am quite envious, I assure you.''

''Thank you, ma'am,'' said Hetta, uncertain of who the woman might be.

Lady Anthony apparently had no such difficulty. "It was kind of you to invite us, Countess Lieven. I am persuaded that we shall all enjoy ourselves enormously."

"That is what one hopes, naturally. Gentlemen, my heartfelt greetings to you. I shan't detain you a moment longer, for there is the Marquis Lyons! Pray excuse me." Their hostess swept away.

"I venture to guess that we have been given permission to join the revelry," said Captain Trevor humorously.

"Oh, yes, let's do! Peter, we simply must go to the card rooms, for I am certain to win tonight. I hardly ever lose when you are with me," said Lady Anthony, her blue eyes wide with excitement beneath her mask.

"I am naturally at your service, ma'am," said Captain Trevor as he gave her his arm.

Edward Strappey executed a flourishing bow to Hetta that set his red domino swirling around his figure. With mock formality, he said, "Pray honor me with the first dance, my lady."

"I would be delighted, kind sir," said Hetta, inclining her head as she bestowed her hand upon him for the first of several dances.

The dancing proved to be hot work in such a crowd, and a cry was soon raised for the long tall windows to be opened wide to let in the cooler night air. A few couples slipped through the windows onto the balconies that overlooked the garden.

After a particularly strenuous romp, Edward left Hetta to procure a glass of lemonade for her refreshment. A very tall gentleman in a scarlet domino who had watched patiently for his opportunity seized the chance to approach her while she was alone.

Edward chanced to glance back as the gentleman went up to Hetta, and a quick frown touched his face. Indecision tugged at him, but at last he continued on his way with the determination to return as quickly as possible to spare Hetta that fellow's company.

Hetta was surprised to find Sir Rupert greeting her with a bow. She looked at him from under arched brows and her voice was cool. "I am amazed that you care to seek me out, Sir Rupert."

"I am never one to ignore the charming ladies of my acquaintance," said Sir Rupert smoothly. He saw by the contemptuous expression in her eyes that she was not to be taken in by his flattery. Abruptly his manner changed to one of conciliation. "Dear Miss Stanton, I am justly in your bad graces, but pray grant me a moment's favor. I have made bold to approach you for but one reason, and that is to beg your indulgence in hearing out my humble explanation. The unfortunate conversation you overheard between me and Markham was not all it seemed."

"Was it not? I thought it remarkably plain, Sir Rupert," said Hetta shortly. She turned to walk away.

Sir Rupert stepped into her path. "I beg only a fair hearing, Miss Stanton."

Hetta hesitated, unsure of her course. It was difficult for her to reject anyone who appealed to her sense of justice. She gave him a searching glance, but the mask he wore concealed his expression from her. She gestured impatiently. "Very well, sir! A moment only."

Sir Rupert glanced about them hesitantly. "Could we not discuss this in a more private atmosphere, my dear? There is nothing more uncomfortable than to discover a stranger's ears pricked at one's shoulder. Perhaps this balcony?"

Hetta reluctantly allowed herself to be ushered toward the curtained alcove. Sir Rupert held back the heavy draperies for her to pass through onto the unlighted balcony. She turned as he let the curtain fall behind him. "What is it you wished to say to me that demanded such privacy, Sir Rupert?"

Sir Rupert smiled, but it was not he who answered her. "It is I who actually wished for your company, fair cousin."

Hetta gasped and took an involuntary step backward. From the black shadows beside the stone bench emerged a figure she knew well. "What do you want, Jonathan?" she asked sharply. "You know that I no longer wish conversation with you of any sort."

"Ah, yes. That was made so unpleasantly clear by our dear Lady Pelborne, was it not?" asked Markham with a faint sneer. "But one should not allow the dictates of a doddering old woman to weigh overly much with one's own wishes."

Hetta rounded on Sir Rupert, her voice accusing. "You have deliberately led me astray, sir."

Sir Rupert crossed his arms and leaned against the stone bricks outlining the curtained doorway. He smiled with suave arrogance. "My dear Miss Stanton, it pains me that you react with such dismay. What else could I do, after all? Your poor cousin was barred from your delightful company when he desired nothing more than the opportunity to persuade you to become his beloved bride."

"I am betrothed already, as well as you both know!" Hetta took a step toward the curtain and Sir Rupert. Her head was held high. "Let me pass instantly. I do not find the present company at all to my taste."

Sir Rupert made no move to leave his station and Markham gave a soft laugh. "My dear cousin, pray forgive me if I seem an uncongenial companion. It is hardly my intention. Indeed, I hope to make of this moment an enchanting interlude to be recalled with pleasure for some years."

"I think you mad," said Hetta with conviction. A sense of danger feathered her spine and sharpened her voice. Her hands stole to the heavy amber brooch at her breast.

Markham read fear in her gesture and laughed. "You shall stand with me before a clergyman, and quite willingly I may add, before many more hours have passed, Hetta."

"Never! Never willingly, cousin," said Hetta. "And do you think that my godmother would have nothing to say to it? She is my guardian, after all."

Markham's smile was strangely undisturbed. "Believe me, dear cousin, even the overbearing Lady Pelborne will be persuaded of the wisdom of our marriage." He snapped his fingers and a large figure materialized from the shadows behind him. Hetta met the man's cruel black eyes and her fingers tightened on the brooch. "I believe that you may recall a previous encounter with my man Lucus? He does not easily forget you, dear cousin, for it was his unfortunate brother whom you shot dead that evening," said Markham softly. "Quite extraordinary of you, to be sure. It was remiss of me to so misjudge your spirit. I had not expected such bloodthirsty purpose in a female. I assure you it gives one pause for reflection."

Hetta bolted for the curtain, at the same time letting loose a piercing scream. Sir Rupert calmly stepped to one side as Markham lunged for her. Hetta twisted in his hard hands and stabbed the sturdy pin of the brooch deep into his shoulder. He jerked back with a vicious curse. Hetta grabbed hold of the curtain, her breath coming fast.

Lucus swung his fist to the side of her head. Hetta's world exploded into fragments of light and she crumpled instantly to the tiles. The amber brooch rolled free of her numb fingers.

Sir Rupert raised his quizzing glass to observe her still figure. "An efficient but rather crude method, surely?"

Markham was inspecting the small bloodstained rip in his coat and glanced over at him with contempt. "We'll be leaving with her now. Do set about the tale we agreed upon." Markham smiled, his eyes rather hard, and said softly, "She shall have me yet. Give me but a few hours alone with her in an unfashionable inn and my dear cousin shall be only too willing to tie the knot and redeem her tarnished reputation."

Sir Rupert laid hold of the curtain. "One is obliged to wish the groom all happiness, but I suspect in this particular instance it should be wasted."

Markham gave a short laugh. "Do not be anxious on my account. I take a certain pleasure in she-cats."

Sir Rupert shrugged. "There is no accounting for tastes, of course," he said indifferently, and disappeared through the curtain.

Lucus threw a black cloak over Hetta to cover the glimmering sheen of her silk domino before lifting her up to lay over his wide shoulder. He put a leg over the balustrade and tested the vines on the adjoining wall, then started to climb down with Hetta swinging limply from his shoulder.

Waiting idly, Markham suddenly heard the murmur of a voice and Sir Rupert's mellow reply. He leaned over the balustrade. "Be quick about it," he hissed. The man grunted acknowledgment. Markham watched intently until he saw him reach the ground. He took hold of the vines in his turn only to feel them give away slightly from the wall. He waited a cautious moment to test their strength before he began to work his way down the hall. By the time he reached the ground Lucus had already put Hetta's still form inside a waiting chaise and climbed onto the box beside the driver. Markham checked the chaise door to be certain that it was securely locked. Satisfied, he untied the waiting horse at the back of the chaise and mounted it. He gave the signal to the driver to start up the team.

When Edward returned with the glass of lemonade for Hetta, he did not immediately perceive her but noticed Sir Rupert stepping from behind the draperies concealing a balcony. Thinking that Hetta may have retired to the balcony for fresh air, he approached Sir Rupert, who was in the process of reclosing the curtain. Sir Rupert turned and gave a violent start at sight of him.

" 'Evening, Sir Rupert," said Edward casually with a noticeable lack of deference for the older man. "Do you know by chance where Miss Stanton may have gone? I thought I saw her with you but a moment ago."

Sir Rupert made a show of raising his eyeglass and leisurely examined him for a moment. He let it fall only when an angry flush crept up from under Edward's collar. "Strappey, isn't it?" He smiled somewhat unpleasantly. "Indeed, you may have seen Miss Stanton with me. Alas! The lady has foresaken my company for another's. I myself have never considered the Honorable Jonathan Markham to be a particularly charming companion, but the female heart is curiously incomprehensible at times." He glanced toward the curtain with a faint smile curling his lips. Ignoring the younger man, he sauntered off.

Edward stared after him, his brow furrowed. He sensed something exceedingly strange had happened, but he could not quite put his finger on it. He had known for several days that Hetta did not receive Markham and it seemed odd that she should suddenly acquiesce to his company. Hetta had always seemed to lack the capriciousness of other ladies of his acquaintances. With burgeoning suspicion he eyed the curtain and abruptly swept it back. Light from the ballroom illuminated the dimmest corners of the deserted balcony. He was turning away when his eye caught a flash of brilliance near the stone bench.

Setting down the lemonade, Edward bent to lay hold of the object and straightened with it held to the light. It was a very old brooch set with a piece of amber that held a bee caught forever in its depths. Edward gave an exclamation, immediately recognizing it and remembering that it had been pinned to Hetta's gown. The sturdy pin was bent so sharply that it no longer closed.

Edward's jaw hardened and he swept the deserted alcove with a second more searching glance. His sharp eyes spotted the disturbed vines on the brick wall and he leapt to the balustrade. Below in the darkened street a chaise escorted by a single rider was rapidly disappearing down the street. The entourage passed under a lighted streetlamp and in the brief instant of illumination Edward recognized the rider's mount.

He swung back into the ballroom. He had no difficulty in picking out Sir Rupert's tall figure among the masked crowd and his smoldering eyes bored a hole into the back of that gentleman's head. With the brooch clutched tight in his hand, Edward went in search of his friend Captain Trevor, who would know exactly what was to be done about Miss Stanton's abrupt disappearance.

A few moments later he found Captain Trevor and Lady Anthony just emerging from one of the card rooms. Completely ignoring his cousin, Edward thrust out the brooch toward Captain Trevor. "Look what I have found, Peter. It belongs to Miss Stanton. I feel certain that she has been abducted."

Lady Anthony gave a trill of laughter. "Oh, Edward, such nonsense!"

Edward threw her an impatient glance and a quick retort sprang to his lips.

Captain Trevor hastily intervened. "Why do you believe Miss Stanton has met with foul play, Edward? She may simply have dropped the brooch."

"Just look at the pin. It is almost bent in two and I did not see it before, but I think that may be blood. Besides, I last saw her with that fellow Sikes, and if ever there were a loose screw, it is him," said Edward with an excited light in his eyes. "Come on, Peter. We cannot stand here jawing all night. I tell you I have just seen the chaise leaving the grounds with Markham riding alongside it. There was no mistaking his brute's gait!"

Lady Anthony had turned white and she clutched at Captain Trevor's arm so tightly that he glanced down at her in surprise. "Oh, my God, Rupert has run off with her."

"Not Sikes! *He* is here! Haven't you been attending at all?" exclaimed Edward impatiently. "In fact, it was he who told me that Miss Stanton left with her cousin Markham, but why should she? I mean to say, she doesn't like him in the least."

Captain Trevor, who had also observed Hetta's distaste for her cousin and drawn conclusions of his own, now stared thoughtfully at the brooch in his palm. "You may have something in all this, Edward."

"What is this I hear about Miss Stanton and Markham?"

The three turned, and Lady Anthony greeted the Earl of Davenchester's appearance with marked relief. "Michael! It is Hetta. I thought she had gone off with Rupert, but it is not the case at all."

"I am happy to see you, my lord. You come in good time," said Captain Trevor gravely. "Young Edward is positive Hetta has been abducted. But according to Sir Rupert Sikes, she went off willingly with her cousin Markham."

"Damnation! I should have guessed. The masquerade

would be the perfect opportunity,'' exclaimed Lord Anthony, anger hardening his voice. The false engagement had forced Markham's hand, as the earl had known it would, but he was furious at his own lack of foresight. When Lady Pelborne denied Markham access to her goddaughter, the man had no avenue left open to him but abduction. Markham had naturally seized on the masquerade as his last chance to snare Miss Stanton. He would have had time enough to lay his plans, for the masquerade had been the hottest *on-dit* for a full month before the gilt-edged invitations were received by the *ton*.

Lord Anthony was chilled by a thin edge of fear. He knew what Markham was capable of, and the knowledge was not easily borne. If Miss Stanton was harmed, he knew that he would kill Markham with his bare hands.

Captain Trevor broke into Lord Anthony's thoughts. ''I take it that Edward's suspicions are not groundless, then.''

Lord Anthony gave a bark of laughter. ''Miss Stanton's cousin is not above an abduction, believe me. I have observed him for some months now and he would do all in his power to have Hetta in his hands.''

''Then we must go after them. If we delay much longer, they shall have too much of a start on us,'' interjected Edward with eager impatience.

Lord Anthony put up his hand. His mind raced. ''I believe it behooves me to first consult with my esteemed cousin. You did say, did you not, that he had expressed an opinion on the matter?''

''Of what possible use could that paltry fellow be?'' asked Edward with a fine contempt.

Captain Trevor had taken note of the purposeful gleam in Lord Anthony's eyes and stepped forward. ''Allow me to accompany you, my lord. I may possibly be able to lend you assistance.''

Lord Anthony laughed. ''Do you think so? Come if you wish, I shan't stop you.'' He strode off with Captain Trevor at his side. They were followed swiftly by Edward and an unusually silent Lady Anthony.

Sir Rupert's unusual height made him easily located among a small group of masked acquaintances. He lifted his thin brows when he saw the delegation converging upon him and he had no difficulty in recognizing his cousin despite the enveloping black domino and mask he wore. "Well, Davenchester, to what do I owe this unlooked-for pleasure?" he drawled.

One or two of the group recognized Lady Anthony by her ash-blond hair and greeted her in a friendly manner. She returned their salutations with a forced gaiety, throwing an anxious sidelong glance toward the two cousins confronting each other. She turned back to her acquaintances and, laughing shrilly, drew them away with a vivacious patter of chatter.

"Pray do me the favor of accompanying me to a private room, Rupert. I have something of import to discuss with you," said Lord Anthony, his voice quiet.

Sir Rupert glanced down at the lady on his arm. "Really, cousin, you are incredibly *de trop*," he complained. "I have but this moment made the acquaintance of this delightful lady and I desire nothing more than to worship at her dainty feet."

The lady at his side, her figure voluptuous even beneath the concealing folds of her bright-pink domino, made a pleased sound and tossed her head coquettishly.

"I fear that I must insist. I feel certain you will feel the urgency as well, Rupert, when I say that it concerns your future," said Lord Anthony with deliberate emphasis.

Sir Rupert looked at him sharply. Lord Anthony's eyes were hard and bright with menace, and Sir Rupert stiffened. His shrug was a study in indifference. "Of course, if you insist." He bent his head to the lady beside him and raised her hand to place a lingering kiss on the soft tips of her plump fingers. "Until later, my dove," he said in a low voice, bestowing on her a look of smoldering promise. The lady's eyes widened with excitement beneath her mask.

There was an audible snort of disgust as Sir Rupert turned away from the lady to accompany Lord Anthony. Sir Rupert darkened with annoyance as he entered the private room Lord Anthony ushered him into. He flicked a black glance at Edward. "The puppy offends me, Davenchester. Pray get rid of him. I have little desire to associate with infants.''

Edward took a hasty step toward the older man, his fists bunched. Captain Trevor caught his tensed arm, and meeting Edward's furious glance, he silently shook his head. Reluctantly Edward gave way.

Lord Anthony ignored Sir Rupert's request. He was seized with impatience. Time was passing. ''Edward has imparted to us the tale of an elopement, Rupert. I was naturally shocked to hear of my fiancée's lapse in etiquette. Perhaps you would be good enough to enlighten me of the truth in it.''

Sir Rupert glanced at Edward's flushed face and a faint smile touched his lips. ''So the puppy ran to you, Davenchester? Blind devotion is such an enduring quality, is it not?''

''Sir, we have little time for pleasantries if the tale is true and Hetta has indeed eloped with her cousin,'' said Captain Trevor gravely.

Sir Rupert hitched a lean buttock onto the edge of a card table and held out his toe to admire the gloss on his boot. ''I do not pretend to be entirely in Miss Stanton's confidence. However, I may say in all truth that I last saw her in Mr. Markham's company. But discretion forbids me to remark on the circumstances, for a lady's reputation should be sacred. I am certain that you understand.''

He was suddenly thrust backward onto the table. With startled eyes Sir Rupert looked up into Lord Anthony's furious face. An ungentle hand gripped his throat. Sir Rupert read the cold purpose in his cousin's eyes and cold sweat sprang up on his marble brow. ''Really, Davenchester! Have a care. My cravat!'' he bleated.

Lord Anthony spoke through his teeth. ''Give me the round table, Rupert, or I swear that you'll not live to meet your inamorata this night or any other.''

Sir Rupert rolled his eyes wildly to the side to find Captain Trevor. ''Sir, I beg of you! He has gone quite mad. Pull him off.''

Captain Trevor, who watched the scene with the unemotional air of an interested spectator, turned his head to the younger man who stood rooted beside him. "Edward, pray see that no one disturbs the earl and his cousin for a few moments."

White-faced with shock, Edward looked from him to the tense pair sprawled across the foot of the green-baize card table. Swallowing, he managed to nod and duck out of the room.

"Obliged to you, Trevor," said Lord Anthony shortly, never removing his eyes from Sir Rupert's appalled face. His steely fingers flexed tight around his cousin's throat. "Now, Rupert, I shall not ask you again," he said silkily. A strangled sound issued from the man under him and a long arm flailed briefly, then fell limp. Lord Anthony straightened slowly, easing his hold.

Sir Rupert wheezed and coughed. He put a trembling hand up to his mangled throat. The glazed look in his eyes gradually cleared and he regarded the relentless face above him with horrified fear. After making several attempts to clear his throat, he gasped hoarsely, "You're mad!" He felt the steely fingers slide suggestively back over his throat, and hastily said, "Markham abducted her. He mentioned an inn, but I don't know where."

"The name of the inn, Rupert."

The sweat beaded fresh on Sir Rupert's gray face. "I swear I don't know. Believe me, Davenchester." He watched Lord Anthony's expression darken and he pressed back against the table, babbling with fright. "Markham said only that it was unfashionable. One—one gathered that it was near London. He means to tie the knot, but he wanted a few hours with her before."

A furious oath escaped Lord Anthony. His eyes were twin points of blazing green flame as his hands closed hard once more around Sir Rupert's throat. Sir Rupert's eyes started from their sockets and the blood pounded heavily in his ears. He thrashed in desperation, his hands feeble against the strength of those steel fingers intent on choking the life from him.

Captain Trevor took hold of one of Lord Anthony's wrists with a crushing grip. "Enough, man! He is worthless to us. It is Hetta that we must think of now." For a moment he feared that he had not been understood, but by degrees the blind rage lightened in Lord Anthony's eyes.

The earl straightened to his full height and with indifferent contempt turned his back on his gasping cousin.

Sir Rupert lay sprawled spent and sick on the card table, his scarlet domino flowing over the edge of the table like broken plumage.

Lord Anthony's breath came quickly as though after a mild exertion. He made an attempt at a smile. "You are a sensible man, Trevor."

"I endeavor to do my best, my lord," Captain Trevor said mildly. He held back the curtain so that the earl could pass from the private room and, with a last glance for Sir Rupert Sikes, followed him. He dropped the curtain and chanced to notice Edward's swift anxious glance toward the private room. Captain Trevor caught his eye and gave him a reassuring nod. Edward visibly relaxed and the boyish look in his eyes began to return.

Lord Anthony wore a forbidding frown. "Damnation! I had hoped Rupert was more in Markham's confidence, but as it is, we hardly know more than before. There must be a dozen such inns within easy distance of London where Markham could be taking her."

"But at least we now know his destination, my lord, and young Edward was fortunate enough to witness the direction they took," said Captain Trevor.

Lord Anthony shot a piercing look at Edward. "I am in your debt, Strappey. When this business is done, remind me of it. We have tolerable good hunting in my part of the country, which I think you might enjoy."

"Michael?"

Lord Anthony turned as Lady Anthony came up with an unusually troubled expression marring her lovely features. "Oh, Michael, it is awful! Positively everyone is saying that Hetta has eloped. It is Rupert's doing, of course. There is no mistaking his monstrous sense of humor. If she does not make an appearance soon, her reputation will be ruined."

"I shall have her back in time, never fear. I am leaving immediately," said Lord Anthony. "Edward, a word with you."

Lady Anthony grasped his arm, hope dawning in her face. "Then you know where they have gone? Rupert knew?"

"Rupert knew only enough to give us a starting point for our chase," said Lord Anthony before he turned away to speak in a low voice to Edward.

Lady Anthony stamped her foot. "But Rupert dissembles so expertly that one can never trust him."

"Sir Rupert was in no position to dissemble, my dear lady," Captain Trevor said with a trace of humor in his voice.

Lady Anthony looked up at him and her eyes widened in comprehension. "Oh! Was Michael a perfect brute, then? How marvelous!" She gave a delighted trill of laughter.

Lord Anthony clapped Edward on the shoulder and the young man walked swiftly away, his domino swinging. Lord Anthony turned to his sister-in-law and Captain Trevor to say shortly, "I am off. I have charged Edward with a message to my aunt. She shall wish to be informed."

Lady Anthony whirled to block his path. "I am going with you, Michael! Hetta will need a chaperone."

The earl laughed recklessly. The familiar queer excitement he always experienced before a battle had begun to pound strong in his veins. "You're not going with me, Loraine. I intend to fly. Believe me, you would not find it a pleasant ride."

"If you have no objection, my lord, Lady Anthony may accompany me, for I will be following shortly after you," said Captain Trevor. He smiled as Lord Anthony's brows rose in surprise. "I hope that I may provide a sobering influence upon you in the heat of the moment. I would infinitely regret the necessity of your hurried flight to the Continent if you were to murder Markham, however much the man may deserve it."

Lord Anthony laughed. There was a friendly warmth in his green eyes. "As you will, Trevor. I cannot deny that your presence this night has proven helpful." On these words he strode purposefully away, his black domino billowing gracefully around his tall figure.

Captain Trevor bowed to Lady Anthony and offered his arm to her. She accepted his escort with a grateful sigh. "Thank you, Peter. You know just how to make yourself indispensable."

"So I should hope, my lady," murmured Captain Trevor as he led her from the masquerade.

15

Hetta had been awake for several minutes. She sat stiffly in the farthest corner of the dark chaise as it bowled swiftly through the night. The air had chilled and she had wrapped herself tightly in the too-large cloak that the man Lucus had tossed over her. She was alone in the carriage, and for that much she was grateful. She did not think she could have endured her cousin's company.

On waking, she had immediately tried the doors but both were securely latched from the outside. As she expected, the pistol holder above the window flapped empty and a thorough exploration of the dark chaise yielding nothing else that could conceivably be used as a weapon.

Hetta waited in apprehension for the end of the journey. She occasionally glanced through the window in hopes of glimpsing a possible landmark, but the moonless night defeated her. Once she glimpsed the silhouette of a rider behind the off wheel of the chaise and she guessed that it was her cousin.

She was stiff in every limb and a dull ache throbbed in her head. Her nerves were stretched taut with dread, yet she dropped into an uneasy doze only to start awake again when the chaise slowed.

The chaise came to a stop and she heard the murmur of voices above the stamping of hooves. The chaise door swung open and Markham thrust in a lantern. He smiled when he saw that she was awake. "I see that you have rid yourself of the mask. That is fortunate. One hopes that you fare well, cousin."

"Very well, thank you," said Hetta politely with outward calm as her thoughts darted quickly about, seeking possible avenues of escape. She knew that Lucus would not be far from his master and therefore she could not possibly duck free from the chaise at that moment. If she could but have an opportunity . . .

Markham chuckled softly. "Your fortitude is remarkable, dear cousin. We have reached our destination for the remainder of the night. I had taken the precaution of informing the innkeeper that my wife was indisposed in the event that Lucus' rough method of persuasion still affected you. I am happy to see that you will require nothing more than my able escort." Her expression must have altered, for he shook his head. "Do not think it, dear cousin. I have only to throttle you senseless and may carry you in as easily as not. I am certain that you would much prefer to maneuver for yourself."

Markham held out his hand to help her from the carriage. As Hetta descended to the ground, she threw a quick glance around her surroundings. Her heart sank. They were in the dimly lighted courtyard of an inn that had obviously seen better days. There was scarcely another vehicle in sight except for a farmer's cart and a broken-down coach. Unless the rough exterior of the inn lied, she could not hope to find within its walls a respectable stranger who might champion her cause against her cousin.

Under Markham's watchful eye and with his hand heavy on her arm, Hetta quietly entered the inn at his side. Upon seeing how the innkeeper bowed and scraped to Markham's quiet orders, she felt another flicker of hope die. Hetta thought bleakly that he would not readily offend the most prosperous patron he had obviously seen in some time, even at the plea of a lady in distress—nor would the few customers in the taproom for Lucus sat among them, and glowered at all who chanced to meet his black gaze. Hetta therefore allowed Markham to escort her upstairs to the rooms he had bespoken for them, hoping that once they were private, a chance to outwit him might present itself.

Markham glanced down at her as they entered the lowraftered parlor. He was amused by her meek manner, suspecting that it hid emotions that were far otherwise. "Still so distant, Hetta? I had hoped for a warmer reception when we were at last alone."

Hetta coolly pulled away from him and turned. The dread that caused her heart to race did not show in her face or voice. "You forget yourself, sir."

Markham closed the door and, shaking his head tolerantly, strolled to a side table. He unstoppered a brandy decanter and poured himself a glass. "Come, come, my dear. We are near enough to an understanding that we may do away with this charade of conventions."

"Your arrogance astounds me, cousin," said Hetta. "I have yet to encourage you by word or deed. Indeed, I have been at vast pains to discourage you."

"True, but we shall wed one day or another. Of that I am certain," said Markham. He threw back his head to toss off the brandy.

Her brows came together in a faint frown. "I do not understand. Why do you persist?" Impulsively she approached him to lay her hand on his sleeve. She looked up at him with a straight gaze. "You know that we should not suit, Jonathan. We could never love each other, so why have you done this?"

He stared down into her upturned face. "Gad, you're lovely," he said hoarsely. "A man could do worse than to bed a high-stepping filly like you."

Without thought for the consequences, Hetta slapped him full across the face. She backed away, her fists clenching. "You are foul, sir."

There was an ugly look in Markham's hard eyes, but in a moment it dissipated and he laughed. The mark of her fingers burned red against his cheek. "I shall enjoy taming you, fair cousin. But we will put off that pleasure for a while yet. For the moment I shall be content with the dinner I have ordered. You are naturally invited to join me." As he spoke, there was knock on the door and at his command to enter, a waiter and his fellow carried into the parlor serving trays bearing several covered dishes. They laid the table and Markham dismissed them with a short word. When the door had closed and he was again alone with Hetta, he looked over at her with his hands on the back of a dining chair. "Pray allow me to seat you, ma'am."

Hetta warily accepted his invitation and sank into the chair. Before he stepped from behind her, Markham strayed his fingers across her neck and involuntarily she shuddered. Markham laughed as he took his place outside her. "I find this a pleasant interlude, do you not, cousin? We have not dined together since our days at Meldingcourt."

"If we were at Meldingcourt, I should at least have Cheton's presence to make this horrid meal palatable," said Hetta, surveying with distaste the hastily assembled meal.

"Ah, yes, Cheton." Markham's hard eyes were bright. "I shall take great pleasure in his expression when we return to Meldingcourt as man and wife, and even greater when he is given his notice."

Hetta looked up, sharp words on the edge of her tongue, but she bit them back. It would not do to anger him unduly. She knew his temper now and could guess how far she could safely push him. She needed time, if only to postpone the inevitable. An opportunity to escape must surely present itself. Surely Markham must grant her a few private moments for her toilette. Perhaps then would come her chance. She needed only enough time to run to the stables for a mount before her escape was discovered.

Markham was watching her with narrowed eyes. "You do not eat, cousin."

"I have no appetite," said Hetta with perfect truth. "Indeed, I do not feel at all well."

He shrugged indifferently as he took a large piece of meat from his fork. "You must naturally suit yourself, cousin. I myself find the dinner to be excellent." He went on with his meal, ignoring her.

After a few minutes Hetta took up her fork and managed to swallow a few mouthfuls of what she afterward considered the most tasteless meal she had ever been served. She told herself that sustenance would be needed if she were to keep her wits about her.

Hetta watched Markham as he ate. It occurred to her that she still did not know his motives for abducting her, for she knew well enough that love did not enter into it. "Jonathan, why have you been at such pains with me? Truly?" she asked curiously.

Markham looked up and seemed to give her question serious consideration. There was a curious expression in his eyes. "Why? Because upon first sight I knew that I had to have possession."

"But how is it that I made such a lasting impression? Before Papa died, you had never laid eyes on me," said Hetta, bewildered.

Markham looked at her almost with amazement. "You? Make an impression on me? Pray don't be absurd." She straightened almost with indignation at his genuine surprise. "It was never you, but Meldingcourt! From the moment I clapped eyes on it, I wanted the estate with all the desperate hunger of a starving man. When I learned how things stood and that it was an unmarried daughter who was to have it all, I decided wedlock was a small price to pay. And so began my pursuit of your nondescript person."

Hetta was chilled by his coldbloodedness. "But why would you be driven to such lengths simply for an estate, Jonathan? You have wealth enough of your own—a respectable fortune, in fact!"

Markham's laugh was scornful. "Cousin, wealth means very little by itself! Obviously you cannot conceive what the possession of a few acres means to a man of my ambitions. Once I have Meldingcourt, I shall become one of the landed gentry and it is they who control England." Passionate greed rang in his voice and his eyes glittered.

Hetta stared at her cousin, recognizing at last what passions drove him. She felt almost a sense of incredulity for her own blind naiveté. She had believed that she was the object of his ambition when all along it was her beloved Meldingcourt. The notion struck her so suddenly that she gasped. "Jonathan." She grasped the edge of the table and leaned toward him. "Jonathan, what if I were to give you Meldingcourt? What if I were to sign it over to you now?''

"What? What are you talking about?"

"I could sign Meldingcourt over to you this instant. Only write out the agreement and it is yours—in exchange for my freedom," said Hetta urgently.

Markham stared at her for a long moment, his eyes hardly seeing her. Slowly he said, "Almost . . . you almost tempt me." She waited with slow-pounding heart, hope beginning to flutter in her breast. Markham shook his head. "If it had been a month ago, then perhaps. But you have become a worthy prize in yourself, cousin. No, a respectable wife is a political asset these days and I could do worse than to tie the knot with Hetta Stanton." He lifted his wineglass in a toast to her and drained it in a single swallow. He reached out for the wine bottle to pour himself another glass.

Hetta was numb. For a fleeting moment she had been certain that he meant to agree, and the taste of defeat was bitter. She felt the hot sting of tears and lowered her lashes so that he would not see. Her eyes fell on the dinner knife beside her plate. A wild desperate thought darted through her mind. With a quick glance at her cousin, she touched the linen napkin to her lips and then laid it briefly over the knife. When she returned the napkin to her lap, the knife was clasped hard between her fingers. Hetta took only a couple of mouthfuls more before she put down her fork and laid aside her napkin. "I should like to refresh myself, Jonathan. Am I permitted to attend to my toilette?"

Markham waved his hand toward the door to the next room. His other hand cradled a half-empty wineglass and his face was flushed. "By all means, cousin. I shall be joining you presently after I am done with my wine."

Hetta rose from her chair, her limbs quivering with tension. It was but a few steps and she must pass her cousin, who sprawled at ease in his chair watching her. When she came near him, she drew the cloak close around her with a slender hand and gave him wide berth. He threw back his head and laughed loudly. Color stained her cheeks, but otherwise she ignored him. She was almost past when he reached out lazily with one boot and pinned the dragging hem of the cloak to the carpet. Hetta turned, her breath catching. Apprehension was mirrored in her dark eyes.

"Do you actually think that I would hand you the chance to barricade the door against me?" asked Markham with heavy contempt. He straightened in the chair and, without removing his eyes from hers, put down the wineglass. "I think it time we set aside these cat-and-mouse games, Hetta, when we both know the end." He reached out for her. She spun free of the cloak and quickly put the table between them. Hetta faced him, a beautiful cornered vixen shimmering gold in the candlelight. She was poised for flight, her breast rising swift and uneven beneath the silk domino.

For a moment Markham remained seated and admired the picture she made. When he stood, his pale eyes were glittering. "I would not have thought it possible, but I desire you more than I have any other woman. And never more than when you are angered or afraid, as you are now. You are quite spectacularly beautiful, cousin." As he spoke, he advanced on her around the table. A smile curled his heavy lips as he derived enjoyment from the deepening expression of haunted fear in her darkened eyes.

Hetta whipped out the dinner knife from beneath the domino. "Pray come no closer, Jonathan."

Markham paused at first sight of the knife, but then he laughed. His voice was low and caressing. "But I intend to come much, much closer. The chase has but whetted my appetite, my little love. Fight me if you must. It will make it all the better for us both. I promise you that before I am done you shall desire nothing more than to feel my hands once again on your body."

Hetta was sick to her stomach with a churning fear such as she had never before known. She backed away from him, exclaiming, "You're mad, Jonathan." She threw a wild, desperate glance toward the parlor door, but it remained closed.

Markham loomed in her path. Her cousin's laugh was hoarse. "Aye, mad for a country wench. I shall possess you at last, Hetta.'' He lunged at her, catching her wrist and wresting the knife out of her hand. He sent it clattering across the table. Hetta tried to sidestep him, but too late she realized that he had backed her into a corner occupied by a couch. Markham caught her up in his arms despite her desperate struggle. Ungently he took hold of her hair and yanked her head back at a painful angle. Tears smarted her eyes, making them glimmer like dark jewels. Breathing heavily, Markham said, ''Please me, girl, and I will post the wedding bans before morning's light. Then none need know of your fallen virtue.''

Hetta was hardly conscious of what he said. ''I beg of you, Jonathan. Pray let me go,'' she gasped, flailing wildly in his grip.

For answer Markham took her mouth savagely. Hetta twisted in his arms, tearing her mouth away from his. Markham cursed venomously. Swaying, locked together in conflict, they fell sideways onto the couch. Markham fell across her heavily, pinning her under him. His hand pawed at her body and there was the sound of ripping silk.

A single piercing scream of despair tore from Hetta's throat. ''Michael!'' Then Markham's brutal mouth came down on hers, silencing her.

The parlor door crashed open. Markham half-raised himself, his face black with rage. ''What the devil!'' A snarl distorted his features at sight of the grim-faced intruder. ''Davenchester!'' He leapt to his feet just in time to meet Lord Anthony's charge.

Lord Anthony crashed into him and Markham staggered. The earl followed up his advantage, stepping in with a savage body blow. Markham sagged, his breath hissing, and met a powerful uppercut to the jaw. The sharp crack of bone was loud and Markham was flung heavily against the side of the plank table. He half-fell across it, sending dishes crashing to the floor. He hung there with his knees buckling under him. Markham's breath whistled in shock.

Lord Anthony stepped back, flexing his hands. His hard eyes were murderous in expression. ''Stand up, Markham! I intend to pound you into the floor,'' he said savagely.

Hetta scrambled awkwardly from the couch and stumbled past Markham to safety beside Lord Anthony. Her eyes were huge with a fright that hardly lessened when she looked up into Lord Anthony's cruel face. She pulled the tattered domino close about her with a dry sob. He glanced down at her. The flicker of a smile lightened the harsh planes of his face. Strangely reassured, she managed a wavering smile of her own. The shy luminous glow in her eyes caught and held his gaze. He drew a sharp breath, his eyes searching her face.

Markham's fingers curled around the rim of a serving bowl. He suddenly came away from the table in a crouching dive and flung the bowl's contents at Lord Anthony's head. Hetta uttered a scream of warning.

Lord Anthony leapt to one side, more in reaction than to avoid the cascade of new peas and scallions. Markham closed with him, swinging a vicious blow to the head. Recovering, Lord Anthony caught the other man in a wrestling hold. Though Lord Anthony was the taller, Markham's stocky build proved surprisingly strong. The two men strained together, grappling for advantage, then suddenly breaking apart to circle each other warily. Their labored breathing was harsh in the parlor.

Grunts of pain were wrung from them as they exchanged a round of punishing blows, but neither man gave an inch. The murderous glitter of their eyes did not dim, but seemed to only to leap hotter with each passing moment.

Hetta watched the primitive contest in mesmerized horror. In all her romantic fancies she had never dreamed that a fight over her honor would be so ugly. She forgot fear for herself or even that her fate hung on the outcome. She wanted only for it to end. "Dear God, stop it. Someone stop it," she whispered hoarsely.

It seemed that Lord Anthony heard her, for he suddenly drew back his fist and threw a flush hit directly to Markham's jaw. All the strength of his powerful shoulder was behind the crushing blow. Markham flew backward to sprawl onto the carpet and lay there, awkward and unmoving. Lord Anthony swayed, gasping for breath. He stumbled forward

and half-fell into a chair next to the table. Letting his head
fall back, he closed his eyes.

"Oh, my lord!" Hetta started toward him, reaching out
with a trembling hand. At sight of his bruised and bloody
face, her heart seemed to constrict in her chest. Tears
sprang to her eyes and she whispered, "Oh, my dear
Michael!" A flicker of movement caught her eye. She
turned her head and screamed.

Lord Anthony started up in alarm, but before he was
fully out of the chair Lucus was on him. The chair crashed
to the floor with the two men. Lord Anthony caught the
swiftly descending arm, barely curbing the plunge of the
dagger into his heart. He held the deadly blade at bay,
suspended between him and his assaiiant. His arm shook
with effort and yet the long blade slowly began to descend
toward his laboring ribs. The dark face above him split in
a twisted grin of triumph.

Hetta looked around wildly and her eyes fell on the wine
bottle. She caught up the bottle from the table and smashed
it down across the man's skull. Wine and glass splinters
flew over the carpet. Lucus shook his head, dazed. His
deadly strength slackened.

Seizing the opportunity, Lord Anthony heaved mightily
and rolled free. He staggered to his feet and prepared to
meet Lucus, who pivoted to face him with his dagger to
the fore. Sweat trickled into Lord Anthony's eyes and he
hastily swiped it away. His body ached in protest of the
punishment it had taken, and he knew with sudden clarity
that he could not expect to win this contest. "Hetta, my
chaise is before the door. Take it now," he commanded
harshly.

Lucus advanced toward him, crouching, the dagger swinging in a slow arc before him. Lord Anthony retreated a
step. He was acutely aware that Hetta still stood behind
him. His voice came as a whipcrack. "Leave now, Hetta!"

Hetta was trembling, her agonized eyes on Lucus. "No!
I shan't leave you here alone," she gasped.

"Damn you, woman!" In desperation Lord Anthony
caught the back of a dining chair and flung it hard at his
enemy's knees. Lucus was taken by surprise and leapt over

it awkwardly. He landed off balance, his rough boot heel sliding from under him on squashed peas and scallions. His arms waved wildly in the air and with a bellow of rage he crashed to the floor. Lucus started to rise, then collapsed with a sigh. He did not stir.

Lord Anthony approached him warily to nudge him with his boot. There was no response and he bent down to roll Lucus on his side.

Hetta drew near. "Is he dead?" she whispered.

Lord Anthony's mouth was grimly drawn as he nodded. "He fell on his own knife." Hetta swayed and Lord Anthony rose hastily to catch her against him. She turned her face into his coat and with one hand clutched at his lapel. Murmuring softly, he gently stroked her hair.

"Davenchester! By God, it appears you have had a time of it!" Captain Trevor stood in the doorway calmly surveying the wreckage. He came into the parlor and Lady Anthony came close behind, fluttering and exclaiming. The innkeeper was in tow and wrung his hands as he protested shrilly that he kept a respectable house as anyone could tell the gentleman and lady. The sight of two men lying apparently lifeless on the carpet robbed him abruptly of speech. Blanching a sickly green, he beat a stumbling retreat.

"We ought to send for a magistrate, I suppose," said Captain Trevor in resignation as he nudged Markham's body with his cane. A groan issued forth in response. He threw a delighted grin at Lord Anthony, who still stood with Hetta within the protective circle of his arms. "He isn't dead, then. Accept my congratulations. I quite thought that I would be forced to arrange your safe passage to the Continent."

Lord Anthony put back his head and abandoned himself to laughter that brought tears to his eyes. Hetta looked up at him with a soft tremulous smile.

"Really, Anthony!" Lady Anthony stamped her foot in vexation as Captain Trevor joined in. "Peter, it is not at all the thing to amuse one. Do not dare to laugh also. What are we to do with Markham now that the horrid man is awake?"

Markham had swayed to his feet and stood facing them. His face was a contrast of bruises and cuts while his left eye was swelled nearly shut. Captain Trevor's knowledgeable eye took immediate note of Markham's misshapen jaw. He glanced with startled respect at Lord Anthony. The earl had to possess a devastating punch to have broken the man's jawbone. Markham spoke with obvious effort. "You have won her, Davenchester. My cousin need never fear that I shall trouble her again."

Lord Anthony nodded in acknowledgment. His eyes had once more hardened. "The Continent may prove to possess a healthier climate for one of your stripe than England, Markham. I strongly suggest that you waste no time in setting out."

Markham attempted a sneering smile. The result was unfortunate, for his face was stretched oddly askew. Hetta shuddered at sight of the grotesque mask. "Do you then exile me, my lord?" he asked with a touch of sarcasm.

Lord Anthony's expression was harsh. "English magistrates do not look kindly on the abduction of gently born ladies, Markham."

Markham recognized the underlying threat in his voice. He was defeated and he knew it. He bowed with the barest travesty of his old arrogance. Then he turned and walked stiffly from the parlor.

"Well, that was rather tamely done," said Lady Anthony, disappointed.

"Would you rather we had shot him and put him out of his obvious misery, my love?" asked Captain Trevor, smiling down at her with a fond light in his eyes.

Lady Anthony stared at him. "Peter! What did you just call me?" she asked breathlessly.

Captain Trevor's face reddened. He shot an uncomfortable glance at Lord Anthony. "I fear that I have betrayed myself." He sighed and said, "Excepting his lordship's presence, I should now plead my cause most earnestly with you, Lady Anthony. My dearest sweet lady, you can have no notion how long I have held my tongue, or how I have cursed your admirable devotion to Edmond's memory. Edmond, who was the best of friends to me! I had hoped—''

"Oh, Peter!" Happiness blazed on Lady Anthony's face. Captain Trevor flung out his hand toward her, his own expression altering. Lady Anthony abruptly became aware of her brother-in-law's incredulous expression and the light went out of her eyes. Her voice came as a broken whisper. "I cannot, Peter."

Captain Trevor stared at her, bemused. "Loraine!"

She averted her face, her pretty lips trembling. Her fingers twisted together painfully. "Pray do not ask it of me, Peter. Pray do not."

For a stunned moment Captain Trevor was still, his disbelieving eyes on her lovely profile. Then the hope died in his eyes and his hand dropped to his side. "Forgive me, my lady. I shall not broach the subject again," he said in a low voice. "I think it time that I spoke with our nervous innkeeper. The man must be having apoplexy."

Lady Anthony stood with a frozen look in her eyes and watched him go out of the parlor. A pair of crystal tears rolled slowly down her white face.

"Oh, Loraine!"

Hetta would have gone to her, but Lord Anthony held her back. She looked up at him questioningly. He addressed his sister-in-law in a gentle voice. "Edmond has slept peacefully, Loraine. You are a bigger fool than I ever thought you if you allow Trevor to walk out of your life."

Lady Anthony gave him a startled glance. She flushed suddenly. Whirling, she ran from the room. "Peter! Oh, Peter, pray do not go."

Hetta watched her go with a smile shining in her eyes. "I am so glad for her. She has been lonely, I think, for a very long time."

"I had not realized that my opinion had so strongly overshadowed her life," said Lord Anthony soberly. He turned a chair upright and settled into it with a sigh.

Hetta looked at him with a softening expression. "Loraine holds you in not a little awe, I think. You have a manner about you that influences those around you despite themselves, my lord," she said. Her eyes slowly traced

each feature of the battered face that had become so dear
to her. She knew now why she had hesitated to accept Sir
Rupert's offer and the reason his lovemaking had failed to
arouse her. She had betrayed herself when she had called
out Lord Anthony's name in her most desperate moment.
Hetta marveled that the knowledge of her love could so
change her perception.

Lord Anthony showed his white teeth in a flashing grin.
"You flatter me, my dear."

"Oh, no. I have particularly noticed it," said Hetta, a
slight flush rising in her cheeks. Her heart was beating so
oddly and she felt a new shyness with him that she had
never experienced before. She trembled at the thought of
the confession she must make to him.

"At the least I was successful in influencing Markham,
though I admit I was almost at a standstill when you
chanced to announce our supposed engagement. I saw at
once that it would suit the purpose admirably," said Lord
Anthony with tired satisfaction.

Hetta regarded him, startled. "What do you mean?
Then you knew of Cousin Jonathan's importunities?"

Lord Anthony apparently felt that some explanation was
in order. "My aunt was distressed for you, you see.
Markham had to be flushed out into the open and I found
the situation to be an interesting one. His possessive attitude toward you gave me the clue how it could be done."

"And—and our engagement was the sort of tool you
needed," said Hetta, turning away, her hands to her face.
She was remembering the attentions he had paid her on a
hundred occasions during the Season, how he had smiled
and teased her. She could hardly bear the thought of his
sensuous lovemaking. It had all meant nothing. It had all
been a ploy to drive her cousin to such desperate measures
that he would ruin himself. Hetta was faint with the pain
that twisted her heart.

Lord Anthony regarded her bowed figure with a gathering frown, not understanding her obvious distress. "I realize that this Season has not proven altogether enjoyable for
you, Miss Stanton. For that I must bear a great share of the

blame. My actions were on occasion unpardonable, and I must apologize to you."

Dropping her hands, Hetta turned to face him, her eyes feverishly bright. "Oh, no! Pray do not feel that you must apologize, my lord! On the contrary, my first Season has been most—most enlightening. I have learned a great deal, far more than you can possibly know. As for our engagement, sir, allow me to formally dissolve it, since it has served its purpose so admirably."

Lord Anthony had straightened in his chair and was regarding her with an unreadable expression. "Hetta—"

Lady Anthony tripped into the parlor. "Are you ready to return to London?" she asked. The cheerfulness of her expression turned to sympathy as Lord Anthony smothered a curse. "Poor Michael! You must be sadly pulled. But there! When you are returned home, I know that your manservant will draw you a hot bath. It is just the thing to restore you."

"I for one am quite anxious to leave this place and never return," said Hetta, drawing together her torn domino and joining Lady Anthony at the door. She did not glance back at Lord Anthony, fearing he would somehow read the pain that she felt must be naked in her eyes.

Lady Anthony's eyes fell on the dead man's body and she shuddered delicately. "I am sure it is no wonder, Hetta! But we need not worry, for Peter has arranged all as proper as it may be. The innkeeper did not make the least push to help, only whined in the most disgusting way about ruin and the magistrates. A stupider man I hope never to meet."

Captain Trevor came to the door and Lady Anthony gave him a dazzling smile that made him blink. "Here is Peter now, Michael! He shall explain it all. Hetta and I shall go down to wait in the chaise." As the ladies left the room, her voice gradually faded. "This is truly the most horrid place imaginable. Can you believe it? I espied the cook positively slinging a bottle of spirits down his throat. It's a wonder that he knows his ladle from his apron."

The gentlemen exchanged grins. Captain Trevor came

farther into the parlor, shaking his head. "She is the dearest of creatures, at once exasperating and lovable."

"I wish you joy of her," said Lord Anthony with sincerity.

Captain Trevor looked at him with a steady gaze. "Do you mean that? I had somehow gathered the impression that you did not approve of her remarrying."

"Loraine is entitled to happiness, and neither I nor anyone else could wish anything better for her than this marriage," said Lord Anthony, stretching out his hand.

Captain Trevor flushed. "Good of you!" He took Lord Anthony's hand in a warm grip and noticed at once when he winced. Releasing his fingers, he asked sympathetically, "Broken knuckles?"

"Bruised only, I think," said Lord Anthony, flexing his fingers. He grinned suddenly and his eyes danced with wicked mischief. "One wonders how long Almack's would buzz if the Earl of Davenchester were to appear tomorrow with a set of split knuckles." The gentlemen laughed together but they quickly sobered again. Lord Anthony got to his feet. "Would you convey assurances to my aunt of my continued health, Trevor? It would be unwise of me to show this battered face in London. I have little desire to touch off further gossip."

"Of course. I shall be honored to do so," said Captain Trevor, turning to accompany him as he began to walk from the parlor.

"The devil you will!" exclaimed Lord Anthony, suddenly grinning. "If I know my aunt, she will read you a scorching rake-down for daring to appear without my person in tow."

"Stoicism is one of my several virtues," said Captain Trevor blandly, a smile lurking in his eyes.

Lord Anthony gave a crack of laughter as they went out the door.

16

Two long weeks had passed since Hetta's abduction. She had returned to London in company with Lady Anthony and Captain Trevor, who were fortunately too absorbed in their mutual happiness to realize her own wretched state of mind. Later, when she was alone, Hetta shed long bitter tears that left her bleary-eyed and had Lady Pelborne exclaiming that she could personally thrash Markham to within an inch of his life. "For depend upon it, Loraine, the chit is having nightmares, and no wonder! One could wish that Michael had murdered the maggoty blackguard," said Lady Pelborne wrathfully.

"Oh, no, Aunt Beatrice! Do but consider. Michael would then have had to flee England. Dear Peter gives it as his opinion that Michael behaved quite prudently under the circumstances," said Lady Anthony.

Lady Pelborne looked at her resentfully, but she reluctantly conceded the point, though she did so with a bad grace when she thought of her goddaughter's subdued air.

The rumor of Hetta's elopement was short-lived when she was seen in Lady Pelborne's company the following day. It was noted that Miss Stanton appeared somewhat wan, but that was put down to her indisposition of the night before when Lady Anthony was said to have escorted her home from the masquerade with the headache.

Mild speculation arose over Sir Rupert Sikes' abrupt departure from town. Those who were knowledgeable about such things asserted that he had done so through a belated sense of prudence. Lady Pelborne had not unnaturally taken offense to learn that the rumor of the elopement could be laid at his door and had been overheard to say that she held him in the gravest disapproval. Those who looked on Sir Rupert with detestation smiled when they heard it, for they saw the beginning of the end of his social acceptance.

Lord Anthony did not return to London. It was generally known that he had been unexpectedly called away to his estates on business, and disappointment was great that the earl would not be finishing out the Season.

As for Hetta, she could only suppose that he preferred to avoid her so that all that had passed between them could be allowed to fade from memory. She did not know whether to be glad or sorry for it. Her feelings were in such turmoil that she suspected that if she were to meet him, knowing that he did not care for her, she would immediately burst into tears. For that reason she was grateful that he had gone, but it was a torture to her as well. She found that she looked for him at social gatherings and was strangely disappointed when his tall figure did not appear. More than she would have believed possible she missed the outrageously warm expression in his eyes and his provocative teasing, which roused her temper.

She did not sleep well, but tossed in her bed so restlessly that she rose more exhausted than when she lay down. She spent more time riding and constantly urged Firefly to her fastest pace, as though she could outrun her bruised heart.

Alarmed by her mistress's feverish existence, Maggie attempted to remonstrate with her in the old scolding manner. Hetta rounded on her fiercely with blazing eyes. "I shall thank you to keep your infernal meddling to yourself, Maggie." Thereafter the Scotswoman kept her concern to herself but muttered darkly about the cursed town life that had brought her poor mistress to such a pass.

The Season was drawing to a close as summer began to make itself felt. Several acquaintances had observed that Miss Stanton had grown thin and pale with the heat. It came as no surprise when Lady Pelborne announced that her goddaughter would soon be returning to her home in the country. A few days later Hetta left London with the good wishes of her godmother and friends ringing in her ears.

Once back at Meldingcourt, Hetta let herself slip quietly into her old routine. Lady Pelborne had made her a gift of Firefly and she donned her riding habit whenever the opportunity offered. The fleet little mare carried her flying over the fields for hours, and for that time Hetta could almost feel herself free of the oppression of spirits that had plagued her since the night of her abduction. The fresh air and exercise began to have their inevitable benefits. Her sleep became sounder from sheer physical exhaustion and her appetite steadily improved, partially due to the efforts of Cook, who tried to tempt her with all her favorite dishes.

Hetta's old friend and mentor Cheton had been appalled by her listless appearance, and he rejoiced when she began to regain her vitality. Yet he remained perturbed by a change in her that he sensed was fundamental. Hetta seemed graver than before she had gone to London. He was at a loss how to account for it. He did not dare to tax Hetta, and Maggie had kept her own council on the matter.

The Scotswoman's hawkish eyes had caught an unguarded expression at times on her mistress's face that she had little difficulty in reading. Maggie's heart was wrung with pity, but she only shook her head, for she knew that there were some ills that only time could heal. She would, however, have given her eyeteeth to discover which gentleman it had been that had so gravely wounded her mistress so she could give him a taste of the backside of her tongue.

It was August and almost a month since Hetta had left London when a visitor was shown into the flower garden where she was busying herself pruning faded blossoms with a pair of slender scissors. A familiar quick step sounded on the flagstones behind her. She whirled in disbelief and dead flowers tumbled from her basket. Numbly she watched the tall figure approach. Her face was completely whitened when Lord Anthony at last stopped before her. She stared up at him as though at an apparition.

He smiled somewhat hesitantly, unsure of his welcome. "I apologize if I have startled you, ma'am."

Hetta started at sound of his deep voice. "Oh, no, no," she exclaimed in some confusion. Hastily she set down the basket and scissors to strip off her cotton gloves. "I did not expect a visitor and I fear that I am rather untidy. Have you—have you by chance seen my dear godmother since the Season ended?" Self-consciously she smoothed back her hair, aware that rebellious wisps clung damply to her perspiring brow.

"I am the bearer of letters from both my aunt and Loraine. She and Peter Trevor are to be married in the fall," said Lord Anthony. "When Loraine discovered that I was to come to Meldingcourt, she charged me most strongly with the task of urging you to be her maid of honor."

Hetta jerked her gloves between her fingers. She said bravely, "I shall be most happy to do so, of course. It shall be a most happy occasion for—for all concerned." Her voice held a tragic note that Lord Anthony did not seem to hear.

"I must confess at the first that I have come on an errand of my own as well, Miss Stanton," said Lord Anthony. She looked up at him questioningly and he indicated a nearby stone bench. When they were seated, he said gravely, "You know, of course, of the renovations that I had set in motion at Davenchester. It has at last reached completion and I now find myself in a quandary, for I do not know how to go about refurbishing the rooms. And so I have come to you for advice. I would be most grateful if you would take the task in hand."

Gazing unseeingly over the garden, Hetta heard him out with pain and astonishment. In other circumstances how happily she would have set about such a task. Tears stung her eyes and it was with difficulty that she maintained her composure. "I am truly honored, my lord, but I fear that I must decline. It would be most improper of me to do so," she said quietly.

"I quite understand, of course. It would place you in a position certain to create awkward speculation," Lord Anthony said.

Hetta bent her head and began to make neat pleats in her muslin skirt. "As you say, my lord."

"Perhaps if we resumed our mock engagement?" he suggested. If Hetta had chanced to look up at that moment, she would have seen the tender gleam that lurked in his eyes as he studied her straight profile.

Long lashes veiled the expression in her downcast eyes. Hetta's voice trembled slightly. "I could not possibly consider such a thing, sir."

Lord Anthony reached out to lay his strong browned hand over hers, stilling the restless movement of her slender fingers. "Could you not, my dearest love?" he asked quietly.

Hetta's lashes fluttered and she stared up at him with a startled wonder, unsure of her own ears.

He brushed the soft hair back from her brow with a hand that trembled slightly. His laugh was uncertain. "When you look at me just so, I cannot help but recall a bewitching vixen with moonlight entrapped in her eyes and her hair. I fell desperately in love with her, quite finally and irrevocably." Lord Anthony's voice dropped lower and softened. "I desire above all things to persuade her to marry me. Dearest Hetta, do I dare hope that she may do so?"

"Oh, Michael!" The aching pain was suddenly gone as the last pretense was stripped from her heart. Her eyes glowed with an intense joy that made Lord Anthony draw in his breath sharply. The next moment he swept her into a crushing embrace and his mouth hungrily sought hers. His kiss was thorough and savage in intensity, but Hetta submitted to it with an eager passion that told him all he needed to know.

Some minutes later Hetta emerged breathless and disheveled from what she considered very satisfactory treatment. Opening her eyes wide, she said teasingly, "You take much for granted, my lord. I have not yet consented."

"Vixen!" he said appreciatively, and caught her close once more.

SIGNET

The sensuous adventure that began with

SKYE O'MALLEY

continues in . . .

**He is Skye O'Malley's younger brother, the handsomest
rogue in Queen Elizabeth's court . . . She is a beautiful stranger . . .** When Conn O'Malley's roving eye
beholds Aidan St. Michael, they plunge into an erotic
adventure of unquenchable desire and exquisite passion that binds them body and soul in a true union of
the heart. But when a cruel betrayal makes Conn a
prisoner in the Tower, and his cherished Aidan a harem
slave to a rapacious sultan, Aidan must use all her skill
in ecstasy's dark arts to free herself—and to be reunited
forever with the only man she can ever love. . . .

**A breathtaking, hot-blooded saga
of tantalizing passion and ravishing desire**

Coming in July from Signet!